PENGUIN B

THE MULTIPL
OF RAINSHADOW

'There has never been a better moment for this book'

The *Age*

'Astley is formidable … uniquely provocative, acerbic
and glittering. Not an easy ride, but the dangerous rides
offer the greatest rewards.'

The *Australian*

'Astley has rarely left us so moved'

Adelaide Advertiser

'*The Multiple Effects of Rainshadow* – Astley at her best.'

Australian Book Review

'*The Multiple Effects of Rainshadow* throbs with as much
passion, brilliance and originality as the best of her previous work.'

Sydney Morning Herald

ABOUT THE AUTHOR

Thea Astley was born in Brisbane where she studied at the University of Queensland. Since 1958 she has published fifteen works of fiction and is one of Australia's most celebrated writers. Three times she has won the Miles Franklin Award – in 1962 for *The Well Dressed Explorer*, in 1965 for *The Slow Natives*, and in 1972 for *The Acolyte*. She is also the recipient of the 1975 Australian Book of the Year Award (presented by the Melbourne *Age*) for *A Kindness Cup*, the 1980 James Cook Foundation of Australian Literature Studies Award for *Hunting the Wild Pineapple*, the 1986 Australian Literature Society Gold Medal for *Beachmasters*, and the inaugural Steele Rudd Award in 1988 for *It's Raining in Mango*. In 1989 Thea Astley won the Patrick White Award. In 1996 she was awarded the *Age* Book of the Year Award and the FAW Australian Unity Award for *The Multiple Effects of Rainshadow*, which was also shortlisted for the 1997 Miles Franklin Award.

Thea Astley held a position as Fellow in Australian Literature at Macquarie University until 1980, when she retired to write full time. She now lives in the hills on the south coast of New South Wales.

Also by Thea Astley

Girl With a Monkey
A Descant for Gossips
The Well Dressed Explorer
The Slow Natives
A Boat Load of Home Folk
The Acolyte
A Kindness Cup
Hunting the Wild Pineapple
An Item From the Late News
Beachmasters
It's Raining in Mango
Reaching Tin River
Vanishing Points
Coda

THE
MULTIPLE
EFFECTS OF
RAINSHADOW

THEA
ASTLEY

PENGUIN BOOKS

Penguin Books Australia Ltd
487 Maroondah Highway, PO Box 257
Ringwood, Victoria 3134, Australia
Penguin Books Ltd
Harmondsworth, Middlesex, England
Viking Penguin, A Division of Penguin Books USA Inc.
375 Hudson Street, New York, New York 10014, USA
Penguin Books Canada Limited
10 Alcorn Avenue, Toronto, Ontario, Canada M4V 3B2
Penguin Books (NZ) Ltd
Cnr Rosedale and Airborne Roads, Albany, Auckland, New Zealand

First published by Penguin Books Australia Ltd 1996
First published in paperback 1997

1 3 5 7 9 10 8 6 4 2
Copyright © Thea Astley 1996

Designed by Jo Hunt, Penguin Design Studio
Typeset in 10.7/15 point Berkeley by Midland Typesetters, Maryborough, Victoria
Made and printed in Australia by Australian Print Group, Maryborough, Victoria

National Library of Australia
Cataloguing-in-Publication data:

Astley, Thea, 1925-   .
The multiple effects of rainshadow.

ISBN 0 14 026755 7.
A823.3

ACKNOWLEDGEMENTS

This book is based loosely on an incident in north Queensland over sixty years ago. All characters are fictional.

Impulses came from Compton Mackenzie's *My Life and Times: Octave Six*, Henry Reynolds's *With the White People*, Bill Rosser's *Dreamtime Nightmares*, John P. Maguire's *Prologue: A History of the Catholic Church as seen from Townsville 1863–1983*, and Renarta Prior's *Straight from the Yudaman's Mouth*. The *Kuku-Yalanji Dictionary* compiled by Lynette F. Oates was also useful.

Special thanks to Professor Elizabeth Perkins of James Cook University; Geoff Hadrill, Reference Librarian, of the Nowra Municipal Library; and Meredith Rose, editor.

The author is grateful for the Arts Fellowship that helped in the writing of this book.

The blue fire, he said. This blue. Burn my heart it jump like fish jumpin straight down sky. Marl-gan! Sky-fire! Cum-oo, he said. Water. He yelled, Go-ah go-ah go-ah! Rain! Talking Gungganyji. Talking language. Talking migaloo, whiteman talk. Made talk migaloo after the big wind at the Heads. Shacks blew down. All shacks. In the mornin after they creep out from behind the rocks where they shelter all night, the bodies. Mumma, he whimper, mumma, stickin his pink and brown paw into hers. Uncles killed. Tribal cousins. Even the boss big house scatter along rain-soaked grass and the rain still comin and no one to tell them what to do.

Did they need anyone to tell?

Mumma, he ask in language, what we do?

Find your dadda, Manny. That what we do.

1

And later that morning with the steam rising and already the stink starting, there had come his father down from the hills, trailed by Jericho and clutching Billy wrapped in a bit of old blanket and yowling fit to bust.

Boss dead. Wife too. Crushed under a ten be eight beam, huge beam hold up his house. Must've gone hide downstairs from the big wind, dadda say, they all say, looking at the body of this once boss/ruler. Silly man, dadda say.

They know better. You can't hide from the wind. You close doors on the big wind it get angry, shake your bones, your house bones, body bones, little sticks it think, it know little people sticks. Flesh fly away like grass in big wind.

So they live like that, build up grass humpies, one week, two, dadda fishin, helpin the other men bury the dead, shelterin under bits of tin left from the boss house and then one day the bullimen come, the gubbamin men. They round them all up – like cattle, mumma say, under the Dog Act – and they put chains on dadda and uncles and make mumma and all the kids march behind to the beach and then they put them in a boat and won't tell nothin.

Where we goin? mumma keep askin. Where you takin us?

You shut up, Mary, they keep tellin her. Mumma's name not Mary. It Lou. He know that. Grandma Rosie, she keep crying. But the men won't say and they frighten all day on the boat roll roll in the swell made by the big wind and all the time chains on dadda and uncles rattle. All night too they rattle and the smells get bad in the little place they sit and he wet himself just thinkin.

The littlies they won't stop howlin.

A night of closed rolling.

The blue fire spits and stabs but in the morning, blinded by light, they are taken up on deck to see in a bracelet of small islands that other bigger island that will be home.

This island swims north like a platypus, beak and tail peninsulas clutching beaches, the island's back humped to mountain size while all the suckerfish islets cluster as if they had come up to gulp for air. The boat moves closer, another remora, and draws gruntingly in to a jetty where the knotted green slopes rush down to the water. They see strange black men standing there with two migaloo and one of them, one white man, slender, youngish, watches as they stumble down the gangplank, chains rattling a grief song.

This man step forward, his eyes that crazy migaloo blue, and he act bulliman, act boss, his voice givin orders too fast while he slap his side with a shiny stick.

But a smile now and then.

That we-ra, mumma say, that wind. It bring us here.

THE WORLD IS FULL OF MORAL DISAPPROVAL

THE WORLD IS FULL OF MORAL DISAPPROVAL. I have always tried to run a respectable establishment: clean rooms, clean linen, no drunks, no nonsense in the gentlemen's rooms of an evening – I mean girls, of course, and even boys. (Oh yes! I'm aware!) But since that terrible morning last year I seem to be thrown into a worm-pit of confusion. What is right? What is wrong? After that murderous Monday who can judge the reason for things? There is more forgiveness, Father Donellan told me in that hopeless hopeful voice of his, than we can ever assess.

You might have thought I could see it all coming.

But how? With my boarders to look after? Landladies get very possessive. And my daughters? But look after them I did, despite the appalling blanketing heat, the jellied air of monsoons that never hatched. Arguing often as not with that military martinet who ran the place. It wasn't easy. Nothing is easy.

Rollcall: Doctor Quigley, Matron Tullman, Misses Starck and Weber. Briefly, schoolmaster Vine. Then even more briefly that misfit Morrow. (I couldn't help liking him.) To say nothing of my girls: Claire still wrestling with correspondence lessons, refusing to stay at boarding school on the mainland; and Leonie at that older, troublesome age, so difficult, realising she is truly the hostage of biology.

There isn't anything sadder than the educated poor.

Us.

Sometimes I find myself repeating those words of Mother's, uttered grimly over some meal in the stewing Brisbane summer, flies whizzing around the unscreened kitchen in that whistling timber house on the edge of Moreton Bay, whizzing to be captured on dangling treacle-coloured fly-catchers that hung their golden mobiles from ceilings. Caught and buzzing. The sounds of summer, waiting for the Trades to blow up across shoaled waters. I watch her hand, the wooden spoon, the endless stirring of cake batter, while the veins stand out under her papery skin. For we ate like our forebears, heavy food in heavy weather, frightened to step out of cultural line, idiot ties dragging us backward twelve thousand miles to memories of cold-climate fodder.

Mother was the widow of a pub owner who lost everything on a race at Ascot. 'Everything?' she had asked the foolish chap. 'Almost,' he had replied with a flash of his old spirit. 'You've still got me.' Did he realise that wasn't enough? He voluntarily removed himself, as Mother put it delicately. A messy business with a

8

shotgun. Despite widowhood, instant poverty and a breathtakingly boring job in a school-of-arts lending library, Mother was determined I would have contact with educational refinements – a little French, a little music, non-inflammatory poetry.

It was all wasted.

We moved north. Inn-keeping must have been in the blood. Mother found work as a station housekeeper on a sheep property west of Townsville, and those four years of boarding in a second-rate school on the coast left me with nothing except an ability to tolerate flies, stodge, and to recite excerpts from Browning's 'My Last Duchess'. (Applause from baffled parents on speech nights.) And all of that, mark you, all of that to be thrown away on a curly-headed pub-keeper's son (I told you I had inn-keeping in the blood!) ten miles down the line who married me with Mother's grudging and pettish blessing and taught me how to serve beer and spirits in his daddy's bar and still remain a lady. Trapped in the rainshadow.

I wasn't really suited. Not for ages. A little Browning is a dangerous thing.

When his father died, Liam took charge. By then we had two small girls in danger of becoming bar-room pets as they trotted in and out, kitchen to lounge to bar, ignoring liquor regulations, along upstairs verandahs peeping into the stale tobacco-smudged rooms of com-mercial travellers and bank clerks. Then Liam went to save all this for Britain by spilling his guts in Flanders. (Forgive me if perhaps I'm crude now and then. It's the bar work.) I was left to cope.

Cope is a soother of a word. That round sound supports.

'We must learn to cope, girls,' I would instruct my children as the money dwindled. 'We must manage on what we have.' Hearing them mock my words with a passable but bitter imitation as they wrestled for possession of a shared toy, I would tiptoe away from the not quite closed door of their room trying to reassess.

By this time Mother had forgiven my wasting a little poetry and French and, though declining to move in with me and share the running of a country hotel, saw us regularly enough on visits when she tried to persuade me to sell up and move south or at least to the coast. She spent her visit days with us constantly trying to fan away the climate and the flies while she dreamed of blue water. She infected the children with her dream.

What is the derivation of happiness?

About that time I was summonsed for a minor breach of the Liquor Act's trading hours. (Let's be frank: I'd refused to lock the local constable inside after ten p.m.) Mother returned south and faded quietly and then, in the late twenties, I heard of this boarding house for lease on Doebin Island, a place called Shippers Vale bang in the middle of a government reserve for Aborigines. And why not? I thought, counting pence, realising that life amid bottles was not for me, especially not for the girls now trembling on the unfurling of frightful prettiness.

Yes, I can call it that: Leonie with her passionate hair and troubled troubling mouth and a way of playing Rachmaninov that was too disturbing altogether and did nothing for the bar trade. And Claire, not quite finished with schooling (a convent on the coast), but able to cope – there's that word again! – with the grammatical rules of being beautiful.

My enterprise was thwarted by the Church who purchased ahead of me but was happy enough to see me installed as temporary chatelaine until a missionary settlement could be established.

I was ripe for a change, a weather-turn that took me bouncing across September water for hours, it seemed, in those last months of 1929, the girls with their faces set toward unknowns, the crew, eyes downcast, being bullied all the way over by the foul-tongued skipper of the island motor launch. Still, the girls had heard all those words before in the bar of the Taws Railway Hotel. Their ears ignored; their eyes were moist with expectation.

A tiny bay. A tropic landscape Gauguin might have lusted after. We trailed behind blacks who lugged our bags through a world stuck and strangled with leaves to Shippers Vale. A glade. A hillock. A low sprawl of a building. A windmill. Water tanks.

'It's different,' Leonie said, Claire said, the three of us remembering the claypans dust drunks dogs whiteant-eaten main-street shops of the Taws. On the island jetty the departing landlady had swept past with barely a blink. Could there be a worm in this tropic bud?

Waiting for us on the verandah was a slender, boyish gentleman in starched whites and pith helmet. An inner febrility fired him. A twitcher. A foot-mover.

'You understand,' Captain Brodie, superintendent of Doebin reserve, hoped after the sketchiest of greetings and barely a glance at my wide-eyed daughters, 'that your ... um ... management is properly under the jurisdiction of the Church, who will be paying your salary. You are, as it were, caretaker here. However,' and he paused and we paused with him, 'because this establishment is part and parcel of the settlement – some of the staff board here – you will have to conform to the regulations governing the settlement. Just laying down a few of the ground rules, Mrs Curthoys. My little kingdom.' Quirkish smile. Apologetic. 'My deputy will explain things later. You do understand?'

I told him I understood. I was longing to sit down and plagued by wondering if the Rangoon creeper that rioted along the verandah had attempted serious invasion of the inner rooms. Tendrils tongued at shutters.

'Let me show you through,' the superintendent suggested. 'My wife usually ... not too well, I'm afraid.' His mad eyes, I note with later knowledge, were wildly blue. Leonie and Claire kept fiddling with the cigarette-shaped flowers of the creeper. Then the superintendent dismissed the boys with a jovial shout and their silent presence was replaced by two shuffling housegirls who giggled and rubbed bare toes against stork-poised legs, palming grins behind hand flaps and lowered frizz. They kept snatching shy peeks at my daughters who were now pretending the pink flowers were indeed cigarettes and making the correct hand movements, puffing petal and air while the black girls stuffed back titters before their righteous – I could tell – boss who said reprovingly, '*Quisqualis indica!* Surely you're too young to be smoking.'

Suitable blushes. I hadn't taught them that!

'Come,' Captain Brodie invited, one arm gesturing towards the french doors. We followed demurely.

A wide hall cut straight through the building and opened onto the green light of a garden. Doors stood ajar left and right of this hallway: a large dining-room, a sitting-room, six small bedrooms, a kitchen at the rear and next to that a fernery and wash-house, showers and lavatories. Across the shaggy grass, swamped by that green luminescence and tucked beneath trees, were four sleeping huts for casual visitors to the reserve. Later I discovered that launches brought stickybeak holiday makers across from the mainland and that native curios were sold, small boys dived for pennies, tribal dances were performed under duress.

Administration pocketed the profits.

'Casuals,' Captain Brodie said, indicating the huts, 'or for those who prefer more privacy. Mr Vine, who is teaching here temporarily, has that end one. Matron Tullman often stays up at the hospital annexe and when we organise her rooms better will probably be there full time. Then there's the doctor.' His mouth tasted something unpleasant. 'And the missionaries. It's only a small family for you after all. Your daughters mightn't mind sharing for the time being.' A blaze of blue eye from them to me

13

that would not stay for an answer. 'In any case the whole situation is . . . well, temporary.'

Mrs Stopgap, there to caretake until mission staff took over! And then? I asked myself. For the moment, heat forbade thought.

Rollcall: Quigley, Tullman, Starck, Weber, Vine.

Starck and Weber, I understood, were rival proselytes but the speed with which the Church expected them to depart, two middle-aged maiden ladies lugging their fundamentalist baggage, seemed less than Christian, the speed tempered only by my employer's inability to persuade suitable (read 'correct') religious to take up an immediate apostolate. (Are you surprised I know all the jargon of evangelist zeal?)

The superintendent's feet were itching to be gone. He kept swapping positions on the polished floorboards, now minimal courtesies were done, and went to poke his head into the kitchen, suggesting the housegirls make tea for the missus. Then, slapping his thigh with a swagger stick, he strode off abruptly through curtains of leaf and heat. Snappy! I settled my daughters' belongings in one room and my own in another and left the pair of them to rest on their camp stretchers, dazed by the suddenness of this new future.

Do I admit the smallest twinge of resentment at Captain Brodie's charmless manner? I am what is known as a fine figure of a woman.

Start as you mean to go on: Mother. (Pity she never did.)

There was full rollcall at dinner. I inspected my charges over tough steak and salad. Briefly, they inspected me. Eyes lingered longest on my daughters.

Rotund handsome Doctor Quigley. Flashy big-breasted Matron Tullman. Annie Starck and Mitzi Weber in shapeless cottons and scrubbed dedication. Schoolmaster Vine, a silent angular man with a sharp carved profile under a sandy thatch. A Mr Morrow, staff supplement, would arrive shortly.

There were careful smiles on introduction, I had noticed, but no small talk, Doctor Quigley having quickly assessed my social position as had Matron Tullman whose observant black eyes already interpreted, in intersecting glances, Doctor Quigley's interest in Leonie and Claire.

I had my vowels to support me.

While my daughters are beauties, I am, I repeat, a fine figure of a woman. Upstanding, some have said, with deportment classes behind me, memories of stately walks, head balancing a textbook (Palgrave's *Golden Treasury*) along classroom aisles, with Sister Virgilia's voice a caustic goad. I stink with respectability. Sorry about that word. The general reserve of my charges maddens. Only the missionaries, Christian to the core, seem disposed towards friendliness.

'Very nice, Mrs Curthoys,' Miss Starck complimented me as she and her partner left the dining-room. They had sat at the table slightly apart from the other three, near the french doors leading to the western verandah where there were glimpses of an ominous sunset. 'Very

15

nice indeed.' Somehow I had whipped up a trifle from stale sponge, mango and custard. 'I'm sure you're going to manage very well. We'll be sorry to leave. We're under notice, you know.' She gave a little smile.

'It is only my job, Miss Starck,' I assured her with stately reserve. 'I believe in coping always.'

'Too true,' she said while Miss Weber nodded and nodded and my girls smirked. 'One must always do that.'

It would take me some days to learn the running of the kitchen, the capabilities of my helpers, Essie and Peg, the pantry stocks, the times for ordering supplies on the mainland launch, the ways of the kitchen garden and the idiosyncrasies of my boarders.

Doctor Quigley, after the most cursory of nods, had taken a newspaper into the sitting-room and, despite Matron Tullman's pursuit and attempted conversation, pretended immersion. In shallows. Under the flickering light from the generator.

'That paper is two weeks old, Doctor,' I pointed out, following him. 'I brought the latest over with me today on the launch. Would you like to see it?'

He looked up over his glasses (your friendly concerned GP) and I was halted mid-thought by the juicy quality of his lower lip now stretched into a smile.

'Very kind indeed,' he said in his rich brogue. I must say it was affecting. Matron Tullman called after me, 'And the mail if there is any?' (Everyone lived here in a state of expectation, I soon realised.)

I tossed a reply back over my shoulder – there was something about that woman! – 'Sorry, Matron, nothing for you I'm afraid,' and kept my face steadfastly turned to the office near the stores so I could not see her reaction.

We were cut off on Doebin and wed to each other.

Pen portraits are in order. Perhaps you have decided on your own already.

The lady missionaries achieve fadedness as well as vigour. Strange. Partly, one supposes, because of the climate and perhaps because a drab zeal is to be expected from orthodoxy. ('You're so biased!' Leonie chides.) In fact Miss Starck is a hefty and highly complexioned forty-year-old with sturdy ankles, straight brown hair cropped short and worn with a dogmatic fringe. She is excessively good-natured, almost aggressively thoughtful and adores the blacks, spending hours hiking from one family to another, visiting the girls' dormitory, running Bible classes, and administering capable first-aid to those who live at a distance from the main settlement. These are small scattered groups, often a few miles apart. Mitzi Weber, fair and genuinely washed-out, has, despite that, a wiry tenacity that can also tramp the same formidable distances as her companion. In a way their work supplements the hit-and-miss arrangements of the island school where Mr Vine is briefly employed. No one bothers about their education after the children reach eleven.

Matron Tullman is in charge of the six-bed hospital/

shed. ('Not enough! Not enough!' I hear her complain to Doctor Quigley who administers treatment of an altogether other kind.) I interpret irregular early morning returns of the doctor from the hospital annexe where Matron Tullman shares alternate supervisory duty with a trained island assistant. I translate the giggles of Essie and Peg as they slyly serve the matron at mealtimes. The missionaries' eyes speak a different language that shames my prurience. Mr Vine counts the days until he leaves for a mainland posting.

A world of our own.

Easily I settle into the routine. My eyes have never sailed over horizons, that giddy tipping beyond the ledge into the vortex. There are no great unassuaged departures within me, more's the pity, but I have come to terms with my own stolidity of purpose.

That Leonie! That Claire! They tackle me for my rigid respectability. They laugh secretly in their room and when questioned turn butter-smooth, milk-innocent faces towards me and conceal books whose titles I cannot catch. Who is supplying them? There is a piano in the sitting-room where Leonie spends much time on the salt-rackety instrument pounding out études and sonatas, a storm of notes like leaves. She tends to perform after dinner, quite deliberately courting the delight of Doctor Quigley who sometimes sings to her accompaniment, one plump hand on the piano lid. He has a rich and romantic tenor. Too rich. Too romantic. Leonie has a way of looking up at him as he throbs to a diminuendo in a fashion that drives Matron Tullman into silent and jealous fury. I get more pleasure from watching the matron than listening to my prodigy of a daughter. Perhaps my principles are foundering.

Picture this!

And picture this building crouched under palm and strangler fig and barringtonia thickets on a knoll a few hundred yards from that shattering ultramarine with its endless white scrolls. Bougainvillea tears relentlessly at trellises. The *Quisqualis indica* invades windows. Allamanda shouts through. And picture us. I sense my daughters speak in riddles.

'How is it,' Claire asks idiotically one morning at breakfast, the doctor arriving late and flustered from some earlier assignation, 'that waves break on our beach one way and break in exactly the opposite direction on the mainland?'

I would have thought the matter self-evident.

I watch Doctor Quigley smile. We sit separately from the guests but his ears are always a-quiver for any opportunity of speaking with the girls. We have, after all, become an informal little group, though first names are not yet bandied.

'I don't know, dear,' I say. 'Being ignorant of geographical physics.'

Claire wrinkles her nose so adorably that Doctor Quigley sets down his knife and fork and saunters over to our table, rolling ever so slightly. For a man not yet forty he has a tendency to corpulence, his flesh an amusing contrast to that clutched-at doctor dignity, though a diminution of it as well. Matron Tullman –

exhausted? jaded? and also late for breakfast – smiles over-brightly across the room and inclines her head graciously, straining after non-concern at her lover's easily distracted attention.

The good doctor hovers. He places his teacup beside Claire's, queries me May I? with raised eyebrows and pulls a chair over from one of the empty tables. The missionaries nod and smile and nod.

'Of course.' I think my vowels have confounded him, brought him to social heel, as it were. Was he expecting some rough-voiced hag of a landlady in early morning hair-curlers with a vocabulary to match? (Stupid man, I say inwardly.) His graciousness has increased markedly over the weeks.

'You see –' one pudding hand rests for the smallest moment on Claire's shoulder, insisting he is a teddy bear of a daddy for the poor fatherless girl, and then flies to his cup over which he gazes comically, 'it's a question of tides. Very basic. Ebb from the mainland brings the sea washing here on our western beach. High tide takes the water onto the eastern mainland, breaking there. Understand?'

His eyebrows crinkle like those of a concerned teacher during a pedagogical crisis. Claire is prettily flushed with this attention. 'And there's the slope of the seabed as well, the shelving up each way, here and on the mainland. It all –' At last he takes a sip from his cup and replaces it gently and does ignorance-admitting gestures with drolly spread fingers.

'Not quite. Not really.'

Doctor Quigley gives a sigh.

'Never mind, my dear. It will inevitably proceed.'

That nominative of address flutters across the room to rest lightly in each of Matron Tullman's busy eyes.

What would I know about expectation who have none beyond the present? As I say, my eyes have never sailed over horizons. But if. But if.

I might have seen into the future along with those flitting black shapes who drifted through trees about the settlement, apparently ignoring the white faces of authority. I try to know them. Sometimes I believe I have the trust of my housegirls. Their brown skins shiver with pleasure when I give them discarded dresses Claire and Leonie no longer wear. 'You mustn't spoil them,' warns Captain Brodie. 'They will take advantage. You should talk with my wife.'

Late afternoon. Set the scene. There has been a sudden rainstorm battering the leaves, the iron roof, the Rangoon creeper.

Through the open shutters the pith helmet sported by the superintendent slips busily above the crest of the shrubs lining the path to our verandah. That helmet, his tropic badge of office, is dented and sloppy with rain. But he persistently wears it, boss regalia. Even when he's closest to standing still, the old twitcher, there's a swagger to him but this is lost somehow when he moves faster, as now – business afoot – in a kind of menacing glide.

There are island rumours.

He's a tosspot.

He's a flogger.

He's a power-drunk despot at loggerheads with his deputy and the doctor.

Alternatively, the blacks are fond of him. His aloofness is reserved for staff.

He's devoted to his wife.

He adores his children.

Menacing? I'm wise after the event.

His wife is a self-effacing woman – I could have said hangdog – absorbed in her children, Davey aged twelve and Barbara a year younger. She makes gentle amends to the blacks for the jocular bullying of her husband, the intemperate rages of Jardine at the workshops, the meanness of storekeeper Cole on ration days.

And she is pregnant.

The overtones of this place refuse summation in a simple melodic line.

We're a dumping ground, a kind of island penal colony. What a mix comes here: half-castes snatched from fringe settlements around back country towns on the mainland, petty criminals, syphilitics, lepers *en route* to U-millie's lazaret across the water, and those unfortunates who've served time for drunkenness or simply for flight from white interference. Leonie and Claire are being confronted fast with the facts of democracy but remain good-humoured and outgoing – sometimes I think too outgoing. Leonie is outspoken for her years. This place has made her cynical.

How do I explain away slavery to girls brought up to believe they live in an egalitarian all-mates-together paradise? Who own dog-eared history books with accounts penned in sanctimonious horror of the evils of the British slave trade?

'We need a Wilberforce here,' my angry Leonie announced one day after returning the superintendent's children to their bungalow in Coconut Avenue where she had heard their father shouting at young Danny Tombo who was mowing the lawns. Why, she had asked the superintendent, is there still slavery on Doebin when Britain abolished it in all her colonies just one hundred years ago? (The poor child was ahead of her time. She didn't know women weren't supposed to have opinions.) Behind Captain Brodie's angry smile, instant reprimands for sauce swarmed and struggled for release. 'His face,' she reported with satisfaction, 'became rather twisted.' Ignoring cautionary nudges from Claire, Leonie maintained features of innocent puzzlement that maddened further. 'Do not,' she reported his replying, 'meddle in things you do not understand.' Then he had added somewhat irrelevantly, 'The then Prince of Wales would travel miles to hear Wilberforce sing, did you know?'

'I think he's quite mad,' Leonie said.

For a week I discouraged the girls from visiting, despite the protests of Mrs Brodie who was grateful for the respite their presence gave. She was confounded by masculine command as well as heat. To say nothing of her pregnancy. Daily she had grown paler, and instead of blooming with prospective motherhood looked dreadfully ill.

Yet the week after, there was a surprise for us all.

Father Donellan arrives by Church launch, the *Little Flower*, to celebrate Mass at the settlement and chivvy the lady missionaries into departure.

A first Mass. Imagine it! All those wondering marvelling blacks clustered around the makeshift altar in the sitting-room where my girls had been arranging chairs that morning. The magic of vestments! The alb. The green chasuble. The chalice. The consecrated wafer. Do the islanders link this ritual in their minds with the god of the big footprint on Cape Grafton? Is it a songline they hear as Father Donellan chants the Latin? Davey Brodie who is home from a Brothers' boarding school in Townsville explains what is going on. More or less. He is acting as altar boy as well. The blacks love his red and white, his scrubbed face, his hands bearing the cup. The soft water-beat of ancient language is not so much translated into the dust-mutter of our own island pidgin as paraphrased in a whispered account. Davey's cheerful face is snubly serious.

Does the little gathering understand the juju?

Do I? Do any of us really? Only the old hands of the Roman rite are absorbed by something, I realise now, I had missed for months: the calm of predicted and predictable prayer.

Mrs Brodie, whiter than death in the morning heat despite a seat near the open doors to the verandah, leans weakly against the wall. She has been bed-bound for a fortnight and Doctor Quigley seems unable to do more than move her through a variety of useless potions and advise rest. Captain Brodie has kept his Protestant self away with the excuse that he must inspect two family groups on the eastern side of the island. The far side.

And then the hard rain battering in waves outside this room, drowning the soft rain of Latin inside, and suddenly the weakest of cries from Mrs Brodie, swaying, dropping forward from her chair during the *nunc dimittis* with the blood running down her legs to the floor, the terrible red of it, her face drained as the body drains and her daughter clutching an arm to help her stumble out before Father Donellan can raise his hand in the final blessing.

An omen of chaos.

Of course I try to help. Of course I try to propel her to a bedroom. It is as if she is determined on martyrdom, whimpering with pain and bleeding, bleeding, as my own girls rush with umbrellas and send Barbara off ahead. Doctor Quigley also has trotted after the group, shouting for carriers from the alarmed congregation. But the men are unwilling. Female blood horrifies, is tabu. Furious, he gathers frail Mrs Brodie up and with my daughters protecting the pair from sky-gush flounders down the slope to the road and up towards the tiny hospital.

I was torn, I admit it, between womanly and social obligations.

Father Donellan's bemused uselessness has won. He will call on her later and define his embarrassment and sympathy with well-meant Christian platitudes and even while he murmurs, appalled and flummoxed, about the

25

matter, he is busy with vestments, the satin sheen of chasuble, the unbloodied whiteness of alb, until he reappears in clerical black to the twenty or so wondering black faces. Davey Brodie, too, is running through rain, still in his altar boy's cassock, stumbling after his mother.

Has the Mass been ruined? Or is this another, a parallel, form?

Something is marred. Father smiles on the shy hands of children who reach out to touch or stroke the silkiness of maniple, of stole. 'Och, there now,' he is saying to me and to them in his begorrah voice, 'there now.'

My mind is blotted by the memory of Mrs Brodie's white and gasping face. And the blood. As I serve tea, another sort of communion, I try to ascertain how long it will be before once again I have to uproot my family, but Father Donellan is religiously vague and keeps assuring me I am doing a wonderful job.

'It's the ladies, you understand, the missionaries . . . um . . . Miss Weber and Miss Starck. They really must leave by the end of the week. The bishop insists. Good women but a different faith. Yes. Good women.' Silence falls. 'But misguided perhaps. Still, one mustn't . . .' Et cetera, et cetera. Is this bigotry? I am glad outspoken Leonie hasn't heard his ripe Irish rationalisations. I let him dither against the wave-sound of rain. Thinking of Mrs Brodie. Sipping our tea. Sipping and possibly bleeding. 'They mean well but surely it's better, indeed I have to believe it is better,' a wry smile in my direction, 'to introduce the one true faith rather than a variety of Christian . . .'

26

Exasperated I suggest we are all on the same road ultimately and see only the superintendent's wife racked on her road to the hospital, hoping that by now she is safely sheltered, intelligently cared for. I can think of little else.

Father Donellan regards me with a speculative eye.

'Now, that's not what I like to hear from a good convent girl like you. Goodness gracious, whatever has got into everyone?'

And a second surprise.

Miss Starck and Miss Weber depart. I will miss their honest to God good-heartedness, their sensible sandals, washed-out sacks of dresses, their rigid refusal to gossip. The islanders will miss them too. In their place arrives Gerald Morrow. He is supposed to be here to assist Jardine, the handyman who looks after the boats, the generator, the building programme. He would need lessons in coarseness to cope.

Someone has made a terrible mistake. He doesn't know a hammer from a spade. Captain Brodie strides by frowning, scowling at bureaucratic incompetence. The mainland office is to blame. Mr Morrow, of course, appears indifferent to the upset. He helps Mr Cole on ration days, handles the curfew bells, calls roll for the work lines. At mealtimes he shares a table with Mr Vine and they indulge their temporariness in quiet exchanges

27

I can never quite catch. Leonie and Claire assure me I'm not missing a thing. 'It's Mr Jardine you should hear,' they giggle.

Bells punctuate our days. They need explanation.

At seven-thirty to rouse the blacks. Again at eight to line them up for tea and damper. Then they work: men on the government gardens, on the roads, cutting cordwood in the mangroves, building; the women are housegirls, cleaners, they help at the clinic. Wednesdays are free for the non-paid workers to spend at their bladey-grass huts. Rations come to bells when the islanders line up for portions of sugar and flour, bully beef and rice. Ah, paradise! They cannot marry without permission from the superintendent. I have visited the boys' and the girls' dormitories, even the dungeon-like detention cells, and have seen the filthy blankets, the cockroaches, the stains of despair.

As if that weren't sufficient chastening, there is the more formal kind. Leonie tells me that while she was out walking with Claire they came across a young man, Willie Omba, handcuffed to a tree. He kept asking them for water and they ran all the way back to Shippers Vale to fetch a canister, but when they returned Captain Brodie was waiting and angrily ordered them off. And the women! Last week Essie turned up with her head shaved to the skull. Between her sniffles and tears I discovered: she had crept out from the dormitory after curfew to be with her boyfriend. She's lucky she wasn't put to sweeping the streets like that, a practice common enough. 'Mother!' Leonie cries furiously, 'Why is it only the women who are punished?' I cannot answer that age-old question. Essie was so humbled she couldn't look at me for days.

Is this a Christian settlement? It is hard to believe so in this nearly arrived decade of the 1930s.

Diversion. An odd thing happened this week.

Doctor Quigley has been bringing a book with him to breakfast each morning the last few days and, though I have strenuously discouraged my daughters from such unmannerly practice, he sits there, letting his breakfast cool, snorting and chuckling.

'Have you read this?' he asked Mr Vine, sauntering across, one plump finger marking a passage, and forgetting his cooling breakfast. '"Leaves from a Squatter's Journal".' He suddenly shouted with laughter. 'Leavings, more like it! Well well well! Laundered vignettes of life in the far north-west. *But,*' here he laid the book flat on the schoolteacher's toast and leant over him, 'do you teach a kid called Billy Cooktown? You do? Well, I must tell you his grandmama was fucked by some of the best upper-class blood in England. Ah, England my England! Well, not mine, precisely, being county Galway, but ... So the next time you and Brodie speak discourteously to Billy and especially his grandmama, Rosie, try to remember, old chap, that Billy's grandpapa was a Rugby boy!'

Of course I can't have language like that in the dining-room though my girls, strangely enough, are taking it in

their stride. (Mr Jardine, no doubt.) And making a fuss
would only emphasise. I shall, I decide, speak privately
to him later. In the meantime, Doctor Quigley is
embroidering his fantasy. How he would love, he is
booming across the table, to take old Rosie Cooktown
and Billy back to England and escort them to Billy's
grandpa's old school. Especially on old boys' reunion
day. 'I wish,' he parodied, 'to see my grandpa's school!'

Mr Vine coughs with embarrassment. 'Billy's a good
reader,' he says. 'A bright lad.'

'It's that dash of privileged blood, doubtless.' Doctor
Quigley winks at smiling Leonie and comes back to his
inedible eggs.

Cultural bias. I share it with him. What else have I
been taught in a country that enslaved those whom it
didn't murder or exploit sexually? I must ask Father
Donellan about these irreconcilables when he next visits.
Or should I? I don't want to be put off with pious blarney.

'Indade you don't,' comments perceptive Leonie who
can read my thoughts.

Meanwhile Doctor Quigley is saying loudly in our
direction, 'You must forgive me, ladies. The verb I used
is of uncertain Middle English origin, possibly 'fuken',
doubtless derived but unproven from the German *ficken*,
to strike, the Latin *futuere*, the Greek *phytuein*, and the
French *foutre*. Mr Vine will support me in this, I have
no doubt.'

Mr Vine refuses the bait.

His days are numbered here. He's a time-filler before
leaving for his mainland appointment at a small failing

boarding school that concentrates on pupils from grazing properties in the Gulf country. Here he is, a graduate from St Andrews, currently teaching reading and addition on Doebin Island. There's a certain idiocy in this. He seems to have no notion at all of how to deal with primitive educational needs. 'I entertain them,' he apologises, edging his tall gaunt body, hedging enquiry. He tells us little about himself. 'After all, it's only till the new year. I'm obliging the government. Morrow and I are both mistakes.'

Well, what can you say to that?

My daughters have been swallowing their laughter as Doctor Quigley gives his little lesson on word origins, chattering on beneath the chattering tin roof, uninhibited by his position or the threat of a gliding topee. He holds forth robustly on the heinous properties of the Act.

In the meantime bells ring for roster parade and a mile away Mrs Brodie lies gasping and bleeding in her airless bedroom at the residency.

Let me tell you more. With asides. I'm coarsened by all this in a way I never was at that hotel in the Taws. Perhaps it is because we are a minority group of privilege at bay, really at bay, despite the hunched and brooding power of the law. It is that which holds us hostage. Protocol. Custom. The small-minded niceties of a lower-class élite. In particular I feel unable to do other than repress natural feelings of sympathy and concern because of that. There is no fear of the unfortunates we guard or tend, only reluctance to outrage the island's equivalent of suburbia.

This place has been called a penal colony but really it's a rubbish tip for government guilt. Here there are men who have committed murder in payback according to tribal law but whom the white authority does not know how to punish, or even if it should. There are station hands who have cheeked head stockmen, girls who have served their sexual purpose and are sent here with gonorrhoea and babies. There are runaways, alcoholics and the old. Doctor Quigley insists on relating a belief widespread among white males about gonorrhoea. Over the coffee! What a dinnertime subject! 'They think,' the kindly doctor tells us, 'they can rid themselves of sexual disease by having intercourse with a young gin. If they pass it on, the disease leaves their bodies. I wish,' he adds with his whimsical smile, 'medicine had other cures as simple as that.'

'For Heaven's sake!' I cry in protest. 'This is . . . is barroom talk. My girls! Please!'

'Nonsense, dear lady! Nonsense!' the doctor says, twinkling.

He makes weekly visits to inspect the lockup where refractory workers are sent for weeks at a time, with black police helpers doling out the daily food ration of damper and tea and an occasional supply of *nikki-nikki*. He hears tales.

Although the doctor is only thirty-six, a fact he let

32

drop on Leonie's sixteenth birthday which we celebrated a few days ago, he looks and acts in a much older way. Already he is developing an importance round the waist, a deliberate manner of walking and delivering his words that makes me think of that liturgical phrase I grew up with – *ex cathedra*. Leonie, however, hangs on his every utterance. He lets her hang.

After Doctor Quigley's uncovering of distinguished connections for Rosie Cooktown, I have to admit to wondering how many more of these bladey-grass dwellers have manorial ties. If I don't watch myself I'll be scanning for evidence of chinlessness and that god-of-the-earth, you-owe-me-everything saunter. 'Feudalism,' Mr Vine announces unexpectedly at breakfast, 'is merely a breath away.'

If you happened upon this island, sails bellied and straining to a landfall, as you balanced on deck with your eyes gummed to this mountain humped above riffled reef waters, you would be enchanted by that necklace of white beaches, foliage growing almost to the sea in a density of plaited vine, aerial roots, leathery green leaves and palms waving casual welcome feathers. Now and again as the boat rocked, an enchanting white-wall glimpse, the glare of a roof, the spurious domesticity of a cooking fire. God love us, you might say as Father Donellan said that morning of our one and only Mass, what a paradise of a place!

The girls' dormitory! The boys'! They'd slap you awake.

Slab buildings, airless, small-windowed, bolted at night to prevent hanky-panky, earth floors scoured with lime to kill lice and fleas. Peg and Essie live in the dormitory, as do helpers at the clinic (Mrs Brodie is still bleeding) and the school. This is what is known as a 'dry' island. None of the blacks is allowed liquor. Nevertheless the men have to help unload the crates of whisky and wine for white staff and I wonder how deep their resentment is watching Captain Brodie dispense sundowners at his weekly get-togethers for the white bosses on the residency verandah. On special occasions at Shippers Vale I serve sherry or port, a small indulgence allowable, I think, for one who runs a respectable establishment. The doctor and the schoolmaster keep bottles of whisky in their wardrobes, the housegirls tell me, giggling behind pink palms.

'You must keep it locked away,' I had to reprimand both men, 'otherwise the housegirls could be tempted – I don't say they would – but they could sample it or give it to friends.'

Another little watchdog chore. I'm becoming fat with righteousness.

A few nights ago an inexplicable case of drunkenness when Jericho Cooktown and Joshua Friday were heard singing loudly and shouting obscenities at midnight in the main street of the settlement. Blacks are not allowed there unless they are working. It would be interesting to know which misdemeanour of a possible four was the most repellent to our gliding superintendent: the theft of liquor, breaking the curfew, drunken behaviour or trespass in the sacred territory of the whites.

I plump for the last.

Yet Captain Brodie is doing his best. New dormitories are being built on stumps with wooden floors and decent rainproof iron roofs. Only the women will still be caged – there is no other word – from the sexual attentions of the young men. 'They're just animals,' pronounces Mrs Storekeeper Cole panting with propriety and a sherry-loosened tongue. Her mean-fisted husband nods agreement. (Mrs Brodie is still confined to bed while her husband plays host over his worries.) 'Nonsense!' Brodie roars. 'Bloody rubbish!' Behind him in his living-room is a photograph of the Doebin Island rugby football team with the superintendent proudly sitting centre row, three team members away from Billy Cooktown's older brother Manny whose white ancestry comes through nicely on this camera portrait. Manny is nineteen.

Doctor Arnold would have been proud of him.

This week at breakfast Doctor Quigley is reading *Salammbô*. In French. My convent school had given me enough of the language to recognise Flaubert, if only as an occasion of sin. Perhaps *Madame Bovary* had been placed on the Index and we had blushed our horror as we took furtive peeks at Gustave's plump mustachioed face in an encyclopaedia of European writers.

After years behind the bar I am beyond shock and was not opposed when the doctor offered to help Leonie and Claire with their French. 'A little conversation,' he suggested, thickening his brogue lovably. The Irish always have better French accents I had noticed, recalling baby-faced Sister Pascale who made us take parts in *Le médecin malgré lui*. *Malgré moi*, or in spite of some tinkerings of warning – sexual, of course, having been brought up in a religion that seems to regard sex as the only sin and a matter of female responsibility – I agreed.

The woman tempted me! our visiting convent pastor would thunder at retreats. A tiny statement that appeared to absolve males from all blame. Y'see, m'dear, he would croak at one or all of us urgent for pastoral advice, men can't help it. It's the nature of the beast, for goodness' sake! It's up to the women, not the men at all at all.

The trouble was, we believed him.

I writhed.

We all writhed – the world and its crime on our young shoulders – but mocked the old fraud later with passable mimicry.

'Maybe,' I heard Claire whispering to Leonie at supper, 'if all the women in the world ceased trying to look attractive – no pretty clothes, hacked hair, pimples, filthy nails – there'd be no problem.' She seemed to have Matron Tullman in her sights.

'Oh tosh!' her sister hissed back. 'That never worried cavemen. Muscle power! Don't you see? It's the structure, the deliberate structure. We have to find poorly paid jobs or a keeper. Ergo, as Mr Vine would say, we have to turn into shop window goodies. I swear I once heard Mother say that marriage was legalised prostitution.'

Now, those were ugly words, especially to one who had worked non-stop since that long ago exchange of vows and rings. But she had a point. I could see that.

I could see that. Despite shock.

Starck and Weber are missed. They departed in a flurry of psalms and good wishes, to take their mission to the desperate flatlands beyond Cloncurry. They forgot to take with them the large jar of boiled lollies that bribed piccaninnies to join their Bible classes.

I mustn't make fun. I mustn't belittle. They had few possessions beyond their clothes. They had endless kindness. Whatever money they had, they spent on extra bandages and proprietary medicines that they lugged with them on their evangelist trips to the far side of Doebin. The blacks called them Jesus fellas. 'She bin Missus Jesus, that one,' Essie told me once over the washing up. 'She bin kind all right.' Thank you for that, Essie (whose hair has almost grown back). I stand reproved.

But their well-meant amateur first-aid infuriated Doctor Quigley.

'Will you leave it alone, woman!' he snapped peevishly one morning at a startled Miss Starck. 'You've done entirely the wrong thing for Jobie Friday. It's not an infection, for sweet Jesus' sake! It's an allergy.'

His blasphemy routed them. It was a week before they left.

But he is not Doctor Cure-all. Mrs Brodie is bleeding to death.

Matron Tullman has radioed for help from the mainland in this chancy weather so close to Christmas. The heat builds in great buttresses against a drained blue sky. At night sulking clouds roll across gritty moonlight.

No help arrives. The doctor and matron spend whole days with the superintendent's wife trying to arrest the bleeding that ends, finally, in the weakened scream of a premature birth, the baby unformed, the mother gushing out her life into packed towels.

'She's gone,' unshaven Doctor Quigley announces at breakfast, his thumb marking the place he is up to in *Salammbô*. 'We tried, my God! Matron and I did try.'

Not hard enough, Brodie was to screech at him later that morning, but now the doctor is wagging his head from side to side as if confronted with an imponderable problem. 'No eggs, this morning, thank you,' he tells Essie. 'Just tea and toast.' And he dives head-first into Flaubert.

Heartless or simply professional? He has, by the way, lent his over-thumbed copy of *Bovary* to Leonie. Is he a cultured man or a cultivated one? He is given to odd

38

jest. Only last month he was seen leading a pig by a string along the main road to the hospital. His public explanation before putting down the animal was that it was diseased. His private, that Jimmy Kadura, the pig owner, was a *burri burri* man.

'A tiny bit, now, of cultural history,' he said over dinner, addressing Leonie, all curls and flush. 'I must introduce you to Tristan Corbière. Have you heard of him, m'dear?' And to her shaken head, 'Ah, no matter. A desperate melancholic who once painted eyes on his forehead – that's what Brodie needs, eh? – donned a mitre, the profane lad, and strolled pig-a-hoop, in evening dress – the poet, that is – through the streets of Rome.'

Leonie was clearly enchanted by this bit of literary gossip. And is even more so when, on this terrible morning of Mrs Brodie's death, he looks up suddenly from *Salammbô* and says softly, 'Ah, poor Captain Brodie. *"Tais-toi, tais-toi. On n'aime qu'une fois."* '

'And who wrote that?' Leonie asks.

'Jules Laforgue,' and 'Matron Tullman,' the doctor and I answer as one.

The doctor regards me with drained eyes. 'You mistake me, dear lady. You mistake me.' And he closes his book abruptly and leaves the table.

The high seas and the rain. The outer whirling edge of a cyclone that has struck the coast one hundred miles north of here. Trees around Shippers Vale assume grotesque shapes, green hair streaming. Verandahs are lashed by delinquent creepers that are torn to rags and disintegrate in air. Sky is water that batters and batters in one monstrous waterfall.

We buried Mrs Brodie yesterday, committed her to earth without formal blessing, for it was impossible for Father Donellan to reach us until the seas lost muscle. Surely our own goodwill meant more. Davey and Barbara sobbed but their father was dangerously quiet as deputy superintendent Leggat read aloud the service for the dead and we all recited the Lord's Prayer. Rain fell unendingly on watchers, grave, and flowers gathered by the black women whose tears – they were forced to stand at a respectful distance – increased the deluge all about. Amen, we all said. And then my daughters sang the twenty-third psalm while Davey and Barbara rubbed relentlessly at their eyes.

There was no wake in the Irish sense of the word but I did invite the superintendent and his children, the deputy and his wife, the storekeepers and even Mr Jardine back to the boarding house for refreshments.

Poor Captain Brodie could barely sip his tea, moving agitatedly between rain-slashed shutters and the doors open to the verandah. Conversation broke into mono-chrome phrases like the glaze on a plate. Useless words. From our angled eyes we watched his sad erratic pacing, his pauses to stare out from the windows towards the bay and the jetty no boat could reach in that wind-rucked surf which rose in giant pleats, doubled on itself and crashed violently on the beach. Sky and sea became one blot of shouting grey.

Suddenly Captain Brodie spun about to face us all, fixing a manic glare on Doctor Quigley and Matron Tullman.

'You killed her!' he shouted. 'You two simpletons killed her! You pair of bloody know-nothings!' He flung his head back and screeched his pain and horrible loss at the ceiling. A gecko scuttled. There we all were with faces frozen like stricken saints. 'Oh God oh God! You inefficient bastards! You useless murdering bastards!' Then he slammed down his cup and strode jerkily into rain that instantly soaked and flattened his clothes and moulded his skinny frame against the keening wind.

Before the doctor could open his mouth Matron Tullman, her handsome face haggard from sleeplessness, was energetic with rebuttals: all we could possibly ... the weather ... drugs didn't ... too weak already with months of ... refusal to go to the mainland when she ... absolutely not their fault. To end with a savage coughing/ weeping fit that distracted the lot of us, allowing the deputy and his wife, the Coles, schoolmaster Vine, an embarrassed Morrow and boatman Jardine to mumble apologies as they sidled out. Thank goodness Brodie's children had already gone home directly after the graveside ceremony.

Doctor Quigley strengthened himself with a large whisky, lowering his portly form into an easy chair. Now and again he flapped a there-there hand at the sobbing matron.

'Understaffed, you understand, Mrs Curthoys. All of us here understand, I would hope. The only authority that doesn't is the government. Over four hundred natives, one qualified sister, four unqualified native assistants; limited medicines, equipment. Dear God, what can one do, I ask, eh?' He leant back and began a list. 'Every sort of social disease, begging your genteel pardon, Mrs C. Syphilis, gonorrhoea, Hansen's, tuberculosis, Weil's fever, to say nothing of the childhood ailments and accidents – the gashes, fractures. All this apart from the results of domestic violence. We haven't even proper isolation bays, only quarantine laws the native police boys can't quite enforce, despite the curfews. Do you see all that?' He gulped the last of his whisky in one searing draught. 'I am only, as the poet says, a lunar reveller who makes circles in pools.' His delicious French accent took over, slowly, distinctly. ' *"Je ne suis qu'un viveur lunaire/Qui fait des ronds dans des bassins."* '

'That makes me cry,' Leonie whispered, gazing at the harassed doctor over the rim of her teacup. And promptly began shedding tears. But they were for everything.

' *"Tais-toi, tais-toi"*,' he said softly, and held his consoling and hovering hand in check after assessing Mama, to say nothing of Matron Tullman, riddled with professional defeat, offence and jealousy, who heaved herself majestically up and announced her intention of leaving, numbering aloud the cases at the little hospital that required her attention: an old man with a broken leg, a child with whooping cough and a woman about to give birth.

'One departs, one arrives.' The doctor's sententious remark was in poor taste, I felt, watching the pair as they fussed about for raincoats and umbrellas still dripping on the verandah. Leonie observed them through damp lashes.

Those hustled goodbyes. To everyone, living and dead.

And it is goodbye for us as well in a way.

We are about to leave our island.

One week. Two.

Captain Brodie has drawn back into his pain like a snail. Gossip limns him. His right hand has begun a terrible tapping, a nervous tic he cannot control. Deputy Leggat finds he is taking over his boss's duties in addition to his own, turning the pre-cyclone eight-hour day into a dawn-to-dusk of patching: roofs, walls, bogged roads, choked drains. What a potch of a business! Leonie has been practising her French and the piano for long alternating periods all day and moons between times about the verandahs and garden saying, '"*On n'aime qu'une fois.*"' I think she thinks she is Emma Bovary. How do I put a stop to such fantasy, to the endless replays of sentimental Chopin nocturnes?

Captain Brodie has locked himself in his house and refuses to speak to anyone, especially on matters of control. His children, confused by loss, tag off along the beach between here and there, faces blank with grief.

43

Their housegirl prepares their meals but the trays outside their papa's door remain untouched.

If these were memoirs in the truest sense, they would still give no evidence of revelation. It is hard to clarify thoughts in this heat.

Last evening, in that strange half-hour before the sun drops like a rock into the sea, Captain Brodie emerged from his locked bedroom, his house, his garden, and was seen gliding along Coconut Avenue past the repaired government buildings, and eventually crossing the footbridge that spans the creek before Shippers Vale. He was moving swiftly, eyes shadowed by that pith helmet he affects, striking out on the bush road towards the dormitories, ignoring the waved hands, the greetings. 'Him eyes funny,' Essie said to me as she lathered dishes. 'I see him. Him eyes real funny.'

Inspired no doubt by tensions of weather and relationships, I decided this morning to keep a journal of these last days. Am I wise before events? There isn't time to write a great deal. The briefest jottings. A skeleton portrayal. Another terrible and unexpected invitation to gather at the residency, the superintendent persisting with the social rituals that preceded his wife's death. A shambles of a gathering. Shouted accusations and countercharges. Blows exchanged. Their rage drives me home. Captain Brodie believes the doctor and deputy are trying to supplant him. Last month there was an official inquiry into complaints made by Mr Leggat and Doctor Quigley. I put all that down. (Half a page, half a page, half a page onward, mocks bright-faced

44

Claire observing mother-at-desk.) To be found at desk is a pretty change after being found at bar, I tell her.

The ceasing of wind and the interminable rain now falling in more or less predictable dumpings has turned the island into a stew-steam with moisture rising from the ground in heavy vapours that make walking more like swimming. There is a constant stink of decaying vegetable waste.

Writing creates maps. Of a sort.

Are maps about people or places?

People and places. That evening, ah!

Mr Morrow, dear man, less than useless, has left without ceremony. Grinner Jardine reports that he has rowed into the sunset. There was a small note left on my work-table and two weeks' board. I am shaken after that turmoil at the residency. It is too hot to sleep. Leonie begins a passionate assault on a Scriabine prelude while Claire watches, twisting strands of hair. We're all deluded by passion in this clamping climate as my daughter's notes or Scriabine's, gutted, almost, from the cheap but resonant upright, hang in the air, linger, create dissonance.

An explosion blasts Scriabine apart. Leonie swings towards me but already I am running onto the verandah when a second boom rocks the settlement. My throat wrenches out a name. 'Mr Vine!' I cry. 'Mr Vine!' Who had gone to bed some time before but is sleepless as well and races to join us where we peer uselessly through the filtered dark. We are one protector less. The doctor and matron have long since returned to the hospital and we test out our fears behind the dripping creepers, seeing, even from where we stand, the first leaping flames stabbing crimson. There are distant shouts, rifle shots, the pounding of feet across the bridge, the sound of running. A woman's scream carves the night then bubbles away.

I want to scream as well but grip my daughters tightly as feet thud down the track again and over the bridge and we glimpse Captain Brodie racing his madness across the garden. He is moving in terrible jerks, a rifle in one hand, his swagger stick in the other. For one moment he pauses and looks up at his chilled audience by the steps and Leonie shouts, 'What is it? What is it?' but his eyes haven't seen or have moved beyond us for he whips about and begins a spastic running back the way he has come, pushing past midnight into a next day, whose air is ruptured by more explosions and new bursts of fire.

Mr Vine takes a torch and strides bravely into the night, into the drizzle which has just begun. We watch his flickering beam wobble across the creek and up towards Coconut Avenue and the fires, separate spires of light. Wary, I douse the lamps and steer my daughters into the shrubbery for safety, where we huddle beneath raincoats until we hear him return, feet stumbling across the verandah boards, voice calling softly to us. Even as he tells what has happened there are two more explosions following quickly, one upon the other, and greater sheets of flame scrawled on the dark.

46

'It's madness,' he says. 'Brodie's gone crazy. He's burnt the residence, the store and the school. He's prowling round the settlement with revolvers and a rifle. His pockets are stuffed with dynamite.' I watch my daughters' eyes widen. 'I spoke to him, just for a minute. Tried to reason with the man. He didn't seem to know who I was. Told me to get off the island. He thinks,' Mr Vine smiled wryly in torchlight, 'there's some kind of revolutionary plot to unseat him. Obsessed, poor bastard. I couldn't find Quigley or the matron. Jardine's skulking in the boatshed and Mrs Leggat has taken the storekeeper's wife and kids to hide in the scrub near the ridge. Maybe we should do the same.'

'I don't know about you others,' indomitable Leonie says in a no-nonsense voice, 'but I'm going to make a very large pot of tea.' And she stalks off through the dripping leaves to the house.

She always was a sassy girl.

I can't bear to remember the rest of that night. The intermittent rain. The mosquitoes. The droning of water, waves, and the unexplained cracklings about the grounds, louder because the whole settlement was now wrapped in a silence thick as felt.

But not for long. In one of those pauses between cloudbursts, nimbus peeled back like stage drapes and a watery moon lit a drama too melodramatic to be believed.

Once more in that ambiguous light we glimpse the superintendent moving beyond the verandah rails, crouched and stalking, it soon becomes apparent, the matron and doctor whom he had surprised, we were told later, in the matron's sleeping annexe at the hospital. Before the doctor could screech a warning to his partner, a shot had blasted a hole in his thigh. Brodie had pushed forward through the crotons outside the annexe window and taken aim at Matron Tullman who was busy trying to lug her portly lover into shelter, but the doctor tore himself free with a cry, 'For God's sake, woman!' just before a second crack of the rifle lodged a bullet in the matron's shoulder. Her thin squawk jabbed through leaves and then she began to run from the annexe, the doctor limping after her. She outdistanced him in no time at all, flopping about in her nightgown, face bloated with fear as she blundered down the avenue through the orange grove towards the little creek and the track leading up to our house.

A filmic quality. In slowest motion.

They created a frieze beyond the garden on the ridge above the creek, the matron panting in front, blood now running down her arm onto the starched white cotton, followed by pyjama-clad Doctor Quigley lurching, staggering, one hand shoved in his spurting groin, and some mad how Brodie, who must have doubled back through lawyer vine, loping after them, his rifle barrel jerking in parody of his movements. Then as we watched, a fourth figure appeared on the ridge-line, deputy Leggat racing with his rifle and shouting at his boss.

A pause. Brodie stopped suddenly and stared not at but through his assistant, eyes plastered on insane distances. He raised the service pistol which he had stuck in his belt and fired wildly to a clicking stop. Momentarily he fumbled in his shirt pocket for bullets, then uttering a shriek of frustration ran back down the hill and began scrambling through trees on the far bank of the creek.

The sequence: I am handicapped here. Leggat, I think, torn between duty and charity, glanced from us to the superintendent's vanishing crashing figure then ran off after him.

Between us we dragged and heaved the wounded pair onto beds. One of the black boys was sent to fetch ligatures and sutures from what was left of the matron's annexe, where Doctor Quigley kept emergency equipment. He tended himself with the help of Leonie who, tight-lipped, handed clamps and sutures, listening to Matron Tullman who lay whimpering with her shattered shoulder and bruised skull. All this, while more shots cut the night, a further explosion and the leaping hunger of fires.

I lit the lamps. What point in concealment? I made fresh tea.

'Mother,' Leonie asked as the three of us sat together in the dining-room playing at heroics, pretending every-thing would pass – her eyes were not quite innocent – 'what was Doctor Quigley doing in Matron Tullman's room?'

When morning grey seeps through we learn more. The deputy and the storekeeper creep down to check on our safety, their sooty red-rimmed eyes marked with horror. Mr Cole had gone rushing to his burning store to find Captain Brodie gawking like a pleased kid at a bonfire night. Madness! Idiocy! 'What in God's name's going on?' the storekeeper asked. 'Oh, I'm just watching it,' the superintendent says, cool as you like. 'I've shot the doctor and the matron and I tried to get Leggat. I missed the bugger but he can wait. And as for you, you'd better clear off while you've got the chance. I'm going to clean up this place. Get rid of the vermin.'

It's a rollcall. It's appalling. It's almost funny.

And the children? Davey and Barbara?

The deputy looks at us and then away. 'That explosion,' he says, 'his house. They were inside.'

We all swim in blood.

There's an end to everything. Two of the blacks set off in a skiff to get help from the mainland. Another rows to the quarantine settlement on U-millie for medical help. The last of the rifles are handed out to police boys told to shoot on sight.

What was it I used to boast? I've always tried to run a respectable place?

As the sun comes up there is another explosion from the jetty below Shippers Vale. The house rocks. Glasses shatter. We trample through terror and blood. It is too much. A nightmare. Goggle-eyed Essie sidles in, Peg trailing, to say that the superintendent has blown up Doebin's launch and in the drizzling morning is heading in a runabout for U-millie. 'Tucker,' she explains. 'He need tucker real bad. Store bin gone.'

He is isolating us.

The day crawls by in tensions. There is nothing to do but wait.

Shamelessly we cringe in the house and live through another night. A medical orderly on U-millie has come over by barge and dressed the doctor's and matron's wounds. Captain Brodie, he says, was given water and meat and set off for Noogoo Island to sit out the day. He spoke rationally, the orderly reports, but kept a revolver at the ready.

'Poor man,' Leonie says surprisingly. 'Poor man.'

In the second dawn we keep watch from our verandah, our eyes fixed on the jetty and the water beyond. The settlement is deserted, the women hiding among the trees near the dormitories. Leggat has mustered the police boys, who handle their guns with reluctance. They like Uncle Boss.

Shame, here.

The white lords retreat as the superintendent in a scarlet bathing costume steps ashore from the runabout holding a rifle. A small wind riffles his hair in an orphan splash of sun. Two of the black boys sent to deal with

51

the crisis are hiding in the mango trees near the waterfront. From our verandah we can see the branches shake as they crawl along the limbs into foliage cover. But a third young man steps forward. It's Billy Cooktown's older brother Manny. His skinny body trembles in his ragged shirt and shorts as he handles with bravado the rifle issued by deputy Leggat. 'Stop, boss!' he cries, inching towards the crazed figure in the bathing suit. The superintendent smiles. 'So they have to send my boys to get me,' he says. 'Where are all those yellow bastards hiding, eh?'

'Please boss,' Manny says. 'Please.'

The superintendent raises his rifle and takes another step along the jetty.

'You put that gun down, eh?' Manny pleads.

The superintendent answers with a shot fired into the moving tree branches and automatically the boy with the rifle replies. Question. Response.

Brodie screams once with the shock of it and falls onto the splintered planks, blood seeping from a hole in his stomach.

It was Leggat's voice I heard before and behind that blast. I would swear to it in any court of law.

'Shoot to kill!' he had ordered.

Where is the borderline between innocence and guilt, that perilous divide Captain Brodie trod?

The police boys brought the superintendent back on a litter beneath cloud that had swaddled the whole island in threat. There was no break in that muffling velvet. They put Captain Brodie on a stretcher in what was left of the charred hospital. Cowards – I include myself – emerged from corners in time for the police launch from the mainland. The superintendent died that afternoon, his lips refusing reasons. His body was taken aboard the *Malita* along with Doctor Quigley and the matron, the storekeeper and his wife and Mrs Leggat, who seemed to have lost her English and was reduced to cries of outrage and grief in German.

At a sobersides meal that evening Mr Vine announced that he, too, would be leaving when the launch returned. Only some foolish sense of obligation kept him here. 'Doctor Quigley,' he informed us as he fiddled uninterestedly with his cold cuts and salad, 'had written his resignation anyway. He told me he'd been thinking about it for some time.'

Leonie raised a flushed face distorted by emotional drench and cried, 'But he can't! All the blacks, poor things. The babies! All those old people!'

Mr Vine looked at her over the tops of his glasses. 'They did very well without us for thousands of years. In fact, my dear, they did a lot better. In any case, there'll be a replacement. We're all replaceable.'

That's the pity of it.

And we too would be gone. There were so many things now I would never fully understand, yet I was resigned to that, to my ignorance of the world. Life is too brief.

But Leonie and Claire had all the time I had wasted and an avidity for understanding. Since I first howled into the light, I have lived through changes that are merely the beginning of things I simply accept, although now my daughters claim that they are dragging me screaming into a new, a different, place.

There they will be, the pair of them, like figureheads against the guardrail of the prow, the salt from speeding waters turning their hair into a mass of briny knots, their profiles carving the wind.

Sitting here watching Mr Vine struggle with his supper, struggling with my own, I am impatient to leave.

Things are always better, I assure myself, somewhere else.

And how do I know?

I know. But that's another story.

Bin clearin, his dadda said. All time bin clearin.

And then the buildin of the bladey-grass humpies and more people come from all over, from up near Cape Grafton where they found the footprint of the first blackman in the rock. Sacred, that place. First blackman. And then more migaloo come, white ladies who talk bout God all the time and teacher show them how to read migaloo.

Chant chant chant.

He gets bigger. He works on the rock gang. They clear trees and roll stones and rocks to load them onto a cart. They blow up dead coral to pound, make lime. They plant coconut trees and mangoes.

No sittin under them trees. Mustn't stay in migaloo place. Uncle Boss he build hospital he call it with timber brought over on the schooner Clyde. But first they build

houses for the migaloo, proper houses with tin roofs. Houses
for the storeman and the new nurse she look out for hospital,
black girls' sleep house, sleep house for boys. And later, eh,
school and maybe little church.

Work work work.

Then more people. Men in chains who were put into
camps and set to clear roads and put up buildings and every
Friday they all line up, his dadda, mumma, uncles, for
tucker rations: flour, sugar, salt, rice, corn beef, maybe,
sometimes little bit syrup.

It was hard. Too hard, sometime. But there was his
dadda and mumma and Jericho and Billy gettin bigger now.
An he got new brother, Normie. Yowl yowl yowl. This
humpy too small, mumma say.

Uncle Boss give out lollies sometime when he feelin
good. An Mrs Uncle Boss a real nice lady. Special days
she let her kids play with him, him and Davey go fishin,
climbin, swimmin. Too bad when them bells went. Crack
your head! That Davey he got so brown couldn't tell
them apart, the missus say. Which one's Manny? she ask.
And laugh. Then Davey he go away to school on the
mainland.

The boss he start football team. Still got photo. There's
me in the back row and Uncle Boss sittin so good-lookin
down front, little smile on face. He train us real hard. The

missus laugh a lot them days, laugh and keep Uncle Boss
sweet till she get sick. Then it all change so fast.

How you keep up?

THERE'S A STORY IN THIS

THERE'S A STORY IN THIS, he told himself, idiot new-chum sailor, his muscles hauling the dinghy through the sinews of water. Blistered hands, raw with salt, blistered face, his burning palms skidding pain on the oars, rowlocks wobbling, tides shoving or dragging. And the sun. The sun the sun the sun over eye-searing blue.

I am porous, he decided, swing dip pull. Porous. How often had he commiserated with, encouraged, sometimes envied those scribblers who had haunted his office in the Great Portland Road with their manuscripts, doggy from too much travelling, long mendicant lines of writers over the work of whose lucky few he had swung dipped pulled with editorial comment that usually offended and shoved them up on their rickety high horses, unwilling to change even a comma.

All this I'll put down.

He would write his own version of those eviscerated thrillers, adventure yarns, travellers' tales he had passed

61

from his desk to copy editor and on to the presses, overcome by the throbbing egos that picked up their newly birthed book with its garish jacket as if it were the Bible Koran Torah that would change its reader's world.

God! He was living all that stuff!

And the land-shelf drew closer hour by hour.

Wouldn't say how he got here, didn't have to, in those days when it was easy to sail in on a British passport, no questions asked. I mean, the accent was enough, not quite Oxbridge but passably rounded and honed from a not very successful private school near Eastbourne – swing dip drag – and not that he had anything to hide except a festering boredom with grubby London, the class pecking orders, people having to know their place. What was his place, for Christ's sake? So he had tried the States first, home of the democratic brave and the free, going straight to the heart of it, New York, staring at the non-compassionate features of the goddess of liberty doing a *matrona caritatis* over the harbour and the stone towers but not offering a living hand.

He'd trudged the streets of Manhattan looking for a job in publishing, which was all he knew, and found nothing as the city built up for the big crash. He was a foreigner, wasn't he, despite the language – his accent marked him! – and perhaps even then the publishing houses could detect the stench of the Depression coming up the East River. Finally he landed a come-down job as proofreader in a fly-by-night firm on West Twenty-third that published cheap westerns and romantic novels

(*Wuthering Heights* with tits, his literate boss told him). Three weeks later they went down the drain together, a terse note from his vanished employer gummed to his locked cubby-hole, and he took a train to the west coast, jotting down notes for the book he was never to write. Mourned, he told himself, dragging savagely at the oars, by those jolly black train stewards who might never read about themselves and the mid-west towns the train rattled through, towns with their lovely clapboard houses and elm-lined streets that would remain the mirage in his skull rather than the adumbration on paper. Ah shit! he shouted to a nagging gull. Shit!

What about now?

There was nothing for him in Los Angeles either, that slick coastal city plunged into its affair with celluloid dreams. He shook his head clear of links with the written word and took a job as a hotel doorman in Beverly Hills, capitalising on the flair of his accent. They liked that and he liked the climate, the unbruised days of sun and sea-waft and hoyden blue above the coastal range.

One day as he swung open the door of a limousine that slid in under the *porte-cochère*, he was surprised to find himself face to face with one of his authors, a self-confident scribe who had never understood the folly of the dangling participle. Eyes met, held. 'Good lord!' the pukka British voice called ripely. 'It is – isn't it – Gerald? Gerald Morrow?'

He had tightened his doorman's aplomb against intrusion and murmured, 'This way, sir,' and snapped gloved fingers (My God! Mickey Mouse!) for a bellhop to take the bags, staring out from the indignity of his epauletted uniform and garishly decorated cap at the palm trees along the avenue.

'Sorry, old chap,' the British voice persisted. 'My mistake.' And winked.

He found he had been tipped a quarter.

But – cheers! – that was the one, the very one who, it had been reported at one of those nasty book launchings (stale cheese nibbles, cheap wine), had stated loudly over a glass of rough red that he was considering moving to another publisher who would at least bring out a second edition. That portly traveller who vanished behind swing doors looked as if his bank balance realised fourth and even fifth reprints. Morrow wished he had shouted after his retreating insolent saunter, There must be a million readers out there who crave boredom! Who love the dangling participle! Who wallow in truisms and fatuous theorisings! You tell 'em, Rim! You tell 'em. Slap in your popular political aphorisms, buddy, but don't make 'em think!

He glared at the frantic glassy morning of Beverly Hills, the boulevard already packed with characters who looked like extras, girleens longing to be discovered, fluttering in deliberately contrasting pairs, brunette with blonde; muscular young men with simulated cowboy rolls (Ah sit easy in the saddle!), and the cruisers in stretch cars examining the scene. One morning on his day off he had gone to a popular breakfast bar patronised by the rich, the gossip columnists, the stars, the would-be stars and the writers who worked for the moguls. The brash self-exposure sickened him. The shrilling from table to table. The self-importance. The dropped names. He couldn't even find it funny. The sadness of it made him gag.

Impulse!

Swing dip drag.

He had, he remembered, slashing at water, looked up and down the boulevard checking taxi and car movements under the *porte-cochère*. The hotel was bustling with guests arriving, departing, under coils of noisy greetings. Almost involuntarily he found himself abandoning his post to walk steadily and flint-faced past reception and head for the small change-room in the basement where he peeled off those Mickey Mouse gloves, tossed cap, circus coat and trousers onto a chair and pulled on his own worn flannels and jacket. Then he stalked back to the front desk and dumped his fancy dress in front of the reception clerk.

'Checking out,' he said. 'Or as you people so quaintly put it, I quit.' To mutterings of outrage, muffled before guests, he strolled casually out the front door past the potted palms, out under the canopy and along the boulevard with the other wackers.

Madness is contagious.

Petrifaction of the spirit. His own diagnosis. Begun, that stony crusting, in the upstairs London offices of that second-rate publishing company on the Great Portland Road, his heart brain soul whatever metastasised as the years whined by, each year itself calcified by bad weather and failed ventures. He burrowed beneath books. The words he shovelled about and out during his working hours were not those he heaped on himself. You and me, Tristram, he often murmured, hauling unwilling feet along the pavement.

Rereading Sterne he identified with the delicacy of mania that could extract magic from banality. 'You and me, friend.' And he whispered it now, heaving his dinghy through the furrowed blue of Halifax Bay. Shandy lay, perilously soggy, on a pack in the bows. This should make the old parson feel good, taking a sea voyage in the Antipodes. All this ozone and salt wind. Just the thing for that groin-stricken uncle!

How he had tunnelled under that comforter of words, or plunged into travellers' tales from antick lands, madmen's memoirs of the South Pacific, the while his wife (yes, he had one of them in those days – inner-London sophisticate with a wild Ancient Mariner eye and flawed morals) chided his dullness, chafed against the cramped flat in Earls Court and the unhoggish quality of his lovemaking that quickly degenerated into a dreaded marital obligation.

He met authors.

He found them a self-adulating crowd, especially those suffering from the print-fever of a first novel, pressing on with febrile flushes that abated only after years of vicious reviews or no reviews at all or the realisation that perhaps it was merely a jobber's drudge and that any glamour attaching to the daily tedium of rubbing words together and organising them into attractive patterns was a glamour created by newsprint about those rare and mythic figures who created blockbusters or intellectual marginalia.

Ooh woo woo! What a little Remington can doo ooh ooh!

Blockbusters, he snarled, rowing. I have invented a new word! Thinking of the mediaeval wooden blocks for the painful processing of religious text upon text. *Ars moriendi!* What a joke! This story, this journey, would crack the wood apart.

He attended readings. He heard poets with poetry voices awed by their own genius.

Godalmighty, he had said, reeling home from that first contact with Sanford Rim still brimful with Pacific island strategy, a latter-day Pierre Loti (where was his poor bugger of a wife?) who was later to greet him in a flash hotel on Sunset Boulevard.

'Really!' his own wife reprimanded. 'Language! You know I simply cannot bear such ...' She was busy burning kippers.

He had glared at her. Already he knew her moral scruples extended no further than her tongue. He suspected infidelity but could never be sure. Not until one evening in spring when he returned home a day early from a publishers' conference in Manchester to discover his wife writhing in the arms of Sanford Rim himself.

67

'And who the hell are you?' he had asked, feigning offensive ignorance.

Rim was struggling with bedclothes and undergarments.

'I could well ask the same thing.'

God! The insolence!

He listened to his wife bleat. She was needing help with knickers. She had wanted, she said, to dissuade Rim from leaving the firm. Her actions, she explained, were more in the nature of public relations. She said.

'You never could spell, could you?' he had hissed.

'I have no idea what you mean.' In snowstorms of bed linen.

'Oh for Christ's sake!' he cried. She was so thick.

He emptied his wardrobe and crammed clothes into bags while Sanford Rim slipped quietly downstairs and the outer door banged after him.

His wife sobbed in triplets. 'He means nothing to me!' she kept saying. 'Absolutely nothing.'

Her words weren't worth answering.

A bachelor flat with a stunning view of gasometers. Divorce. (That was in the whispering days!) He wasn't tempted to remarry. Perhaps his wife had summed up his libido accurately after all. When the divorce was finalised (his presence only in court) he learned that she had joined forces with a soft-goods salesman from Glasgow who had run away from his wife as well. What a coupling!

He made no further enquiries. And he didn't see Sanford Rim until ten years later on that hard yellow morning in Los Angeles.

Flight number two.

This was predating airline terminology.

This was getting to be a habit.

He signed up as galley-hand/steward on the first cargo boat heading west, a lumbering rust-bucket shipping building materials, pumps, generators and primitive refrigeration plants to the Pacific Islands. He resisted the siren quality of Hawaii; he ignored with some difficulty the lush invitations of Pango Pango. He stepped ashore in Brisbane, the first landfall on the great flat plate of the southern continent, surprised that the unfinished quality of the place delighted him. After flashing his British passport and banking accrued pay, he set about exploration in a town that was sticking like a rash along the banks of its river, houses pasted on roller-coaster hills. While he decided what he might do he rented a cheap room in a boarding house in Spring Hill. Really he didn't want to do anything.

He was drunk with anonymity, with being where no one knew him or even cared to know. The heat that October in Brisbane town induced torpor. No one hurried. People dragged themselves off and on the rattling tramcars, straggled across streets, leaned across bars, hunched over café tables. It was a braces-and-singlets town. He thought of Los Angeles and its scurriers with their grim manic race towards personal destinies. Here, no one was waiting to be discovered. Not even the horses waiting with their anachronistic hansom cab outside the law courts. They suitably drooped.

He caught buses south to Cleveland, north to Shorn-cliffe. He ate fish and chips in seedy eateries on the beachfronts and found his restless and curious eyes seared by glinting water, broiling sky. Once he hired a rowing boat and took himself out to the muddy islands of the bay and paddled along mangrove-fringed shorelines, his senses rinsed clean by a rawness of salty air and the Trades scented with supple landfalls. But after, it was always back to the boarding house, now filling up with jobless men who couldn't pay their rent, who sat staring hopeless as they listened to the wireless each humid evening after a day spent tramping the streets.

He felt guilty because he was still solvent.

All day, walking past the soup kitchens, the public halls where community singing was conducted to keep the jobless chipper and their minds off empty stomachs. All day, past the tatty ill-patronised corner stores, and his feet limping under/over blankets of heat down to the Valley and the trains, the deadbeats waiting for the pubs to open, and then the long walk out past the peeling houses to New Farm and the park beside the river where the bums rolled over on the grass under the trees, chasing the shade and wondering behind the bony structures of their starved faces what the hell it was all about. Now and again they remembered fighting for a myth known as king and country. King and country weren't doing too much for them now.

Those who still could hawked up phlegmy gobbets of Flanders and the Somme.

There were no jobs and sometimes when he squatted under the trees with them and talked about it he knew himself a hypocrite with money still in the bank, even though that money was shrinking. But it shrank slowly because he was a careful man and all the time, all the time, there was that itch, the urge to move on, away from the groans and the snores through the thin partitions of his boarding-house room, the mealtime gobblings, the hopelessness of bodies crammed into and with despair.

On the train north he had a compartment to himself during the day, but at night the soot-filled carriage filled up with men who had been riding the roof or the goods van and who sneaked in to stretch out for a few hours. They had to keep moving or the sustenance allowance was refused. Some of them lay awake all night, eaten by hunger, smoking the painfully thin rollies they made with careful skinny fingers. Most of them didn't want to talk. It was the same old story that bored even the tellers.

When Morrow got off the train in Townsville on a wide-eyed November morning, it was into a heat brilliant as glass. Jesus! he whispered under sweat. He found a room at the Exchange opposite the creek and for the first couple of days spent his time in a settler's chair on the wide verandah watching the few cars and the horse-carts rocking along Flinders Street.

Work. He had to keep repeating the word, whipping reluctance.

The local newspaper didn't want him. The one lending library regretted. He began searching the columns of the daily. The pickings were small.

Here he was, a silly bookish fellow, roosted on a pub verandah in a lost town of a lost continent.

One advertisement drew his eye again and again. On an island group thirty miles north there was a vacancy for a works' foreman. Why it had not been seized at once in this town of jobless men jogged enquiry. A kind of island hell, he was told. Almost a prison. Boongs, one man explained contemptuously. If you like that sort of thing . . . Should I not? he asked himself, looking at his useless grammarian hands, looking at his age looking back at him in the mould-spotted mirror above the communal hand-basin at the Exchange.

He filled in the requisite forms. (It was a state government position.) His accent was educated. He lied, just a little, about his experience. After all, were would-be writers in that first flush of publication even as intelligent as those despised indigenes? They were all turning out primitive carvings.

He would never know whether it was desperation or departmental snobbery on the part of the interviewing officer that gave him the job. (Desperation, came the snarled answer as he rowed into late morning across Halifax Bay. And there's a story in that, by God!) For within the week he found himself and his suitcase on a government launch rocking up the coast to Doebin.

Ah, paradise enow! Yessir!

Ashore was syrup-thick with shade trees exotically unfamiliar. Behind, blue acid. Dazed with newness he was guided along jetty and up sandy tracks to the hutlike administration centre by a weedy man with a ginger moustache that so filtered the offered name he forgot it immediately. A frowning black boy toted his bag.

So much newness would splinter memory. Bits. Pieces.

But this was only the beginning to the story.

Swing dip drag.

Should he change to present tense? For trendy immediacy? In his burning swollen paw one oar skidded. He nearly lost it. He decides on the change.

Captain Brodie, superintendent of Doebin reserve, is a twitchy youngish man with a – is it kingly? – assured manner as he stares across his desk at the new arrival and his splendid vowels. The verbal splendour appears to irritate. There is no moustache, but the phantom of it. There is no swagger stick. But there is the phantom of that.

'I don't know whether,' the dapper superintendent says, measuring his words, 'you are really the man for ... What I mean is, did the interviewing panel tell you what it's like here? The nature of the work?'

'Not precisely,' Morrow answers, trying for charm. He gives the regretful twisted grin he had once used on rejected authors. 'No brochure. No pretty pictures.'

The superintendent emits a sharp sigh rather like a hiss. His face is beginning to redden. 'Not just organisational skills,' he tells Morrow, 'but practicality. It needs practical skills. Practical.'

The flush deepens. The fingers clench and unclench fascinatingly on the desk edge and embarrassed Morrow takes time out to observe the room, the wooden shutters that slice a leaf-spattered seascape, the curved shining back of a native hoeing a garden bed, the photograph of a tired woman (wife?) watching them from the top of a filing cabinet.

He murmurs deprecatingly that he thinks he could cope. Does he want to cope? Again he sees the grass houses of the settlement glimpsed as he had walked from the jetty, the black faces of women turning their shyness aside. 'I take it the job is merely supervisory?'

Captain Brodie begins a syncopated and impatient tapping. 'Good Heavens, man! You've got to have some practical experience in a place like this. My God, the things they do to me, those government bastards! Sorry. Not your fault. But do you know anything about road building, carpentry, drainage? Well, do you? Be honest now.'

Morrow coughs and looks directly into the superintendent's crazy blue eye.

'I rather gathered they couldn't find anyone else willing to come here. Perhaps that's –'

'Are you a penitent?' the superintendent demands. His voice becomes terrifyingly soft. 'Oh God, what a shambles! Are you after martyrdom, sainthood?'

Is he? Morrow watches Brodie swallow unpalatable lumps of departmental gristle before he manages, 'Well, not your fault, Mr Morrow. We'll simply have to make the best of it for the time being, until we can get things sorted out.' He repeats the words 'sorted out, sorted out', seeming to become lost for a moment in mumbles. 'Paperwork, perhaps. Returns. Just do your best, eh? You know,' the superintendent leans forward becoming stagily confidential, 'they leave the whole damn thing to me as it is, anyway. I've made this place. This entire place. Created it. It's my . . . well . . . my little kingdom as it were. You understand? That's why I . . .'

The words he might have said ghost out through the shutters.

He met (opting for the past) the other white workers: the doctor, the matron, the teacher, the storekeeper. 'And you know my deputy, Leggat.' Their features, like those of the missionaries, were defeated by the newness of landscape.

And he met his landlady and her daughters in their kingdom across the little bay and unpacked his belongings in a hut suspiciously like a *boi-haus* at the far end of the boarding-house garden.

75

'I'm sorry about this,' Mrs Curthoys (that was her name, wasn't it?) was saying. 'But we are full up at the house at the moment.' She sighed, quite prettily he noticed, and made a regret signal with her handsome mouth. 'But feel free to come and go as you wish. The living-room –' lots of smiles and motherly intent, 'meals, of course. The piano. You'll have more privacy here and the girls, Peg and Essie, will look after your laundry and so on.'

Your daughters? he had foolishly asked.

Arpeggios of disclaiming laughter.

He apologised for missing their names. Leonie. Claire.

Reading? he wondered. There was a kerosene lamp beside the stretcher in his room but he had never worked one before and made useless shruggings until Mrs Curthoys gave him a fast tutorial on adjusting the wick, suggesting, half-whimsy, half-menace, he be careful to turn it out before sleeping. Fire, she warned with plump waving hands. Fire. They were so dependent on pumps and of course . . . Hands flung consequences outward.

'I know nothing about pumps,' he said mildly.

'But I thought . . .'

He shrugged. They exchanged tight smiles.

'My goodness!' Mrs Curthoys said. 'You certainly will need coddling.'

After all, he lasted barely two months in his gestures towards realism.

The clerical work was nothing. The rollcalling of his gangs of resentful black workers took up the early part of his morning as he directed them from one assignment to another, watched by moustache-fondling Leggat whose stroking fingers were implicit with criticism. Morrow marvelled how, in that flattening heat, the blacks could hew, shift rock, dig trenches, lug bags of earth and sand, heave timber. Those skinny legs and arms! Those long-enduring faces! When Leggat took time off to work in his own garden, Morrow helped supervise as well the doling of rations and was overseen on these occasions by a grudging storekeeper.

'They're pitiful amounts, aren't they?' He could hardly believe the single scoops of flour and sugar, the mugs of treacle, the rare small lumps of corned meat.

'Don't gab about what you don't understand,' Cole said flatly. 'We get lots of do-goods like you coming in wanting to change the world. Why don't you stick to what you know, eh? Whatever that is.'

Squashed.

He helped the churlish boatman direct unloadings at the jetty in sprays of obscenity. 'This is your big chance, you silly bugger,' Jardine told him as they watched four blacks stagger shoreward with crates of meat from the supply launch, 'to get off this fucker of a place. No boat now for a month, probably. Longer, if the weather drops.'

'We'll see,' he replied.

And, 'Sundowners at six!' Captain Brodie announced

brightly, gliding up behind both of them. A royal command. Morrow was gummed in by sweat and curling seas, sinking below his Plimsoll line into the stink of rotting fish, leaves, black bodies and his own mortal reek.

That was an order, sundowners, clutched-at colonial bathos, to be taken on the verandah of the superintendent's house, the white *mastas* keeping up the flag, outpost of empire on the no-go area of Coconut Avenue. Already he had attended five of these weekly gatherings, listened to the repetitive gossip, the sly malicious digs, watched with interest the abrasive stirrings of Doctor Quigley, deputy Leggat, and the lower-order resentment of the storekeeper and the boatman who wrestled silently with patronage so that he could sense it stick in their gullets. Wives clustered. The schoolteacher, a sad dilapidated Scot, simmered over a grudging whisky. The bottom ranks got sozzled.

Repetition can provide rhythm and lyric beauty.

Week one. Week two. Week three. Week four. Week five.

Week six brought changes.

Year-end was upon them.

Storeman Cole's wife remained at home. Leggat sulked. Jardine, who was aware that the whole settlement would crumble without his tending of generators, pumps and launch engines, became abusive and told Captain Brodie that he was a bullying prick. Prick? Mrs Leggat had never heard the word. She was Viennese. 'Vot iss prick?' she asked over the teacups. No one answered. Mrs Curthoys pressed her lips together, fighting smiles.

'A failed prison farm!' drunken Jardine was shouting.

'I'd never call it that,' the superintendent said softly, watching his dying wife, more out of focus than the bad snapshot on the filing cabinet, hand round tea to the ladies. Mrs Brodie had been permanently damaged by weather and the unrelenting energy of her husband. Pregnant, Morrow realised, eyeing the thickening waist, the drawn cheeks. In other rooms lurked a son and daughter whose voices played harmonics above this drawing-room ritual so that he was suddenly cowed, wincing over the sharp sherry in his glass, by the merciless progress of decades and the number of his years. How could he believe in the him-ness of self? What proved he was he, chipped at and smoked out in his fourth-plus decade? An age that the unseen young behind those timber walls would regard as having no future, for that was how he had thought at their age: that the world and its prospects ended for anyone older than he was at that precise ripe-for-plucking time.

He decided on desperate small talk with Mrs Curthoys who was holding her cup in a genteel way and enquired about the ages of those unseen voices, though he knew.

'Eleven. Twelve.'

'Ah! The world is their oyster.'

'Perhaps.' Mrs Curthoys appeared hesitant, regretful, not as confident as he'd imagined through six weeks of breakfasts and dinners. 'And for you too, I suppose. In a way. For all of us, really. New beginnings.'

Foolishly idealistic she suggested that the world was

anyone's oyster at any age. Was it possible to throw off prejudices, habits, old sins, old charities and start peeled back in such a place? Sometimes in the last few weeks he had found himself lusting after the stone lace of Lisbon and St Roque, the barley-sugar balconies of Venice, places where unknown language alone guaranteed outer silence and inner, instead of this chantilly of tropic leaves, an unstationary fabric that wove new patterns by the minute.

Stasis. He wanted that, he thought.

And what used you do? they had asked on his arrival.

Books. I was in the book trade.

You write books?

Afraid not.

They lost interest then. He watched jaws drop, eyes flicker away because not even authorial pretension could absolve his uselessness.

Mrs Brodie has died in a welter of blood despite all Doctor Quigley's ministrations.

Overheard half-sentences at breakfast hint at a miscarriage and a physician too much under the weather from the latest sundowners to save mother or child. The matron, it is reported, was sulking at the vital time and had stalked off to walk round Settlement Bay. A lovers' tiff?

Since this tragedy Captain Brodie has, understandably

enough, behaved erratically. He would like to apportion blame, Morrow can tell, but he holds himself in a deadly check that merely aggravates his wretchedness and fury.

For days after the sad little funeral there was oppressive gloom and then he came suddenly to life with irrational tantrums, shouted and conflicting orders, his cringing kids dodging parental demands.

'Must keep going,' he announced in the office at a briskly summoned meeting of staff. 'My wife would have wanted that. Very devoted to this place and what we're doing. Absolutely devoted.' His eyes glanced involuntarily at the top of the filing cabinet. But he had already removed the photo and his gaze drifted away and lost itself in trees.

The men sat in silence not knowing what to say. It was as if the superintendent, launched on private grief, had forgotten they were in the room. The clock on his desk tocked seconds, tocked minutes, and through that embarrassment came the sound of a stifled whimper and the gulp-snuffle of repressed tears.

Deliberately Jardine emitted an offensive belch.

'Right!' Captain Brodie snapped, coming to. 'What the hell are you all sitting about for, eh? There's work to be done. Let's get on with it. I'll have no slacking.'

Then the boatman, head waggling, eyes rolling, semaphored insulting forehead tappings that the superintendent missed.

'Really,' Leggat reproved when they had walked some distance along the avenue, 'the poor devil's had a rough time, Jardine. No need for you to be so bloody rude.'

'You arse-licker,' the boatman said. 'Thinking of taking over?'

Morrow lagged behind them both, unwilling to involve himself in partisanship but sufficiently slow for the pounding feet of the superintendent to catch up with him.

'One minute!' Brodie was shouting. He grabbed a frantic handful of Morrow's shirt. 'One minute, you men!' Breathless, he could hardly puff his words out. 'Drinks as usual, eh? No need to let old habits die. Sunday week. Same time. Joan would have wanted that.'

But that was to be the last party for all of them.

Morrow hated to remember.

An argument had broken out between Doctor Quigley and the superintendent.

'You power-hungry bastard,' the doctor was railing, careful to remain vertical but leaning ever so slightly across his brogue and a fifth drink. 'You might run the island but you don't run my hospital, damn you. You don't run my health programme.' Mrs Leggat was so startled she slopped tea. 'This place needs someone new. New brooms, boy. New brooms. You've been here too long, you power-drunk little man. What the place needs is fresh blood.'

The superintendent's face went white.

'Blood!' he roared. 'Oh God, you allowed plenty of

that! You let my wife die, you incompetent! Let her bleed to death while you watched, you slipshod butcher.' He swung a punch with a hand still clutching a whisky that splattered in the doctor's eyes. Yelps of pain. Female screams. The two men waltzed, locked, onto the verandah where the doctor's nose dripped redly onto the boards along which Cole waddled his bulk to pull them apart.

'A conspiracy!' the superintendent was shouting. 'A conspiracy to take over.' He was marooned between sobs and rage. His voice bellowed down the darkening funnel of Coconut Avenue to the listening thatch of the bladey-grass huts where his work boys sat over their cooking fires.

Morrow had placed his glass carefully on a table and walked towards the steps.

'Don't you bloody go!' screamed the superintendent. 'Who the hell are you to go like this, eh?'

Morrow hadn't known the answer. Who was he indeed!

'I'm no one. Not anyone at all.'

Doctor Quigley was hunched over the rail beside him spluttering mucus and gore.

'I'm the one who'll be remembered!' Brodie shouted. 'I made this place! I created all this!'

'Och, you prognostic bastard!' the doctor roared, swinging about. 'All what at all? All bloody what?'

Matron Tullman kept tugging busily at the doctor's arm. Morrow wondered if venery or concern motivated that over-bright gladeye. 'Come away now, do. Come along, Tom.' She worried the doctor's flesh like a heeler, her fingers snapping at fabric.

Come along, please! To that fruity big Irishman with the velvet vowels which would punctuate mealtimes with a dash of French, a slice of Ovid! For nearly seven weeks Morrow had observed him at breakfast rolling his handsome eyes at the elder Miss Curthoys whose response, he gauged, was not all innocence. Despite an air of white muslin and sprigged flowers, a suggestion of unruliness in the curls, there was an acolyte fervour as she leaned across buttered toast, lips parted to absorb. Morrow had wondered and wondered.

Ah, the mess of things, he thought. The mess when hurtling human comets collide. His heart ached for something lost so many years ago. He was unsure of the exact nature of that loss, and trying not to think of his once wife found himself sleepless in the *boi-haus*, tossing under the mosquito net to the noisy silence of rainforest and the steady applause of the sea.

He walked away from the superintendent's house, shouts rioting behind him and heavy clouds forming a slurry of black surging air that threatened the whole island. He was a dab at symbols. He had had enough. He would present himself the next morning at Brodie's office and, I am not suited, he would say. I don't think this is what I want.

He didn't get a chance to say that.

The superintendent sat restlessly behind his desk, the

ruffled ashy sea behind his own ruffled drink-rotten skull. A hand intercepted Morrow's opening words.

'Please. You mustn't judge us by that little outburst last night. Let me explain myself. Things, well, things are difficult. In the beginning, you understand, I handled this place alone. Did the lot. Ran the boats, supervised the building, looked after the blacks. They like me. I'm fair. Tough but fair. They call me Uncle Boss, you know. God, I've seen cooboos here grow into men and women. Watched them marry, have kids of their own. Twelve years of it. And damn little help.'

Morrow heard him out, all the time pondering the nature of isolation, the difference between withdrawal surrounded by others and withdrawal surrounded by no one.

Abruptly he said, 'I must leave. I'm sorry. I simply cannot stay.'

The superintendent's mouth tightened. 'There's no supply launch for a month, Morrow. You must do this through the proper channels.'

'Rubbish! You have other boats.'

'For settlement business. Not for some employee whim.' He smiled, mouth downturned. We shall suffer together, the smile seemed to say. 'Don't let's prolong this. Shouldn't you be down at the stores?' He consulted a roster. 'Cole is expecting you right this minute.' The superintendent raised his voice and shouted to the adjoining room, 'Leggat! Leggat! Take Morrow down to the ration lines, will you?'

The deputy appeared, coaxing his moustache, his eyes

85

shifting busily. As they left they heard the superintendent lock the door behind them.

In the avenue below the administration office, Morrow shook off the weedy man's arm. He surprised a look of gloating on the features watching his.

'Get your hands off me,' he ordered. 'I'm not staying.'

He strode through the deputy's protests back to the *boi-haus* and packed his bag with the nothings of those weeks. The housegirl who was sweeping the path outside watched him as he stamped past to the boarding house, up over the little hill above the beach and down to Jardine's shed, beyond goodbyes even to those who had been kindest.

The boatman, skin gleaming with grease and sweat and a hot impudence as he stared up at Morrow, was working at a bench, stripping a motor down.

'Need something, mate?'

Exposed, driven, forced to beg favours from this lout!

He said, 'I need a boat. Can you sell me one?'

'Can I what?'

'A boat. A small rowboat. I want to get off here.'

Jardine grinned, his teeth glinting foxily through oil smears.

'Well, this is sudden. Place getting too much for you?'

'Just a simple answer. Can you?'

'It's possible.' Jardine laid down a spanner delicately. 'Anything's possible – at a price.' And, 'Get on with that fuckin job, Sambo, while the boss and me talk business, eh?' Manny Cooktown, face sullen, rubbed his hands on a bit of waste and went back to hammering a sheet of

86

metal, while Jardine steered Morrow out to the uncut grass behind the workshed where untidy piles of pipe and wood scrap foundered in weeds. There was a dinghy overturned beneath a rain tree. 'There's that,' Jardine said, pointing. 'Still seaworthy. Sold it to some drongo a couple of years back. Came to settle on Culgaroo. A stupid bastard. Didn't know a fuckin thing about survival. I got tired of having to go over to help him out of his messes but Brodie was always a sucker for these up-themselves Poms. Said he was a writer. The stupid coot had dragged along a wife and kid. They didn't stay long, mate. Anyway, he was always shooting off and leaving them to fend for themselves. Left the boat behind when he cleared out. I'll sell you that.'

'How much?'

'Thirty.'

'Twenty, and a hand lugging it down.'

'Done,' the boatman said quickly. He gave a gross wink. 'You rowing back to town, eh?'

Although Morrow didn't want to explain, didn't want to exchange the smallest of emotional confidences that might bind him to this fellow, he watched satisfaction spread over the boatman's face – the thought of crossing the superintendent welding quitter and stayer into a vile chumminess.

That same day, a small landfall. Two hills linked by palm

groves. A coral beach and sand-spit at the northern end and granite sea-worn cliffs to the south. Rainforest scrub choked with pandanus and wild banana and lit by the dim candles of orchids. In the heart of the island a tea-tree swamp. Symbols persisted.

He discovered all these things on the first day.

A rusting tin hut still leaned into blue winds and hoarded remnants of the last owner: a camp oven, the pole skeletons of makeshift stretchers and half a dozen invoices for supplies made out to Sanford Rim.

The nightmare of it!

Any thoughts he had of staying fled before those ghost reminders as he inspected a half-filled water barrel, a collapsed cesspit and the middens of oyster shells left carelessly near the hut doorway by the gorging writer. But for that! was his resentful reaction as he kicked through a tangle of weed-choked sweet potato vine. But for that!

He walked down to where he had beached the dinghy and sat looking at Doebin three miles away and the airy ellipses cut by two eagles swinging between the islands, envying the birds their indifference to gravity. His shoulders throbbed from rowing, his middle-aged heart pumped too fast and he cursed himself for folly.

Saint John Bosco, he reminded himself, is the patron saint of editors. A prayer mightn't go amiss on this sand-spit, some cowardly aspiration seeking guidance.

At least rest, the saint, someone, advised. Buddy! Morrow said aloud to the nutmeg pigeons, the gulls.

He listed survival possibilities: a few tins of food, a

waterbottle, a lamp filched from the *boi-haus*, matches and a copy of *The Life and Opinions of Tristram Shandy*. Another night before rowing on? He could not bear the loss of face that returning to Doebin would mean. For the rest of the day he tracked the loathsome Rim's inefficiency as beachcomber, checked his failed gardens, wells, even uncovered lost pieces of manuscript damp with the tears of wife and child hauled off to placate a madman's dream. Was *he* less mad? He totted up the pluses of wilderness that cancelled fog and damp and bedsitters and cold-water walk-ups run by landladies with pursed lips. The addition tottered when he realised he had no can-opener. 'No,' he said aloud to the patron saint of editors and that vanished portly author forever poncing through the swing doors of a Los Angeles hotel. 'No no no no! Not yet!'

He attacked one of the tins with a rock and prised open a congealed mess of mince and vegetable. To be eaten with fingers. And as the evening rolled in he was driven mad by sandflies and later mosquitoes that droned in the recesses of the hut. No wonder Rim fled. Moths drummed against the lamp under rain-shout on iron as he lay sleepless waiting for the squall to pass, only to be offered another, a kind of epiphany, when he walked out into a night noisy with water and filled with a surf of stars.

From across the channel came an explosion, and by the time he ran to the sand-spit there was a burst of flame on Doebin, fire hurdling towards that louring hump of mountain, palms black and ragged against orange light.

Crazily he thought of the Strip.

Silence for a moment as he watched, and then the crack of a rifle shot, murderously clear. And then another.

An excuse, he argued within. A reason to row back, offer help, expunge his pigheaded flight. Resentment and pride and the comfortlessness of what he had done all taunted him on that lonely beach and even as he debated, his self-interest was ruptured by more shots and a second detonation that bucked the shoreline. Other fires flared in the settlement, and across the water came screams and cries and then, more terrifyingly, a stabbing and total silence as if everyone were bolted up in some kind of vacuum. While he watched, the flames rose higher in five separate biblical pillars.

Useless, he convinced himself. You would be useless. A craven's plea.

His conscience, jerked this way and that, wouldn't let him wait for dawn. Back in the hut he scrambled his few possessions together, filled the waterbottle at the tank and took the lot down to the boat. Oh God, he kept apologising as he tripped and stumbled on coral lumps, as he fumbled rowlocks and oars into position and dragged the dinghy across the shallows to the deeper water. He was running away again.

Was there no end to the running?

There was certainly a story in this: fleeing fires, fleeing

rifle shots, constantly rationalising his guilt-panic as he pulled away south, trusting to the archipelagic nature of these land lumps to provide resting places. Thirty-five miles if he could do it, stupidly refusing to doubt he could cover those blinding rocking miles down the coast with the sun all day clobbering his neck. You don't have a choice, Bosco told him. The tide and the currents were with him and the relative coolness of the night while he swung dipped pulled, waiting for Havannah Island to loom through the dark.

The rain started again, heavy marbles of water that blinded and confused. Breather to bail with the jagged mince tin. He plastered thoughts of Phoenicians and Vikings like medallions on his mind-screen, watched long-running silents of the triremes pitching across the Mediterranean or the longboats slicing the waters of the North Sea. A change of programme. He thought of Bligh. How many miles to Batavia? Three thousand from Tofua with only a compass? (*He* didn't have a compass.) And he was flinching at the thought of a mere thirty. (But only one set of clerkly hands and shoulders. No lower-deck swabbers here to share the burden.)

The tide was running him in towards Havannah. Should he let the dinghy drift on the south-east-bearing current or work with it to get beyond that point before daybreak and the enemy of sun? Body muscle against water muscle. Swing dip drag. Tale of an anti-hero.

At first he had been surprised at the ease with which current and boat wedded and at how smoothly he slipped through darkness. In his first fever he had wanted to head directly for the coast opposite, a shorter distance by half, but he knew his chances of landing near a settlement were remote on this unpeopled seaboard. A country without resonance, he said aloud. Or with too much. He looked back to Doebin, now a distant shadow, and the pillars of fire had sagged to red glints.

When the dinghy slid in towards shore at Havannah he was afraid to rest, knowing he had only three hours of tide with him riding the current, racing the dawn. He shipped oars briefly, uncapped the waterbottle and took a gulp. He opened his mouth to the rain and let it drive into him. Then he started rowing again, his skinned palms screaming with every drag of the oars.

After another two hours he could see the bony ridge of Rattlesnake Island watching his folly. The horizon grew a bloody rim through storm cloud. His watch had stopped. Tristram and Uncle Toby paddled for their lives in the water-slop (where's the good doctor?) in the belly of the boat. As the rain eased, the light hardened and he kept pulling on the oars, pulling, bracing himself with chants, with muttered shanties that robbed his breath. To go back, he knew, were tedious as to go o'er.

O blow the man down bullies, he croaked, blow the man down, to me way hey, et cetera. Moving into, There's fire in the cabin and in the fo'c'sle too, to me way hey hee hi ho, accented with each plunge of the blades. Capstan songs. Songs for lowering the sheets. Work songs. But the effort of pitting his voice against the void exhausted, though irony helped.

Deliberately he thought of that fool Rim and his quarter

tip. Rage kept him going through an agony of back and shoulders, the screaming tendons of his neck, the blistered hands now bandaged in pieces of torn shirt. There was little time left before the tide swung around to nudge his boat back the way it had come. Nature's malice. Swing dip drag with the tide turning, his whole body an automaton of pain. Overhead clouds spread canvas without effort, sometimes obscuring the sun and offering a blind to the dazzle of moving waters. He closed his eyes and pulled.

In the late afternoon his boat washed in to a beach at Rattlesnake. Here the mainland was so close but offered only a line of scrub miles from anywhere. He'd never make it on foot. An hour before, he had seen a busybody launch (checking catastrophe?) bouncing north towards Doebin, too far away in the roadstead for his wavings and shoutings that disintegrated in air. Syllables fragmented. The book he was writing, should be writing, broke into chapters, paragraphs, phrases, a litter of unconnected consonants and vowels.

On the beach he dragged the dinghy up above the tide line, drank another two inches from his waterbottle, upturned the boat and crept underneath to sleep.

Soldier crabs crawling across his legs woke him in the early dark. Sandflies worked over exposed sunburned skin, even nagging through the stubble of his jaws. Where, he marvelled, was that otherworld sifter of manuscripts, courted by untalented hacks at cocktail parties and book launchings? Here here here, being nibbled by the real cannibals, unshaven, stinking, peeling, with graveyard breath. At the sea edge he sluiced his head and rinsed out his mouth, ear cocked to tide crash and suck. He thought of them back at the settlement: the whites he barely knew, the blacks he had been dissuaded from knowing. Once he had asked the school-master, Vine, about the families of those he struggled to teach in his makeshift classroom. Vine was a silent man who kept his counsel at boarding-house meals, a book propped open beside his plate. He had mumbled vague-nesses in reply. He avoided friendly gestures, often neglected to appear at those semi-compulsory sundowners (lying, I never drink!) and retreated into some inner abscess of the soul. Like me, Morrow had decided, but was unable to probe beyond.

And there's a book in him too, he said to himself.

He rebound his hands with dry strips of shirt, shoved the dinghy into the water and began rowing again.

He swung the prow towards the mainland, a mere few miles away, determined to follow the coastline closely to the first light, the first welcoming glint of roof. But there was nothing except interminable green shuddering into darkness, the bump of small waves and a sickly quarter-moon lost suddenly in rain.

Swing dip pull.

He heard himself sobbing as he dragged the boat south. Dreamt of hot food, soft beds. He was rowing towards a well-set table, starched napery, cut glass, quacking out what was meant to be laughter. He was no mug pioneer like Rim, determined on hunting copy for his dangling participles and lifestyle. But right at that moment he could, he fancied – swing dip pull – face a sherry party, a bit of a shindig with basso women and soprano males, all vowels impeccable, condemning in sly asides his firm's latest offering while the author, hit with the old print fever, the incandescence of the launch, pranced just out of earshot, courting critics.

But the afterbirth!

That sniffing phoney praise from reviewer pals; the bitcheries from the jealous, the offended. Those sheer resenters!

And then the fade-out. As his own boat was blotted by squall.

Everything fluid, sky and earth. He sensed his little-ness, his cork-bob unimportance in unharnessable tides. By ten that night – measuring hours in pain-lengths – the tide was on the turn but now he was in sight of Magnetic's hummock, shadowy as a stage-prop, and his bobbing craft was nudged inevitably away from shore-comfort towards that looming shadow, shoved out to sea by the gutters near Pallarenda and the speeding shallows on the southern side of the point.

Had he slept, despite his raging hands?

He had rowed through the night under a sky black with storm, the sea chopping viciously at the boat, breaking over the gunwales, the bailing tin afloat. He was drifting along the west coast of Magnetic, hacked at by busy water that kept driving him in towards mangroves near Cockle Bay. Through rain and salt came the smell of sand, earth, leaves. And there he was weeping. Him! Laughing with relief. Journey's end. If he could just round that granite spur he would be in shelter, he knew.

The sky was lightening, revealing shapes. He saw he was too close to the point. Waves smashed themselves apart in black and white on the rocks. Black fangs snapped from the sea. Pulling frantically away, thrusting an oar at shelves that threatened in the scurry of tide and current, he thought cravenly of nothing but survival. Even publishing parties became luridly precious as he gasped for the synthetics he had left behind in London. After all this! To be denied so close!

Swinging about on his seat he faced the prow, using his oars like punt poles, shoving and driving and panting as he wrestled water for a glimpse of beach, a slice of sand-white against darkness. The long jetty down which he had strolled, day tripper, two months before, was a mere few hundred yards away and there was a man fishing. He could make out the hunched figure against sky.

Morrow let out what he thought was a yell, was merely a *craark*. Closer. The man's back was turned. Curses and yells in whispers, frightened of washing past the jetty as his arms refused to match the drubbing waves. He closed his eyes and let the dinghy ride the swell. He was sobbing without knowing, his dried mouth hacking out terrible sounds. He couldn't see, couldn't think. One oar fell from his hand and washed away and he bent forward uselessly after it to pitch giddily into the belly of the boat, floating with Shandy in the bilge. The dinghy thudded against a pile, swung about, cracked, and wedged beneath salt-stinking timbers as green sea washed over.

He was beyond caring.

Someone had dragged him out. The fisherman?

Voices making no sense gabbed in gull cries round his water-blocked ears. He was plastered on sand, a wordless bit of sea-wrack, while a rough stranger paw propped his head and a beaker trickled water between his split lips. There were gobbling sounds. His? Arms hoisted. Carried.

He woke on the verandah of the Dagoombah pub, crusted eyelids first opening on the narrow edges of solidity: the cot, the floorboards, a door leading back to voices; then his eyes glanced towards railing and beyond, blinking at a storm-streaked sky and palm fronds nagged by rain. Between the trees mist dangled like cotton candy.

Someone had placed his dried clothes on a chair.

He absorbed these things, closed his eyes, opened them, tested his feet against the sheet, peeled that back and creaked upright, his entire body stiffened with pain. Even dragging on a shirt made him whimper. He limped his way along the inside courtyard verandah to a bathroom and leaned exhausted against the closed door. From across the room his mirrored face frightened him. Years had piled up.

He had slept all day, he discovered, but at supper that evening the pub was full of speculation, the shootings on Doebin, his own bit of jetsam spewed up by the sea. He shoved mashed potato moistened with gravy between ruined lips, avoiding eyes bright with some kind of noxious interest. Doebin? they asked slyly. He said he wasn't there. You're lucky to be here, eh mate? they said. They examined him as if he were a fugitive while he denied any knowledge. Sure, mate, they said. She's right. The police launch had gone over the day before. Pity they hadn't spotted him, eh? Saved him a bit of sweat.

Morrow sucked painfully at his tea, nodding and nodding. He suspected his accent irritated rather than impressed. Could he flatten vowels to match spirits?

The dining-room was a vast bare space fronting the palms, the beach, the turmoil of darkening waters scored by white. Against one wall a piano, its varnish flaking, exhausted by salt air. A barrier of vertical wooden shutters, open to night and wind, sliced the world into rectangles, sliced the conversation about him.

'No ferry till morning,' the pub owner commented. He leant too close, one pally hand on Morrow's anguished shoulder. 'You be right to go back?' Morrow nodded. 'You can stay on if you want,' the pub owner insisted, sturdily curious. 'No trouble. Plenty of spare rooms this time of the year.'

'No,' he said. 'No thank you.'

He went back upstairs and lay down once more on the verandah stretcher. His bag had been lugged up as well from the wrecked dinghy and the contents spread to dry. *Shandy* was a block of soggy pulp that might never cure. It would take weeks for the Coral Sea to dry out. He rolled to the edge of the bed and lit a cigarette, seeing himself reduced to a wraith of that editorial cog who once sifted adventure yarns for dreamers who could never, not ever, touch the actuality of what he had just lived through. The real thing, he thought with stupid pride. He had experienced the real thing. The thought nourished his bones and he dismissed those London years as abstractions, pointless as the words the fronds beyond the railing were scribbling on wind.

Back in his old room next day at the Exchange there he was, a bruised paper-stuffed man who once peddled whodunnits now absorbing fragments of whodunnit speculation at communal mealtimes: shot the lot . . . No, only the doc and his lady friend . . . Cooked his kids, would you believe? . . . Not true . . . He got his, shot in the guts by some trigger-happy boong, told to do it, all the whites pissing their pants with fright, even the dep.

He walked away from these words, and finally found a job at a local radio station (they liked his accent – touch of class!) where he spent his days broadcasting assumptions to a gob-open town of listeners crouched by wireless sets. The irony of it tickled him. His copy of

Shandy eventually dried out. And in the fourth week as he walked along Flinders Street to work, he was surprised to encounter his late landlady flanked by her limpidly beautiful daughters. 'Aha,' she said over-dramatically while the daughters smiled and smiled, 'this is some kind of fate!'

Replies clotted.

As they had clotted his few weeks on Doebin with Mrs Curthoys amicably bullying, genteel above that underlying grain of coarseness, eyeing the doctor eyeing her girls, utterly happy, Morrow presumed, to have her finger laid 'upon the place' – or that of her eldest daughter!

Yet later that week, taking Sterne's suggestion to heart, he paused at Chapter 38, Book VI, took pen and ink, and on the approved blank page of *Shandy* drew his own version of widow Wadman, as unlike his wife as resentment would allow. Something took over. Lines flowed from his pen: sensual curves, concealed mirth. There was a rich swag of hair swept into a high roll, wide absorbing eyes, a mouth with crinkled corners below a straight but impressive nose.

He looked at what he had sketched. It was Mrs Curthoys.

He grow bigger.

Young man now, nineteen, he think.

He come back from turtle fishin with his dadda, Thomas Cooktown, and he see this girl, pretty, all brown shinin, who came over under the Act. She part migaloo, like him. The gubbamin they hate them, these part-whites, most. It remind them what they did to the black women, to his grandma Rosie. Murru! *Shame. Shame. There that girl under the coco palms behind the jetty, gatherin somethin, puttin it in her* dah-loon. *He call out, Hey, you workin hard, eh? and she too shy. She hide her smile. But he see all the same.*

So sometime, those days Uncle Boss let them, he take her out to sit in the long grass and the woman in charge she watch them and she cry, No touchin! No touchin now!

So at night Jeannie sneak out from the girls' dormitory and he take her up mountain and he touch. An even those days when the woman cry out no touchin he manage to wander off with Jeannie and gammon hunt for witchetties under the gidgee trees.

Hunt hunt hunt.

Jeannie she soon expectin and they marry them in a hurry. Big party. All new dresses and trousers. Some visitin preacher Uncle Boss bring over those times and now there's three of them. He call his son Joshua. Big family now, all family. Grandma Rosie, dadda Thomas, mumma Lou and Jericho, Billy and Normie. House too small all right. But happy.

Happy don't last long, mumma say.

I LOVE THE BLACK BUGGERS

I LOVE THE BLACK BUGGERS, he was fond of saying. I love their simplicity, their friendliness, eh? And when you get to know them, their loyalty, their unquestioning loyalty. I love that.

Small-farm, small-town boy, Captain Brodie, army-translated to officer class with a medal or two for bravery on the Western Front. Simple himself. How would he know where disloyalty might spring? But they all thought he was right for the job after the big wind tore out the heart of the settlement at the Heads and it was relocated on a fairytale island.

How he'd worked! No time for sunflower dawns or the floral effects of moonlight. Not much time for the wife he'd taken just after repatriation. And then the children – all impedimenta, he sometimes felt guiltily, despite a stubborn and persisting love. But the island welded them closer. How he'd slaved in this place, helping with clearing, road-making, the building of houses and office, small clinic and school; supervising the bladey-grass huts, the dormitories, and rejoicing in the sweat that rivered out of him in the festering weather. My kingdom, he thought, said aloud, gloated proudly. I've done the lot.

Staff, of course. And not soon enough. A solo perform-ance for months before he got a deputy, a mechanic/carpenter, a storeman, a ragtail procession of casual medicos until . . .! And a hit-and-miss run of temporary teachers unable to cope. They had all joined him gradually. Joined him! He held his cracking head between his hands while the pains raced up the back of his neck and split and spilt into a florid orgasm as if his brain were about to burst. Relief for a few moments and then once more the mounting pressure.

All that. The work, the tightness and closeness of community – fishing with the native boys on late Sunday afternoons, running a football team, bullying, chiacking, watching over them in his own rough-handed way. But loving them. Ah yes! Loving. All of that he had established and survived, and now, my God, now, as he'd suspected for months, plots for his removal, the slimy connivance of deputy and storeman, doctor and matron.

Behind him in the house he could hear his children cough stir whimper in their sleep. He thought of calling his wife and remembered she was gone and shook his head as if remembrance were part of an ugly dream. He'd drunk too much that Christmas evening amid the claustrophobic socialising and the ragged streamers and tinsel and cotton-wool snow of Christmastide stuck up here in the melting tropics. Treachery, he inwardly raved, beneath the mildewed holly and mistletoe, the limp branches of artificial pine, treachery alongside the paper tree with glass baubles sitting crooked in a pot while the whole bunch of them, betrayers, time-servers, bloody Judases, all quietly planned his downfall as their stomachs rumbled for next day's roast dinner.

The pain surged into his head once more and he bent forward, gripping the arms of his chair and vomiting a thin yellow bile onto the verandah floorboards.

He spun beneath memory-flash and resentment. He saw himself shuddering and holding his glass in one quaking hand as he'd rocked backwards and forwards in the living-room of the residency (native artifacts, rattan deckchairs bulging under the bums of staff and wives), all of the party slightly tipsy and reaching that point where universal love would swing to belligerence. It had been 90 degrees in Coconut Avenue. Mrs Deputy Superintendent had begun playing Christmas carols on the gramophone. The thin sounds had fluttered and wavered, mocking the lights as the generator hiccupped.

My island, he recalled saying, my island is a . . . a . . .

Model of its kind? Doctor Quigley had interposed, rising and going to the sideboard to splash more whisky into his glass along with irony.

Beyond the verandah was a blackness no black was permitted to enter. No Christmas lights or candles sparked after curfew. In the small village groups scattered through the bush, natives slept in their huts under palm-leaf roofs

107

waiting for morning white-joy with its extra ration of bully beef.

'. . . the snow lay all around, deep and crisp and even,' droned the turntable, the distorted carol singers like a bad joke.

That's it, he had said thickly. A model of its kind.

And you playing mine host to perfection.

The doctor, pox him, had sauntered across to the verandah doors, staring into hot darkness while the voices on the gramophone petered out but the turntable kept up a maddening click. Its revolutions would die, too, in their time. Deputy Leggat had eased himself up (scratching unembarrassed at his crotch in front of the women, the sod) and joined the doctor. The matron and Mrs Deputy went round once more with culinary pacifiers no one wanted. Somebody had donated mince pies.

He'd been full of braggadocio he recalled, wiping the thin vomit from his lips. Only a fortnight before, there had been an official investigation of complaint: bullying, striking the natives. Someone had reported him. But the inspection cleared him. Lily Friday admitted it had only been a slap on the arm. 'Why, Lily?' the government inspector had asked. 'I called him nogood bossman!' Lily admitted. 'And why would he do that, Lily?' Head hanging. Shuffling. 'I stay out too long with boy.' 'You marry this boy soon, Lily?' Silence. 'You want to marry?' Nodding. 'How long you stay out, Lily? You miss your job, eh?' All night, she tell them. Matron wait and wait at clinic.

I've made this place, he had shouted at the group by the doorway. Me! Twelve years of grind, by God! What would you lot know about it? Slashing the jungle back to the hills, cutting out tracks, turning them into roads, building the houses, the bloody houses you live in, by the way! Hospital, store, school, my God! Say thank you, all of you! Say thank you for the school, Vine! It's all due to me. Say thank you, Doctor bloody Quigley!

Quigley had turned, his face horribly amused and not hiding it. 'You're a bully,' he had said softly. 'Bullies get things done through fear. They're afraid of you out there. It's not your island, dammit. We've all had a hand in it. And your hand has fallen harder than most.'

At those words there had been a ringing in his skull. A voice – his? – asked what did the good doctor mean? Everyone was watching with bright eyes as the superintendent, his body still boyish, swung across the room to fling drink at the doctor's immaculate front – who did an impertinently careless brushing and said, 'Your hand, dear boy, landed somewhat brutally on Lily Friday. She came to me for treatment for bruising. Well, not to me personally, but to Marcia. You're a rough bastard, sir!'

Brodie remembered drawing back a bunched fist and swinging a cruncher that landed on Doctor Quigley's jaw, knocking him into a welter of faded carols and crumbled mince pies into which he too stumbled. The superintendent had hauled himself upright by the sideboard and panted unpleasantly.

(He panted unpleasantly now.)

Then he and the doctor had done a frightful tango onto the verandah where someone had pulled them apart.

'Anyone else?' he'd challenged.

109

No one moved. Wives made time-we-were-going murmurs and the matron bustled forward with her officious bust, her officious vowels, and snapped, 'Come come now, Captain Brodie! You're making a fool of yourself!'

Horrible! Horrible! Shaking her hands off without a glance into that sensual face, he went back to the living-room and saw the doctor's nose had bled richly on the matting, spreading into a crimson map that reminded him of the island. He didn't remember hitting the nose and soon the room, dark shapes lurching down steps and through garden, was empty.

Everyone, he had shouted drunkenly after them. Everyone, happy Christmas!

If Davey Brodie and his sister Barbara found their father strange in the next week, silent, brooding, impatient and over-excitable as though a kind of scrub itch raged through his mind, their father was not aware. He was hardly aware of them at all, or the week passing. Hardly aware of a dead wife except in bursts. Only of aloneness and this bursting skull that paralleled the build-up so that in those monstrous temperatures not even the deep shade of the mango trees along the avenue soothed.

Davey, kid sister trailing, wandered along the crushed-coral avenue in the opposite direction to his father, who was walking with that stupid jerking stride towards the office, muttering to himself. Davey Brodie quailed, pulled his hat-brim low over his freckles, and scuffing at gravel headed towards the hill across the creek where he knew Mrs C and her daughters would welcome him and ask nothing. Since Christmas he had found that the children of the deputy and storeman were being kept away. He was contagious, he imagined, kicking a stone resentfully. He knew all the whispers: mad! Crazy as a galah! Lost control! Doesn't even know we're here!

He began to sob.

Mum, he thought and tried not to think, remembering the wisp of a blood-drained face watching him from the bed in the shadowy front room, the family pictures set all along the dressing-table near her tired old hairbrush with the combings still curling greyly off the bristles. 'Be a good boy, Davey. Look after your dad.'

The nod had vanished in the gulp, the touch of his mouth to her cheek, the awful smell of blood – so much of it, he knew, as they waited vainly for the mainland launch.

That was it. Be a good boy, Davey, and the old man carrying on like one of the black *moodjas* at a ceremonial funeral, carrying on for days, weeks, until as suddenly as the grief started it stopped, and his father, with a new and glaring shell of brassy assurance, took up his duties again with meticulous vigour that bordered on the insane.

He couldn't wait for school holidays to end. Couldn't wait to get away from the great gloomy house and his daft dad. Not even his sister comforted, gone silent since. He was tired of listening to what wasn't said. Suddenly old, he knew he was too young to be listening to silences, to be trying to interpret their sticky voids.

The girls were waving to him from the verandah as he trudged up the path between the crotons. Behind him Barbara whined trying to catch up. As Claire raced down the steps to meet him her bare feet slapped across the boards, her gingham skirt flashing between the wooden posts, while from an inner room her mother's voice, amused, unruffled, admonished, 'Shoes on!'

Gee, Davey thought disloyally, home.

His father, meanwhile, impelled by furies, glided at speed throughout the settlement, visiting the boys' and girls' dormitories, calling unexpectedly at the grass huts of those blacks he had made his special interest. He was touting support. He wasn't touting support. He was compelled. He hardly knew where he walked or why. My people! he kept saying. His wild eyes frightened them.

From behind shutters storekeeper Cole watched with narrowed eyes as later that day Brodie drove his car, the only one on the island, at a slow and elegant speed past the administration block, the little hospital, the school, only to turn about and drive back again. And again. And again. On the fourth trip down Coconut Avenue, the superintendent punished the car by swinging it onto a snigging trail, shoving it along in low gear over the ungrubbed scrub roots and coral lumps towards the family settlements farther out.

Brodie smiled as he caught movement at Cole's window. Sorry, old man, he had said to the storekeeper's suggestion that he, too, might buy a car. Only one car on the island. Can't clutter the place with tinware, can we? In any case the barge has refused to allow any more to be loaded. It was tricky enough with mine.

While he drove he waggled his head with unlaughing glee over Cole's resentment of the privilege of rank. He'd had six boys travelling on the barge with his second-hand Ford to keep an eye on the lashings. Six loyal boys! Six of the best! Thoughts screamed gull-like round his head, dived and pecked.

How had all this threat of settlement decay come about? He'd heard all the arguments from lawmaker to politician, from country farmer to town shopkeeper. The difficulty, they said, the insuperable thing always has been to make those damn Abos want to work! Why should they, perceptive sympathisers pointed out, when they can obtain all they need from a few days' hunting? Then we must remove their means of subsistence, the sheepmen cattlemen farmers said. Then they'll have to work. But what's worse, they said, the buggers have no respect! Don't understand master–servant relationship at all. No concept about who's boss. They go on as if they're doing us the favour when they spend a few days mustering or turn up to chop a bit of wood or clear a paddock.

Well, aren't they? You don't pay them!

Brodie had fallen out with half his old farming

113

community with those words. Nothing more than a few sticks of *nikki-nikki* or a handful of flour. You call that fair pay?

But they argue with me as if they are equals, for God's sake! Don't they know who I –

The gentlemen, the prelates pointed out, seemed unaware that Aboriginal society had been a near perfect democracy with all the concepts of sharing that Christians so assiduously avoided. You've plunged them, they warned in letters to newspapers and parliamentarians, articles in magazines, into a stratified society, a capitalist system. They don't understand. They simply don't understand.

And one weary squatter back of the Taws commented to his fellow moaners, They don't give a fuck.

Well, he did. Captain Brodie had savaged his inner being for them in a kind of benevolent despotism. Perhaps that's what it was. He didn't know what else to offer. He'd worked bare-backed alongside them in the first years, handling a pick with the tribesmen. Okay, the rations weren't so good. He was limited by government funds. But at least they were kept from the floggings and fornication of mainland squatters and their farmhands. He was not a flogger. He was a fanatic.

The car jammed against a fallen log and he got out cursing. His head split, cracked open, the gulls stabbing again and again, and he sagged down in the grass at the trackside. Anyone who starts from nothing with nothing, he mumbled, must be a fanatic. How else create? As he had created, starting off with a few score blacks dumped there summarily by a government feigning care and

114

concern, sixty terrified wretches who could communicate only within their tribal groups but had nothing except sign language to make connection with strangers.

At first he had looked hopelessly at his band of kidnapped: snivelling kids, adults frightened and sullen. But he'd won them! He'd won them!

He learnt words. He said *jawun-jawun* – friends. He said *jawun-jawun ngayu* – my friends. No time for fanaticism. He'd lived in the welter of creation. Or was fanaticism something unanalysable that embraced without one's awareness? Twelve years of unending struggle and the government sending more and more poor-fella half-castes rounded up as if the bullimen were droving sheep.

Doebin became an occasional interest spot for tourists from the mainland, ferries with whites in holiday mode for whom the black women displayed their *yagal* mats, their *mura mura* and *bundu* baskets, while the boys dived for coins or sold pieces of trochus fetched up for hard-eyed mainlanders. His people became curiosities for nosey gapers, as did his kingdom fashioned from cajoling, bullying – yes, even that! – and sweat.

As his head surged with climactic pain he lay face-down in the grass and whimpered. Staff, he moaned on the subsiding waves of agony, nit-picking undedicated time-servers waiting for better appointments. Even the school he had commenced. For a while anyone who could read or write gave a grudging few hours weekly. Probationary teachers from the mainland were blooded there. They didn't last long. Fledgling doctors put in six-week appearances. He wrote ferocious letters to a southern

115

bureaucracy demanding full-time assistance and here he was landed with uppity traitors who had no conception of ... couldn't imagine the difficulties, the ... Liars! Destroyers!

Ah, the doctor! He sobbed aloud. Joan had bled for weeks, her life seeping out to comforting medical rumbles. 'Keep your feet up,' Doctor Quigley assured, who was nothing but bedside manner when it came to dealing with the wives of staff. He was less attentive to blackskins. 'Just rest, my dear. That's all we can do.'

He'd left it too late. They'd all left it too late. Sweet Jesus! he cried into the lank grass. By the time the superintendent took matters into his own hands and had his boys carry his wife up to the little hospital while he radioed for a launch from the mainland, things were beyond help. His wife's thinned and anxious face had looked up from the makeshift pallet as the juices drained away. 'The children,' she whispered or rather shaped with her pallid lips.

He had squeezed her hand. 'Of course,' he had whispered back. 'Don't worry. I'll take care of them.'

The children? He writhed on the trackside and wondered where they were. He couldn't remember. Back at school on the mainland? His daughter? Was she back in the house? At the convent in Townsville? With her cousins on the tableland north? And Davey? Was he away, too? He couldn't recall seeing either of them since that drunken night. He thanked God they weren't here to witness their father's shame. But they wouldn't witness his defeat.

He propped himself up on stratagem. His head whirled momentarily and the pain simmered, rose briefly up the nape of his neck and subsided. He would destroy the whole edifice he had built. His mind-fire would spread out and envelop buildings, gardens, enemies. His thoughts sharpened with the daring of that decision.

For days he locked himself in his office, deaf to knockings, to staff pleas, numbed with drink. His children quivered in the residence in the care of a housegirl. He no longer remembered he had children.

Then unexpectedly he emerged in the flush of madness.

Another part of the forest.

Elderly boyish, despite hangovers, despite forty-plus years, gliding and jerking back through the bush tracks to see Manny Cooktown, his chief boy help. He had seen Manny grow to manhood – having watched him blubber off that first boat with his daddy in leg-irons, a snotty seven-year-old, his nose streaming mucus, his eyes gummed with tears and pus – into a tall muscled miracle fisherman and crack shot when he borrowed the superintendent's rifle to bag bush pigeons for the stewpot.

Yet within yards of Manny's grass hut he swung about suddenly, pivoting on remembered rage and resentment. Calling me that! A drunken bastard!

He grabbed his head in both hands and wobbled it. It wasn't Manny at all. He couldn't get things straight. It was that Irish body-plumber who was reeling with liquor himself, belching and farting and almost spewing over the ladies' cupped hands. A stream of charm and whisky. And not just that! He'd started the investigations, hadn't he? Or was it that slimy Leggat? Someone had brought that prowling official nosing round the island, questioning the blacks, checking on him! A long-beaked, tight-lipped bureaucrat!

The gulls screeched into his skull, stabbing and whirling.

And who lodged the complaint?

I can't say that, I'm afraid.

Afraid? *You're* afraid?

A little smile. Silence.

Tell me. I demand to know. Who was it?

I can't tell you.

Can't or won't?

It wouldn't be right.

Well, let me tell you something then. The lot of them, wasn't it? The bloody lot. Leggat, Quigley, Cole. That louse Jardine with his brood of half-castes no one wants to mention. Oh yes. That lot.

You're putting me in an awkward position.

So you agree? You admit it then?

They all signed. They all complained.

About what?

Your attitude. Your tactics with the natives. Physical violence, I understand.

Once! He accused me of punching a black woman. Me! A mere slap.

(That once! There must be a second and final knock-down for the doctor. One and one.)

His feet rejected contact with – refused to feel – the sandy earth of the tracks. Eyes watching him outside houses slid away. Now and then a voice called to him, Uncle Boss! But he had forgotten how to reply. Eaten up with fury that made him want to vomit, eyes failed to see, ears to hear, body to feel. His wife gone forever, killed by maltreatment. Maltreatment?' No treatment at all. 'Just keep those feet up, my dear, and rest.' His children? He shook his head again. He hadn't spoken to them for days. They had dodged away after meals, shrinking from his basilisk eye. Perhaps they, too, wanted him out. But no, he told himself as the pain raced up from his nape and burst into shooting delicious stabs, they weren't there. They'd gone back to the mainland already for the new term. He was fighting this alone.

And he would show them, the traitors. He would destroy the whole island, everything he had built, everything.

My dears, my lovely roads, trees, houses, buildings, all my –

His brain whizzed with bullets and burst into fire. His glide became a spastic stagger, an uncontrolled hobble, as he went crippled towards the bungalow in Coconut Avenue.

They'd accused him of being a drunkard, a bully, an incompetent.

'Davey!' he shouted through the echoing hall. 'Barbara!' Only the shadows shifted, and the iron roof expanding in the heat cracked replies that drilled into his skull. He shouted for his wife again and again. Why wouldn't she answer? All gone. They'd all deserted.

He dragged himself across to the bedroom mirror to seek his other self, the one he remembered as slim, handsome, not looking his forty-plus years, but saw only a madman in filthy tropic whites who grinned lopsidedly.

Rubbish! He was still spruce, his gear nearly clean, nearly pressed. Everything nearly but not quite.

He poured himself a drink from the bottle he now kept by his bed and tossed it down in one gulp to stop the whizzing of the bullets.

He drank all through that long hot afternoon and into the evening, listening to the shorthand of the rain. Once he looked into his children's rooms to check on them from old habit. Barbara was breathing lightly, her face turned to the wall. Next door Davey slept with one hand outside the sheet clutching a book. The superintendent opened the louvres wider to catch the ragged puffs of breeze that came up from the sea.

He was surprised to see them there. Surely they should be back at their schools by now. Baffled, he rammed his knuckles into his forehead, worrying flesh and conundrum, then went back to the living-room and fumbled himself another drink, spilling half. He took it out onto the verandah and reeled into his settler's chair as his head once more exploded in flames. Sip hate sip hate. He could sense the lot of them down the avenue, listening and waiting.

His mind a scribble-slate, all facts and non-facts, erase, rewrite, erase-rewrite, don't spit, sonny, use your sponge, back then back then. Cancel. Everything to be cancelled.

He dozed but woke to mosquitoes and the dark. Dreams had bitten and he'd scratched at the flesh of memory. He was glad his wife and children were safe on the mainland. He could see their goodbye arms waving from the launch. Thank God for something. But not for the anger that sent him twitching down the steps and along the road blotted with the massive dark of mango and palm. Nothing moved except his body that he felt to be almost too cumbersome for his intention.

There was a glimmer of light in the deputy's house and beyond that the looming slab of the store, the storekeeper's residence and the annexe where Matron Tullman slept and was now, he hated blinkingly, in the pudgy arms of her Irish paramour. And fifty yards on the small armoury, to which only he and the deputy held keys: the gelignite and fuses for rock-blasting, the two rifles kept in case of riot. There never was a riot. It lay only in this cleft skull that even now shattered again with rockets of pain.

The dark and the boundaries of nothing. If he could weep, the humanity he was trying to suppress would overcome the rage. He lusted after the rage, after purging.

Officer material, they had said.

Anyone who'd been to a private school, no matter for how short a time, and understood the rigours of boarding school and self-discipline must be officer material.

Forget those years of early milkings in frozen dawns, the six-mile bike ride to school, the smeared slate, ink-stained copybook. Later, the yes sir no sir of thirty small boys herded into classrooms, cricket teams, football warfare, boiled cabbage dining-halls and tearful dormitories would create officer material. The British lion roared and he was sucked back into its stinking breath and waded through mud in western Europe to return with what was called glory to the farm, to marriage, to a humdrum scratch for subsistence.

He'd leapt at this chance on Doebin. Leapt.

He'd kept his swagger stick, first as an affectation, then as a handy weapon for snakes. See him stride and glide, swagger stick prancing in his hand as he inspects his kingdom. He doesn't know he's even swinging it. He doesn't know it alienates Leggat, Cole and Jardine as an abominable pretension.

He has forgotten it now as he lays the gelignite and fuses beneath the residence verandah, giggles a moment, remembering the Somme, lights the fuse and moves back across the road to watch. It is too late for him to hear or even believe the wake-up panic of his daughter, Davey's startled bird cry.

The whump, the obscenely beautiful blaze and the skittering figure of Uncle Boss racing across a backdrop of scarlet in the spatter of rain towards the matron's annexe brings out like an halloo the braver of his staff, who watch, stunned, and hear a rifle shot and the crash of china toiletries. Another shot and they cannot see, as the invading superintendent sees, the good doctor staggering across the bedroom clutching his groin while a madman takes aim for Matron Tullman's jugular, misses and begins beating her with the gun stock.

The pain in the superintendent's own head drives him out into the night and he is aware of a wall of fire somewhere to his left but cannot connect for the moment. As his head clears, he patters suavely, neatly, back to the roadway and towards the office where he drenches an outer wall with petrol and tosses a match. It's unslakable, this thirst for reprisal. The school's thatched roof is crackling in dream satisfaction.

He stands back smiling.

Leggat accosts him in the thick smoke-filled pall now slashed by busy fires, choking and coughing on questions.

The superintendent shakes his head, forcing down that terrible agony. 'That cunt of a doctor is dead. I've shot him, him and his mistress.' He shutters his eyes with both hands, the rifle dangling, and fights to remember. 'My house, the lot. I'll destroy the whole place before I let you take over.' Recovering, he looks up and glares and Leggat can see nothing but teeth and gun barrel. 'It's your turn.'

His rifle spits at emptiness as Leggat sprints into shadow and back towards his house. Someone is shouting at him. Cole? 'You've killed your kids, you bloody maniac!' And he hears himself mumble through shock and horror, 'They aren't here, you fool. They're not here.'

Are they? He doesn't know. Cannot believe. Better, he rationalises, trying to help himself, they're dead than know their father a murderer.

He races after the fleeing deputy who is shadow now with shadow wife and children chivvied into hiding in the scrub behind the avenue. The night is filled with the sound of scurrying movement, the houses untenanted.

The superintendent pranced like a fire demon, feet high in caracols and curvets, down the rain-soaked avenue, leaving behind him sprouting pillars of fire – residency, store, school. From the corner of his eye he spotted the doctor and the matron staggering into the night, toting their wounds towards Shippers Vale.

He raced after them, swinging rifle and a stick he picked up as he ran. He could hear footsteps thudding behind him but the pain in his head blotted purpose and swung him about, diverted. There were shouts, cries. Now and then he heard rustlings from the hidden enemy, the whimper of children huddled against uncovery, their parents shushing. His madness sped him beyond even that as the rain drummed harder, hammering on leaves, until his ecstatic jouncing took him to the jetty and the government launch moored alongside the hulk of an old coastal steamer and the settlement runabout.

In the cabin of the *Nita*, he dragged off his drenched

clothes and crept under a blanket, insomniac with fire, with bullets, wondering about his children. Cole's shouted accusation had jolted him but he refused to believe. Could not believe.

And then their memory was blurred and replaced by the ranked faces of the foe.

He woke early from his half-sleep, pulled on his scarlet bathing-costume, and elegantly armed with bullet belts across shoulders and around his narrow waist stepped from the *Nita* onto the jetty. He held a rifle and revolver and cut a murderous dash.

How his brain burned.

He had forgotten wife, children, the ashes of burnt-out buildings and years. A small surf fizzed along the beach but he could not see it. In the shoreline scrub a bird hawked and coughed. He could not hear it. He craved havoc like a numbing drug. Racing back he sloshed benzine through the bunkroom and on the decks of the launch, tossed a lighted match down the hatchway, and springing nimbly over the side waded to the runabout. As he wobbled astride the little rocking boat, his rocking brain absorbed fire. The *Nita* went up with a roar.

Fire cleansed. Cleansed.

Beyond that glazed dawnlight he could see the furtive shapes of some of his boys watching from the shelter of the trees. He raised his rifle and laughingly fired into a sky he hoped to bring down, a final curtain. Rain answered. He pointed the deadly eye of his rifle straight at the heart of Danny Tombo who had stupidly ventured onto the beach. 'Uncle Boss!' the fool was calling. 'Hey, Uncle Boss!'

'Here!'

Danny Tombo wanted to slither back to the casuarinas. 'Uncle Boss?' Voice and legs quavered.

'Here, I said. On the double. You come quick, eh!'

The boy came slowly to the edge of the water and paused. The superintendent felt his brain boil.

'I said here, damn you! I mean here!'

Tombo waded out to the runabout, putting one terrified hand on the rocking gunwale. His eyes jittered with terror.

'In!'

The boy kept his face averted from this maniac, watching his big splayed toes in dawn water, his body frozen into stillness until the nudge of the rifle barrel energised him. In seconds he was seated in the stern, dragging on the starting cord of the outboard until it hacked into clatter and edged away from the burning launch, described a wide arc and bucketed off towards U-millie, a shadow sister of Doebin at the end of the superintendent's pointing finger.

Brodie hunched up in the bows, still gripping the rifle, still gripping his rage. The bandolier sagging across his bright red bathers made him not a comic figure but one of eccentric tabu. Spray whipped hair and thought into curls, and his mind, overturned momentarily by the beauty of his seesaw world, relinquished the horror he had left behind, that turmoil of fire and gun-blast, until it was the limpest fag-end of a nightmare that lingered only along the lonely margins of his obsession.

He grinned at Danny, who refused to look. 'Hey,' he said. 'Hey Danny! We're friends, eh?'

He screamed his plans against the wind and the noise of the motor. They would go to U-millie and get food from the lazaret, then head off to Noogoo and camp there for the day.

'Whaffor, Uncle Boss?' Danny asked, keeping his eyes on the nearing beaches of U-millie. 'Whaffor?'

'Until,' the superintendent replied enigmatically. For a moment his blaze of happiness was soused. Across reef waters he could see clouds boiling up on the northern rim. He muttered, 'I will kill them all.'

'What you sayin?' Danny asked.

'I will kill them all,' the superintendent shouted.

'Who, Uncle Boss?'

'My enemies. All of them.' He straightened, tightened his grip on the rifle and made a mock-threatening movement. 'Not you, boy.'

The sun had climbed well up above the lacquer-grey water and lurched behind storm cloud. U-millie loomed – the beach, the huts, the lazaret roof glinting at the back and someone, tall and thin as an exclamation mark, striding down to the landing stage over the rocky pathway.

'*Le bon docteur!* Another!' the superintendent was hissing between teeth. '*Le médecin malgré lui!*' he said, thinking of Quigley. 'Danny, when we ground, go and ask Doctor Clereau for meat and bread.'

Danny shook his head. He cut the motor and the keel grated on sand while he kept watching wavelets slap and break on the side of the boat.

'Too scared, Uncle Boss.'

Whatever threat the superintendent might have intended was erased by the sudden rush of pain dancing into his skull. He dropped the rifle and clamped his head between both palms, whimpering. By now Doctor Clereau had reached the landing stage and he watched as the superintendent bent painfully forward to retrieve the rifle. Its eye inspected him as the superintendent, mad in his bathing-suit, his portable arsenal, glared above the sights. 'I have killed the others,' he announced. 'I have killed that bastard of a doctor. I need supplies. Are you my enemy too?'

Doctor Clereau's lips tightened. He had been half prepared by a garbled and frantic radio message from Doebin. He forced a smile. 'Certainly not.' An infusion of reassurance into his shaken voice while keeping one eye on the trembling trigger finger of the superintendent. 'Of course you can have whatever you want.'

'There's a good chap,' the superintendent said, emerging from spasm. 'You and me, Jean Paul, we could run the place like a dream. Go on, Danny, go with the Doctor Boss. No. Wait. Better still, I'll follow to see you come back. I need you, boy. I need you at the tiller.'

'No need for that,' Doctor Clereau said. Turning from the beach they began to walk stiffly to the settlement and the storeroom in ridiculous procession, with the carnival figure of the superintendent at the rear springing along in his canvas shoes, rifle and now pistol cocked. He was vested in cunning and mind-change. He ordered Danny Tombo back to guard the runabout. Native nurses scurried away as he and Clereau reached the first huts of the settlement. For one terrible and lucid moment the superintendent sensed he carried death on his shoulder like a monkey, monkey fingers pointing.

'So you've killed everyone?' Doctor Clereau asked, realising the folly of words but humouring him as he loaded a lump of beef and some bread into a knapsack.

The superintendent became uncertain. His neck quivered under the premonitory onslaught of that scalding rush.

'The doctor,' he replied. Enumerating. 'That whore of a matron. That leaves you to help me start again.' The pain receded and he gave a charming smile. 'And my kids, of course. They'll help rebuild when they're finished school. I just have to go back tonight and see to Leggat and the storekeeper.'

'Of course,' Doctor Clereau agreed gravely. 'But of course. Will you be right now?' He nodded at the food pack and helped the superintendent sling it over his shoulder, where it nuzzled the bullets.

'As right as I'll ever be.'

But when he rocked down to the beach Danny Tombo had fled to hide his terror behind one of the huts. The superintendent, stumbling on driftwood and gashed by memory, forgot his absence in seconds, dumped the food

129

into the belly of the boat, dragged the anchor from the sand and yanked furiously at the starting cord. Clereau stood by on the beach to watch him leave, stretching out a placating but ineffectual hand. 'Don't touch me!' the superintendent screamed as the motor blasted into life. 'Get your bloody paws off!'

The doctor nodded and waved the little boat into the distance. The sun was well up now, but clouds bellied with rain were sweeping in. The thunder was more in the mind. He ran a hand through his sparse hair and made one last attempt, shouting, 'Let me know if you need . . .' to the superintendent's rigid back. Under his breath he whispered, '*Que le Dieu vous sauve.*'

The superintendent did not turn round. As the runabout swung towards Noogoo he sat in the stern facing a new shore. His face held the blankness of a traveller who had discovered too much.

I am waiting for nightfall, the superintendent told himself, beached in a cove on Noogoo. He told himself many things. Inelegantly he wolfed damper and bit into a slab of corned meat beside his fire. The flames reminded him of something else, though his tortured head had trouble discovering what. A house? A store? Those scarlet petals like a monstrous corolla matched the turmoil in his skull. Flower or fountain? He preferred fountain, recalling sparklings of water and scintilla-like rain, like *go-ah* that now began to fall in the late afternoon and persisted as he huddled under the shoreline scrub. He yelled for Tombo. He could see him out there in the shallows with his *gunbara*, spearing fish, his back in a different storm from the seething lightning within Uncle Boss.

We-ra, Danny Tombo was shouting to him. Wind. Big wind come soon. The superintendent shrank beneath leaves and watched the boy shrug. He knew. Uncle Boss knew. Migaloo bored these people, frightened them. Migaloo bullied, sponged, patronised – everything. The blacks took refuge in their own indifference. They were happy not to be the crazy ones.

The superintendent lay flat in the scrub and tossed fitfully until the dawn.

'Time!' rapped out the superintendent, remembering the Somme. He stood ridiculously to attention on the empty beach, presenting arms in his long, shapeless bathing-suit. He blinked and found Danny gone, the beach empty except for the dot-pictures painted by rain. He stalked down to the boat, militarily correct, one eye on the northern sky. Above him clouds began their slow grumble. He wondered if the racket came from Goon-yah, the first black man speaking on behalf of Da-lore, the good spirit. He shuddered despite heat, despite the bullets of rain which had begun to bite.

'In!' he shouted to no one at all. 'In! In!'

The motor sputtered alive.

He was the motor.

The boat curled out and away, plugging across churned waters to Doebin through rain, through wind-toss.

He was the boat.

He was the motor, the boat, the wind, the rifle, the revolver. He was the punitive avenging force. He sat upright, hardened by the ramrod of his rage.

There was unexplained music in his head.

He remembered times of devastating sweetness.

Listening to Puccini on the gramophone and the doctor joining in with his high Irish tenor. Mrs Curthoys would sit bemused, flanked by her exquisite daughters, his own wife happy with it all. Those were the days before he suspected treachery. Rubbish! Admit it! He had suspected it from the moment he had shaken that plump Gaelic paw damp with sweat. Pulling rank: I'm the new doctor. (Read: you are a mere ex-military bully!) He could still hear the harmonics of that first rich 'Good day to you.'

The blankness of seascape and sheetings of rain that had trapped him on Noogoo to huddle for a wretched night beneath the trees now trapped him tightly within himself. Perhaps he had slept. He couldn't remember as he steered the runabout in the dawn grey, the rain easing back as he chased Goon-yah, the clouds taking their cumbersome load south. He was pursuing storm.

Doebin moved closer. Between body-rack and head-split he could not think beyond carnage. His inner tumult met only silence when finally the runabout grated on sand near the landing-place where the launch and the bulk of the *Koonawarra* moored alongside still gave out small gasps of smoke. He could feel Doebin waiting for him, waiting, despite the seemingly deserted cove.

Stepping out of the boat he waded to the beach, rifle cocked against whatever lay behind the scrub. Sea-rustle behind. Leaf-rustle ahead. Then Manny Cooktown, his fishing-boy, hunter and shooter, pride of his football team, stepped cautiously from behind the trees and yelled his predigested migaloo command, 'Put your gun down, Uncle Boss, or I fire.'

The words meant nothing in the half-lit morning.

He laughed as the pain hammered for escape inside the bony walls of his head. He heard the words again and shouted back across them, tearing them apart, 'They have to get my boys to kill me!' He strode forward hearing other voices behind that screen of leaves, the muzzle of his gun wobbling uncertainly on its target, to receive a terrible blow in the region of his gut and see the wetness of his own scarlet gush onto that of his bathers.

Surprise took him one step more before he staggered and fell face forward into morning.

That night, eh? No one talk about that much.

But he remember. Manny Cooktown remember all right.

Uncle Boss gone crazy they all say. Burn house. Burn store. Burn school. Them whites they runnin scared.

All the island quiet like fish and they wait in huts, wait wait, all day in the hot and no wind and that Leggat, that bagga bones he keep runnin round fussin and givin orders and handin out guns to the police boys and he say, Boss gone now, but he come back soon. You wait down by jetty, eh. You wait and when you see him, you take his guns.

He got guns? he ask.

Leggat nod. He nod and shake.

Why don't you wait? he ask.

I have to look after the women and children, he say. He all importan. There things to do.

135

What about that Mister Cole, eh? He got no store now. He could come down.

Don't argue with me, boy, Leggat say. And he shove rifle hard at him and say, Take other boys with you. Take Billy and Willie Omba, he big enough now. I'm givin you big responsibility.

Then that Leggat he walk away, quick quick and he keep watchin and see him run.

And then the little boat come in across the water and Uncle Boss standin in the prow, holdin tiller, look crazy fella, in bathin suit with belt and gun and rifle tuck under arm.

He and Billy wait under mango trees back from the beach and when the boat come into jetty, Billy scramble up into branches with Willie and hide. Don't blame them none. All hot and still everywhere and Uncle Boss step outa boat and he come down jetty and when he see Manny he raise rifle and point it straight at him, laughin.

Hey, Uncle Boss, he call. Don't do that. You put down gun, eh.

He always like Uncle Boss. They go fishin sometime. They share tucker. But Uncle Boss he keep laughin.

Gotta get my boys to kill me, he yell. Staff scared, eh? Yellow buggers.

Manny remember the word he was supposed to say.

He call, Surrender. He call, Put down your gun.

Then Uncle Boss laugh like mad thing and aim the rifle first time up at Billy who shakin them branches then at him. An he scared too an he fire. He fire an Uncle Boss drop down as he run up and see big red blotch on Boss's belly and the blood spreadin and he cry and say, Sorry Uncle Boss. Real sorry. And Uncle Boss he say, That all right, Manny. Those bastards made you do it.

Then Billy run screamin up to Coconut Avenue and the whites come down and Leggat push him one side and say, The police will want to talk to you about this.

Can't stop thinkin bout it, bout what he done. And what that Leggat done. They carry Uncle Boss up to the settlement but he die and next day they put him on board the police launch long with doctor and matron and take them to mainland.

He keep seein that blood, hearin them words, Why they use you to do their dirty work, Manny?

He keep askin himself why why why.

Two days later more bullimen come back to Doebin to get him and Willie Omba. They say be witnesses. Then they take them both to watch-house and shove Manny in lockup.

One week. Two.

He get angry then at havin to fight whiteman's quarrel. Do their dirty work. An every night he keep seein Uncle Boss's face, see him lyin there. He cry. Didn't know whether he cry for Uncle Boss or himself.

The bullimen tell him he coulda been killed. Brodie's gun jam twice, they say. He was out to get you, mate. You were lucky, eh? Then later he hear in court that little boat loaded with two boxes dynamite. But still they charge him, Manny, an months go by an he worry bout Jeannie an his little boy an he keep havin that dream.

An then they try him for murder even though he save all them others, do what Leggat tell.

He hardly hear when they say not guilty.

'CAN'T SEE YOU NEXT WEEK, 'CUSHLA!'

'CAN'T SEE YOU NEXT WEEK, 'CUSHLA!' Doctor Quigley said breezily to his mistress and Vine's wall-flapping ears. 'I'm getting married. But I'll be down the week after for sure.'

Vine had put aside the essays he had been marking and sat at his table barely daring to breathe, waiting for the hearty cheerie-bye at Marcia Tullman's gulping door.

Twelve years ago, it had all started there. At that moment.

Playing a last Beethoven quartet now in the breezeless inland afternoon he was transported from memories that still nagged or nibbled, lifted up during the *alla marcia* by a threnodic, tidal quality of strings. He wondered how the composer had felt when he'd stabbed down the final note, alone and deaf in his dirty rooms. Just that. At that moment. Like God?

Beside Vine lay another heap of unmarked essays on the spiritual isolation of the Ancient Mariner. (No less than three pages. Quote from the text to support your observations.) 'Le marin, c'est moi,' he said bitterly. And Marcia his albatross. In the kitchenette attached to his senior master's flat he could hear his wife scouring the burnt bellies of saucepans. No black help here as once on Doebin. Really, he preferred eating stew-slop with the boarders because Marcia, resentful about housekeeping on top of being matron to twenty boarders at the school, made a surly production of the simplest meal despite multiple certificates in caring for the sick. (Delicate broths, jellies, tender pieces of chicken in aromatic gravy?)

'I tend the body,' his wife had said stubbornly, 'not the gastronomic whims of teenage boys or, for that matter, Samuel, middle-aged schoolmasters. I can't do everything.'

Point taken. She was above the bedpan, the preparation of invalid diets. But lately when dining-room duty was rostered for him he fled there with relief. Twenty more or less cheerful faces bent over Sunday cold-cuts, forking in shredded lettuce and stringy mutton. Twenty faces, most of which had never seen the sea, let alone understood the superstitions of sailors alone in a riot of blue water. He ringed another misspelling in red ink, laid down his pen and sighed.

Twelve years here. Married for eleven. One two three four, et cetera, et cetera, when fundamentally he was not, he realised, the marrying type. Had he simply yielded to the embarrassed despair of that long-gone conversation winnowed through the thin walls of Matron Tullman's flat to his own timber-quaking room? Doom-shoved by a specious gallantry?

Those pulpy memories.

He had found his nemesis crouched on an inland dust bowl, with its few score of pupils a mixture of idiot snobbery uneasily coupled with a veneer of practicality. 'Our students,' stated the falsetto brochure sent out to prospective parents, 'combine study of literature and the classics with classes in agriculture and animal husbandry.' Pause here to examine a dying vegetable plot and three stringy cows. 'All boys are expected to join a sporting team. The school has facilities for football, cricket, gymnastic and athletic work. A swimming pool is planned.' The pool was still planned. And the classics (*mensa, mensa, mensam*) proved splendidly unpopular. 'The school endeavours to instil firm Christian principles in its students, and boys are required to attend a weekly service within the church of which they are members.'

Well, that was telling them!

Vine had travelled out to the Taws on the western mail, the narrow gauge running parallel to the beef road, his heart sinking a little lower with each arrival at whistlestop hamlets scattered along the briefly tarred road that led to further sprawls moated by loneliness, by distance. The crummiest of ballads. His ultimate destination was a barmy conglomerate of mining-town illusion, the quick-prop scenery of a temporary theatre run that had somehow managed to outlast its popularity: stilt-and-verandah houses lined streets whose business premises had grandiose notions of nineteenth-century classic revival, with an Italianate clock-tower and renaissance banks and city hall. It was the most populous town on the line and a central trading post for the vast sheep and cattle runs that spread north and west to the Gulf and Channel country. Locals fondly called it the World.

(Ah, he breathed now over the unmarked essays, the red-ink scrawls, had I but world enough, and time!)

He had tottered stiffly and sootily into dry sunny air, hauling his suitcase and already worrying about his boxes of books sent ahead a week before. There was no one to meet him. Outside the station he found a ramshackle taxi, one of two that serviced train arrivals. The driver sucked on a pipe and watched speculatively as Vine flung his suitcase onto the back seat. He suggested Vine would be new here and called him mate. 'Where to?'

Vine told him but asked could he see the town first. The driver nodded and the cab rattled away from the station along Enterprise Road and then swung in towards the township. There was a park with a bell-topped bandstand. They passed it and turned into what was clearly the main street. Where now were the tens of thousands of diggers, wives and children who once jostled to buy stores, visit travelling tent shows, cheer for Federation? Jobless men had moved out and on. Others came through humping their swags, driven by poverty and despair. Years later, he would wonder about the long-gone readers in the newspaper room of the Labour Exchange.

The cab was idling past women shoving prams, honking at slow buggies and post-proppers outside the Lucky Chance Hotel. And then it left the shops behind – a moment of a town really – and they were bumping over

144

a dirt road towards his future home? Purgatory? Limbo? He couldn't discover even now.

He went into the bathroom and stared at his noncommittal face in the basin mirror. The flesh was time-thinned, shrunken from back-country summers, but the weathered grey eyes stared steadily out from spotted glass and examined the disappointed mouth, the fastidious nose, the still thick but grey-shot hair. Clinger Vine. That's what the boys called him behind his back. An unoriginal bit of metaphor but it had stuck through all those years at the place, this place, seen through the window that gave him a corner of the playing field and the back end of the gymnasium. He could see the distant figures of small boys tussling near the football oval and watched the ghost of Tony Shell, that too handsome sports master and junior-school dogsbody, emerge with cheerful shouts from the change-rooms. Vine felt hollowness all through his frame.

That first sight of the school: the haphazard spread of converted homestead set in its would-be park behind struggling she-oaks, presenting a simulacrum of St Jim's, the crack of willow on leather (he was still grabbing at fictional exemplars) at the pitch beside a creek, and – lucky! – willows and weeping casuarinas to provide side drops for alfresco afternoon teas after politely cheered matches; the scattered out-buildings – for what? Masters? Dormitories? Domestic staff? How describe now what he recalled? A blur of poetry rushing across his mind-screen: 'a ghostly batsman plays to the bowling of a ghost/and I look through my tears' – yes, tears – 'on a soundless

145

clapping host/As the run-stealers flicker to and fro'. And there was, if not a tear, a sentimental moisture that appalled. The stupidity of it!

Clinger! He lashed himself with the name. Clinger!

The taxi had abandoned him in a spatter of gravel, his luggage dumped at the foot of steps leading to the wide verandahs where two rangy lads in school blazers were eyeing him. 'Need a hand, sir?' Indeed. But Doctor Parsons? Your headmaster? 'We'll tell him you're here, sir. Would you come this . . .' Yes, yes of course.

The wide hallway lit by sun at the far end and the classrooms, he guessed, leading off. There was the buzz of voices, a smell of chalk, and an overlying reek of boiled mutton and cabbage from the rear of the building. The familiarity of it all. Recognition in a strange land. Nothing changed, he decided as he was led to a room at the far end of the building, even though hemispheres might.

'Oh yes!' he had murmured aloud in that flash of affirmation. His guides looked at him curiously. 'Yes!' He had come home.

Had he ever expected such a death's head of a headmaster, such a bag of righteous bones, nose and mouth corners inevitably seeking the nadir of wilful behaviour: the tentacled probings of a God man – yes, he had to use that word – after schoolboy sin? Doctor Parsons – was he still known as Reverend? – had been a missionary in the islands, in the Territory and the Gulf. He was, the redneck board of directors decided, a suitable appointment. Even the name gave confidence. And he had been with the school for five years, a lustrum that appeared to endorse a sense of ownership.

The highly polished table between them gave back reflections of chin, fingers, the worn academic gown assumed to impress this new man, this Samuel Vine, who had, after all, been chosen by the board in his absence at an annual education seminar in Brisbane.

Neither, having observed, really liked what he saw. There was little generosity of spirit in that wax-pale face eyeing Vine, assessing, totting up, but a kind of mulish obsessiveness in the speckled eyes. Behind the headmaster the windows looked out on an ill-cared for garden fenced off from the cricket field. Two boys, supervised by a spectacularly good-looking young man, were rolling the pitch. Vine had a dotty vision of cucumber sandwiches and iced lemonade set out on trestles under elms and could not repress a smile-twitch.

The headmaster's head creaked round to seek the source of the smile.

'Are you a cricketing man, Mr Vine?'

'A what?'

'A cricketing man? We do believe in the moral worth of team games here. Most important.'

Over the headmaster's shoulders, Vine watched the young man ruffle the blond thatch of one of the boys in what seemed an over-zealous encouragement. The hand appeared to linger.

'In moderation,' he lied gallantly. 'I'm fundamentally a grammarian, I suppose. Very dull. Poetry, the novel. My field is English literature.'

The headmaster stared. He suspected an unsuitable flippancy. 'Well, yes of course. Of course. Your degree seems sound enough.' He fiddled with papers on his desk and glanced through Vine's folder of application. 'But there are other things in a school like this as I'm sure you realise from your ... er ... experience at previous establishments.' He went on to explain the obligations of a resident master, priorities with regard to study duty, refectory attendance and supervision, the ... um ... alertness needed for dormitory control.

'Could you clarify?' Vine asked, deciding he might as well be disliked fully. 'Specify exactly?'

Outside, clouds without rain skulked over the oval from which the master (a jocular arm around each laddie's shoulder) and boys were now walking away. Doctor Parsons began an imbecile pencil-tapping on the gleaming wood of his desk – *tuh-tuh tuh-tuh tuh-tuh* – signalling impatience and playing for time as he fossicked for the right euphemism, humming and huffing through 'Er ... friendships of a special ... um ... nature,' avoiding all mention of the flesh. Vine refused to help and looked non-comprehendingly beyond the empty playing fields to those damp stone walls of his own English public school – the hissed demands of prefects, the rustlings in the dormitory at night, the furtive callisthenics in the showers.

'Part of boyhood!' The jovial school curate had dismissed

148

his timid complaint. 'The rough and tumble of the male world, lad.' (Had the curate licked his lips?) 'It's a kind of masculine freemasonry – fraternity as it were – you'll grow out of the moment you enter the world at large. Believe me, boy. Mark my words.'

Not actually scarred for life but with a chilling indifference to genital tyranny of any sort at all, he had plunged into the which-way waters of romantic bards, caught up in the meretricious currents of anapaest and dactyl, the sexual beat of rhyme. For half an hour he had fallen in love with a frail ashen fellow student at St Andrew's who had perched on the edge of a table in the students' common-room and begun to sing *'Die Forelle'* in a high light voice, her face a blurred lovely pale colour, straight blonde lashes blinking above grey, equally blurred, eyes. The downfall of her hair he remembered best and her sideways smile at him before she stopped, just as inexplicably, picked up her book-satchel and vanished. Where? He had never seen her again.

Apart from that two-minute emotional upheaval little had moved him. He finished his degree, found his elderly parents too old to care one way or the other as they wasted quietly in their Lake District cottage, and decided on a new vision, a new world. He migrated to Australia (there were always letters!) and trying to shake off mist and heather found himself trundling down the gangplank of the *India Queen* into a Sydney of summer dazzle and blue tides, and a junior mastership at a small private school on one of the harbour peninsulas that jutted its proboscis into a bustling waterway of ferries.

One year. Two. Three.

'Now the great winds shoreward blow,/Now the salt tides seaward flow,' he chanted, sometimes audibly, as he perched up the stern end of the ferry *Lady Denman* that he took to work. But was in more desperate moments to mutter, 'Now I only hear/Its melancholy, long, withdrawing roar.' If he said, 'Sophocles long ago/Heard it on the Aegean,' that would be to promote himself, Samuel Vine, to peaks of philosophic encounter and egotism. Sentiment made him favour 'Ah, love, let us be true/To one another!' (All that from a school inspector!) It had heartened him and he chucked a particularly terrible assignment from Jarvis, Form II, into the ferry wake and would later say, 'I'm most frightfully sorry, Jarvis, but I've mislaid it somewhere. How about a pass *pro tem*, eh?'

All days become one day, looking back, involving nothing but the sweaty smell of boys, lunch packs, chalk, a life with no edges but the occasional feather-duster of a girl whose hand he clasped between exchanges of caramels in the sticky darkness of some rococo theatre palace.

One edge though. One. Ploughing through Livy's milky prose with three senior students all anxious to matriculate in law, he had countered the boredom, their complaints of dead language, their eternal why-must-we's. 'One moment,' he had said, the whimsical pedant. 'One moment.' And, 'Quintus Horatius Flaccus,' he further said and proceeded to read Ode XII, Book II, watching their glazed eyes as he intoned. He paused for explanation.

'This was written to flatter a wealthy man, Maecenas, and in brief, boys, in brief, friend Horace suggests that prose is for history and poetry for lovers and that Maecenas wouldn't barter a single hair of his wife's head for all the riches of Arabia or the triumphs of war.' He heard a voice whisper, 'My old man would!' and ignored it. 'Try this,' he said, 'for a dead language.' He reread the last stanza:

> *dum flagrantia detorquet ad oscula*
> *cervicem aut facili saevitia negat,*
> *quae poscente magis gaudeat eripi,*
>   *interdum rapere occupet.*

A yawning silence. Impudent nudgings. He smiled. 'Well, here's a translation. Perhaps you'll change your mind about "dead":'

> For when she bends her neck to your hot kisses
>   [delicate stress on 'hot']
> or, playing coy, denies that you should catch
> what she craves more than you, the more she misses,
> why, her mouth's first to snatch!

Later, a parent complained. There had been a summons to the headmaster's office. 'I am broadening their horizons, their cultural horizons,' Vine had said.

'That is not the sort of broadening we require,' the stuffy head replied. 'You will stick to set texts. I must say, I am rather disappointed in you.'

He was disappointed!

Restless Vine longed for new places. Could he plough? Muster? Angle on rocking waters? He needed a frontier challenge unsupplied by the shimmering glass shopfronts of Sydney town that reflected a man in a rut. Not even the war had provided that spurious pre-death sense of adventurous risk. University interrupted, deferred, he had spent the time (weak eyes, flat feet, a persistent pleurisy) shining his pants in the London War Office, reading with grim amusement the military miscalculations of generals and marvelling at the way they carelessly piled up the bodies of young men in Flanders and the Somme.

When he finished his degree he was elderly by student standards, twenty-eight, and already burdened with conventional responses against which he fought and fought. Passengers on the *India Queen* bolstered his belief in the testing qualities of the new land. 'A hard place,' the old hands warned him. 'The heat. The flies.' 'To say nothing of the claypans,' one added who was returning to a drought-stricken cattle property in the far west of Queensland. 'Get yourself a wife, young man.' (Was he young? He felt ancient at thirty-one.) 'You'll find it makes all the difference.'

'Really?'

'The boring bits. You know. Meals. Washing. Shopping. Kids. All that sort of thing. A man hasn't time for that nonsense.'

'Why not a housekeeper then?'

'You *are* green. Costs too much. Marry and you get it for

free. With other things, of course.' The man leered, winking. 'If you want it. You'll learn, mate. But if it wasn't for the boring bits – and God, you do need backup for them – I doubt whether any man in his right mind would contemplate marriage.' He glanced cautiously at his drab spouse who was playing deck-quoits with another farmer's wife. Vine couldn't help thinking the two women looked as if they were having the best time they'd had in years.

He brooded over the grazier's words but no one and nothing disturbed his celibate mould, though he admitted to a continuous searching. He refused to be diverted from the succulent promises of the romantic ideal.

Mug!

Clinger!

That's what his fellow students had called him, and as if by some indefinable process of osmosis that agnomen pursued him across twelve thousand miles of ocean to his post as junior schoolmaster in this antipodean town. He could list his faults: hopeless at sport, no sort of disciplinarian. There was always one pack-leader who selected him for punishment, usually a muscle-bound rugger moron whose attacks were confined to farts, raspberries and the occasional crass one-liner hurled out for the gleeful response of the class. It was, he realised early, impossible to embarrass thick-wits. Brighter boys he could control with his tongue. Only the clever ones got the point.

When he first arrived there had been five men on staff in this school at the Taws: Doctor Henry Parsons, headmaster, B.A., D.D. (where? where?), classics when required; Oscar Pretorius, mathematics and science; Clarrie Somerdew, junior master of almost everything; Tony Shell, second junior master, sport and general dogsbody; and himself.

Himself surprised as senior master in English and history.

Various part-timers employed weekly to deliver choral and art classes, vanishing in dust-wakes on the unsealed road, were the lucky ones who spread their cultural empire over several townships but never endured the abrasiveness of day after day of deadly accountability. And now, twelve years on, there was a woman, her presence graciously conceded by Doctor Parsons, a Miss Laroche who taught French and music, organising choral classes for the indifferent lads.

He looked into the hand-basin mirror, watching his mouth say her name softly. Twice. Three times. He tried not to think of her.

Once more he was running foul of orthodoxy.

'You have radical notions for a history teacher,' Doctor Parsons had reproved only a week before. 'This is not the sort of place for such ideas to be spread among the lads.'

It is not only the rich who matter, he had argued, the privileged, the foreign names of upstart European royals who are, after all, merely the sanctioned descendants of thugs. In all literature, he persisted, head in hands, fingers

154

scratching at thinning hair, for how long had the emphases been on the wealthy as if only they might concern a reader? Only the wealthy could read, Doctor Parsons replied with a crafty smile. Vine ignored him. Even the eighteenth-century writers, Fielding, Sterne, with attachments at least to the upper-middle class of squires, landowners and gentlemen rakes, gave lip-service only to the lower orders except as some kind of comic turn. Until Dickens, say, had had the guts, pardon me, headmaster, to credit the underprivileged with emotions, with humanity. Especially that. Tread carefully, Doctor Parsons warned, locking his fingers to end the discussion. Your remarks in history have been reported. There have been complaints.

Again? Sex maniac? Anti-royalist commo sympathiser?

He stroked the side of his unshaven cheek and stared back at himself in the glass. He heard the thuds as Marcia, heavier with years, thumped along the passage to the sick bay where two first-formers were having bilious attacks.

His awakening, his epiphany, had come during his brief term on Doebin.

There he had drowned, fathoms under, in the poverty, hopelessness, wretchedness, gentleness, kindness and forgiveness of the island blacks. Despite his lack of skill in teaching six- and seven-year-olds who were sent to him to learn to sing 'God Save The King', despite the Protection Act, despite everything, he had learned much from them. They taught, he decided, and he listened. They offered a courtesy rarely extended by the white officials, and in

155

return he managed to help a few of them, at least, read the primitive unsuitable readers supplied by government stock and do the simplest of sums. Back here, on home ground, so to speak, among the unmarked texts, the dried grass of the playing field, the boarders' choir butchering the school song, comparisons crowded him.

As he travelled over from Doebin the mainland threatened, the Great Divide a prune-coloured backdrop to the stage horror. He had wondered what worse could lie beyond those mountain drapes! The others leaving the island with him had sat primly in the cabin, fingers marking, as it were, biblical phrases, minds concentrated on justice and justice's revenge. Since the killings, everyone's lips had compressed into white lines over the inexplicability of evil. A whole family! they had kept saying. A whole family! Vine had not dared suggest that perhaps he understood ... That although he was not a passionate man ... There but for the grace of God ... et cetera. The others might have lynched him.

He had not looked back, not regarded the choppy waters, had ignored farewell assurances from deputy Leggat who was doing the right thing by staying on once the whole desperate event had been examined, his lying evidence sifted. Vine had stared ahead, traversing the claypans to his new posting. He hummed softly, maintaining across those ruffled waters an unruffled gaze that saw only into a future of preparation, supervision and classes of exquisitely mannered boys with public-school poise.

He was wrong.

As if they'd care. As if.

Who? Why, these unexquisitely mannered boys he had not really imagined.

School numbers were dropping in those first years.

'The Depression, of course,' Oscar Pretorius explained over a friendly cup of tea in what passed for the masters' common-room. 'Hard times on the farm, in the town stores. Parents don't have the money for gentleman jinks. They're sending their kids to high school on the coast and boarding them with relatives or friends. Or they're simply taking them out of school altogether, mainly that, and counting their savings. No one knows which way the economy is going to jump. Could I draw you a little graph?'

Mr Pretorius was fond of that phrase. The boys called him Little Graph, a ludicrous bit of misnomer for that bulky pear of a man with his lumbering and deliberate movements and great shiny pate. His eyes glistened with a fierce but good-humoured interest in the world about him, even the tediousness of insolent adolescents. He worked in the most primitive of laboratories, and appeared to have little equipment beyond weights and pulleys, pipettes and Bunsen burners. Despite this he controlled his classes with a glassy jocularity and the sudden springing of novel experiments that caused eruptions of appreciative laughter. Vine envied him. He envied his easiness in the job. He envied his living out. Vine and the too handsome Tony Shell were the only resident masters, apart from the Head. Clarrie Somerdew boarded in the Lucky Chance and rode out on a pushbike daily. 'Just look at us,' Pretorius commented. 'What a grab-bag!'

School numbers had dropped to forty. There were a mere twenty boarders.

'Intimate,' Vine murmured to Pretorius after the first month's lunchtime stews. After all, the seating arrangements in the dining-room made more for the appearance of a large extended family than a boarding school. The headmaster, however, obliterated all hilarity with a prolonged grace before and after meals and an imposition of silence until the pudding.

'We are fortunate,' Doctor Parsons announced one evening five weeks after Vine's arrival to the boys assembled for study, 'in obtaining the services of a fully qualified matron,' (Little Graph had told Vine of a scandal the previous year when a first-former who had broken his arm at football practice was allowed to linger in class for a week before his parents arrived and began shouting and threatening litigation), 'to take charge of the infirmary.' The headmaster paused to allow the importance of the occasion to sink in. 'Notices will be handed out and boys are requested to include these in their letters home. My wife –' a nod to Mrs Parsons who sat plumply mute on his left, 'and I expect that all boys will treat Matron Tullman,' (Tullman? Tullman?), 'with the respect her position merits.'

Should they clap?

His fate was sealed, as they say, at that moment.

Marcia Tullman was installed in the eastern wing of the building which contained a flatette and infirmary with four beds. ('Our lads are well fed and healthy': a smiling Pretorius.) Vine's own small room was on the far side of hers. Oh, the sheer forced excitement of his greetings and the unforced yelps of coincidence from her! Pretorius watched and continued to smile. Tony Shell was bored. Clarrie Somerdew was far too young to care, absorbed by his struggle with a correspondence course at university a thousand miles south. He thought constantly of leaving.

The weekends stretched long in that town. Vine's supervisory duties were sometimes taken over by Mr Shell who seemed eager to relieve him – Shell at his boyish happiest punting balls with the older boys who formed a votary group as he dashed about in fresh creams or raced with them in shorts. There was always the reading room at the Labour Exchange where Vine could have spent time, that lofty-ceilinged place filled with unemployed men in caps sucking at pipe-comforters while they searched the Jobs Wanted columns of local newspapers. There was that. But often he was too tired, too – yes – uninterested to face the long trudge in and the lonely pot of tea in some fly-blown café. And admit it, there was more inducement to stay put.

From his narrow study he could assemble two sets of leaping scandal.

On the second Saturday of Matron Tullman's residence, a car pulled up in a swirl of gravel and disgorged Doctor Quigley who had driven his mended body eighty-odd miles in from the coast to check on his former colleague, to pay court, perhaps, or pick up the slack. Or.

Their audible rough-and-tumble drove Vine out. On the first occasion he had walked to town and calmed himself with steak and eggs at the Inland Rose, timing his return to school to postdate the doctor's departure. To postdate seeing Tony Shell sliding into dusk with the chummiest of the seniors, a blond boy with olive skin and cornflower eyes who made his own teaching life a maze of innuendo. (They were reading what Danny Chalk, master of pudendal metaphor, called *The Frill on the Moss*. 'Sorry, sir. Bit of a spoonerism!') Now he stayed, playing his gramophone at full bore. Could this be connivance? How long before Doctor Parsons suspected and intervened?

There could be no dodging a meeting with the doctor who ingratiated himself with speed, establishing a small surgery in town that he visited fortnightly and eventually – it took one term – becoming honorary medico for the school itself.

The walls between his room and Matron Tullman's were unspeakably thin. Between changing records Vine occasionally heard soft argument after the cries of passion had ceased.

160

Was the good doctor tiring of the relationship? Was Matron Tullman too demanding? And then he had caught those words, 'Can't see you next week, 'cushla,' with a malicious leap of the heart. He had regretted that leap for years.

How was it, he wondered, that light, this white light of the inland plains, could create such darkness. Or was it that his own black hole spread out and obliterated?

Nineteen thirty-two was the worst year, as if the accumulation of poverty since the crash of '29 had amassed its reactions, not only in one little town but all over the country. Each week men on the dole passed through looking for work. There was none. The best they could hope for was a feed. Stores closed. The numbers fell even more at the school and idiotically Vine married.

Perhaps it was the furious campaign Matron Tullman conducted in the aftermath of rejection: those delicious hot meals whipped up in her kitchenette. Perhaps it was the way she sewed buttons on shirts, turned frayed collars and darned socks. Now and then he thought of that beefy grazier on the *India Queen* and realised that one of the most cunning ploys of eugenicists had been to promote male uselessness at the boring bits. Perhaps, too, this increased dependence – she played her cards with skill, withholding the aces – aroused the curiosity of a man who had flirted with sex only a dozen or so times and then as a paid proposition. Clinger!

Other factors suggested themselves. Bachelorhood could be suspect. Tony Shell was dismissed. One of the second-formers spilled the beans, exposing what Vine had suspected since day one. Snap! – Mr Shell strolling off the oval, a bronzed arm carelessly slung about Danny Chalk's shoulders, the pair of them walking like film stars into the twilight of the toolshed. Snap! – Mr Shell prowling the dormitory and showers on weekend duty, acting silly buggers with wet towels, checking lights-out, too long, too lingeringly: 'I say, young Chalk, a brief word.'

'He is sailing,' Oscar Pretorius commented one morning at tea-break, 'too close to the wind. Should one make a complaint purely on supposition?' Vine had shrugged indifferently. The place was speeding downhill. 'If Shell goes that will be one salary saved. Let's be cynical. He won't be replaced. We'll all have to muck in. Now, there's financial wizardry for you. Poor little Somerdew will have to take over.'

It was Mrs Parson's parsimony that undid Shell. A small light burning late in the dormitory washrooms took her insomnia snooping to discover teacher and student locked in sexual oblivion in the communal shower stall. She did the only thing that occurred. She turned on the cold water full blast.

Shell departed, his shame screened by the bland faces of po-mouthed boys. Danny Chalk was recalled to his father's cattle station. Doctor Parsons made no reference to this sudden gap in staff. From his study window Vine

162

watched the wretched Shell, sacked without wages, shoving his few possessions ahead of him in a wheelbarrow, heading out along the road to the coast.

Even as he walked from a Taws kirk with the pulsating Marcia Tullman on his arm he wondered how it had all happened.

Returned to the school late one evening from a local historical society meeting in the town, he had found Matron Tullman in his bed. She resisted his schoolmasterly protests, scoring victory with racking sobs (he had his soft spots!), and after preliminary solace she began to devour him. He was stunned to find what he believed to be his natural asceticism vanish as, after that first recoil, he returned her hunger.

'I will marry you of course,' he proposed next morning over an omelette of exceptional lightness that she whipped up in her kitchenette.

He'd never seen such melting.

'Things will be easier,' Marcia Tullman said, 'for both of us. Two incomes are better than one.'

But only minimally as the country staggered through depression towards recovery in bloodshed.

To give Marcia her due she was, in those first years, an obliging partner: meals, clothes, everything attended to with goodwill and even taste. He knew now why men got married. Yet he marvelled, in his more honest moments, why women would fall for such a poor bargain. Well, yes, they were kicked along that path by poverty wages, few jobs and the sugar tunes of Hollywood manipulation now crackling over his little mantel radio, loneliness and a carefully organised social stigma that applied most heavily to single females.

Wowee! Marcia might have cried, signing her name for the first time as Mrs V.

Well, bless you, Marcia, you've earned it!

And she gave him a son.

The attentiveness of the first year or so was modified for each of them by this new arrival. Both felt pride in Matthew – cuddles, chuckles, yowls, feeding dramas – but at the same time they perceived their own relationship slip into a dutiful politeness from which Vine hid behind teacherly obligations. He gave extra classes at weekends to those cramming for university entrance. Clinger's boys. Never more than three or four, though the numbers picked up at the outbreak of war. Several of his students were more entertaining companions than his wife. He could talk to them about things that interested him but remembering the fate of Tony Shell he was always careful to maintain a distance. The boys thought him an oddball, an aloof dryasbones.

And the itch in the groin?

Even that diminished as he watched his Marcia swagger her full-busted authority as wife of the deputy headmaster at public meetings, especially delighted when she ran into Doctor Quigley on those occasions. The doctor was unmoved and once he and Vine even exchanged complicit smiles. To complete their domestic bliss, Doctor Parsons extended their living quarters by opening up that paper-thin scandal-filled wall between the once separate rooms. 'There now,' the idiot had said while his own admiring wife looked on, 'a proper little apartment. Room to move.'

For twelve years.

That Billy, he the bright one, and Normie. Clever like mumma, like the teacher almost. Billy and Normie they read faster, think faster than any of them others. That teacher who come after the killins, ole Pop Wesley, he say it because they got these white bits, genes he say, tucked into them through grandma and her white husban.

Maybe.

An through his other grandma, too. Your mumma's mother Nellie, his dadda tell him. She small girl, bout nine, ten, say. She taken from one of them camps outside Charco by one of them lugger captains, big Scot, he got more blacks all over the north than you can count, eh? Anyway, she taken, see, an he parade her through the streets of Charco to be busted.

What busted? he ask. What busted say?

It mean raped, Manny, his dadda tell him. You big boy now. It mean she taken by any of the crew drinkin along them pubs in Charlotte Street. Them animals. They all laugh, see. Anyway she grow up. She called Nellie, don't know no other name. Lou, she Nellie's girl. You plenty white all right. An me. Son of Rosie and big whiteman own half north, eh? English bugger.

Yeah. Plenty white.

He didn't like that much. Bitzer. But the island was full of bitzers. They took comfort in each other.

OTHER KINDS OF WAR

OTHER KINDS OF WAR.

A sort of war.

'I'd like you to knock before you come in,' old Pop Wesley said one morning to Doebin's new director who had barged straight into the classroom and begun ranting.

Forty pairs of horrified eyes.

Those days. Old Pop Wesley sailed smoothly through them, content to be surrounded by kids, unanxious for past or future, taking each day as it came, ploughing through the page-curled finger-stained readers, chanting tables, taking the boys for games in his own time in the late afternoon. All the kids loved him. He wasn't too strict but he wasn't lax, either. Above all he was fair and, what pleased the kids and their parents most, he took no nonsense from the new boss.

'What? What was that, man? I beg your pardon!'

Pop Wesley smiled. 'Accepted. Now what did you want? I'm busy.'

Normie Cooktown sat watching, quick to assimilate the structures of power. He was twelve. He was to be the first and only student who had gone beyond the fourth grade, and was so eager he was allowed to prepare for the scholarship exam. The director disapproved. He believed in the caste system. He believed in people knowing their place. He had obstructed the attendance at a mainland high school of the first few students Pop Wesley had proposed. Inevitably the director's fanatic eyes turned to Normie Cooktown, who was the tallest and oldest pupil in the room. As far as the blacks were concerned, the director equated learning with trouble-making. He had never forgotten that old chestnut of Pope's and was particularly impressed by the sequential line no one ever quoted: 'There shallow draughts intoxicate the brain.' He was determined that somehow he should thwart this lad whose older brother Billy was a loudmouth, a critic of the system. A complainer. A black who argued. My God, he couldn't bear blacks who argued.

'Stand up, that boy!' Pointing.

Normie stood.

'So you intend taking the scholarship examination next week?'

'Yes.'

'Yes, sir.'

'Yes, *sir*.'

'And are you well prepared?'

Normie rolled his eyes helplessly at his teacher.

'Answer me, boy.'

Normie mumbled yes.

'What was that? I couldn't hear.' The director did a whimsical feigning of deafness, one hand cupped to an ear.

'*Yes, sir!*' Normie shouted, goaded beyond self-control. Some kids at the back of the room giggled nervously.

The director's face flushed slowly from neck to forehead. His mouth shook.

'How dare you, boy! How dare you speak in that tone! Outside.'

The classroom with its shabby charts, its gecko-specked picture of the king and queen, its meaningless map of the world, was so still Pop Wesley thought perhaps all breathing had ceased. His own small sigh fluttered out like a moth.

'That will be all,' the director snapped. He felt he had lost control and he hated that. 'Back to your work.' He nodded abruptly to Wesley and stalked out of the room to find Normie defiant on the verandah.

'You're confined to the dormitory for a month,' he told him. He smiled. 'You may not attend school. You may not see your family.'

'But the exam?'

'You'll have to miss that. It will teach you not to be insolent. You would have failed anyway.'

The director's starched back jerked boardlike down the school steps. 'Take him,' he ordered the native police boys who accompanied him on all his little official visits, and he stalked past their scowls into a mid-morning bright with his own bile.

173

In the beginning of the new school year after war in the Pacific broke out, an Aboriginal boy appeared at Vine's school. 'We have,' the headmaster announced at morning assembly and making heavy weather of it, 'a new boy in first year.' Fifty pairs of eyes inspected Normie Cooktown who was shuddering in his strange uniform that didn't fully conceal the difference between his skin and all those other skins. His small body quivered and he dropped his eyes in terrible anguish and scuffed the toe of one boot across the floor. He wasn't used to shoes. There were suppressed sniggers.

The missionary zeal that had sustained Doctor Parsons in his apostolate at the Cape and on the islands was prodded by egotism. Tracking a peculiar logical sorites he attached the infallibility of the Lord to himself. He was never wrong. He was determined that his attempt at scholastic aid for the blacks would extend the influence of the Good Book which he had preached to bemused natives in the Kimberleys and on the coastal fringes of the Gulf. They were gentle with him. They had impeccable manners – they didn't want to offend a bore. And more than that, accession to the rules he had laid down meant blankets, tucker, and occasionally *nikki-nikki* even though he preached against the vice of tobacco.

'Those boys misbehaving will see me at the end of assembly.' He raised his voice, permitting an oratorical richness to vibrate through the hall. 'I cannot and will not tolerate unchristian antics.'

Behind the headmaster the seated staff stirred uncomfortably in their seedy gowns. Little Graph released a

174

hideous sigh he covered with assumed coughs. There were waxen smiles. (Memories here of recent unchristian protests from Church elders and parents, of white tribal grunts.) Fifty voices rose in a variety of cracked trebles announcing that the Lord was their shepherd and they would not want. Then they saved the king and were dismissed to classes.

It was as if the chalk dust had entered not only Vine's lungs but his veins. And the clogging of familiar smells: boarding-school meals, packed lunches from the day boys' satchels – bananas, orange peel, pencil shavings, erasers, ink. He could know nothing else. This was his desert peopled by – what? Half-humans? Part-people? Later that day, doing playground duty at the rear of the toilet block, he came upon a knot of shrilling lads and to the muted hisses of 'Here comes Clinger!' he parted brawling arms to discover Normie Cooktown dribbling mucus and tears. His new shirt was torn and someone had plastered a mudball on the side of his face.

At a staff meeting some weeks later, 'There should have been *two* lads from Doebin,' the headmaster admitted. 'Two. At least friendship, you know, a commonalty of culture and experience.' The sententious old bugger wagged a regretful head.

'The lad's a great little runner,' Clarrie Somerdew said flatly. 'He'll make out.'

'Do you really think so?'

Mr Pretorius interrupted, his voice harsh. 'Of course. There's enough patriotic hatred occupying all their minds these days without their having to waste time loathing the indigenes.'

'Oh, I hope you're right,' the headmaster said. 'I do hope so.'

War had reached the Taws. School windows were blacked out with brown paper. Slit trenches had been dug on the perimeter of the football field. There was air-raid practice every week. And every week, day after day, American planes droned overhead, taking off from the coastal air base for the Coral Sea or for the strips on the Cape. Townsville filled with GIs, and those boys who had managed a weekend in town with parents who had not fled south resumed school with fake Yank accents, chewed gum and called each other bud.

Vine found himself taking as much interest in the progress of Normie Cooktown as in that of his own son, now a second-former and top of his class. After Normie bloodied the noses of two classmates who persisted in calling him Darkie, he enjoyed a passive acceptance and was avoided until his agility on the sportsfield and in the gymnasium where he quickly outstripped the lot of them won their admiration. Watching that skinny fluidity on the vaulting horse and parallel bars, his form-mates became fair-minded at last. They had to admire. How could they not when he treated his skill with such indifference? 'It's easy,' he'd say, grinning at achievement. 'I'll show you. Look.' And he would bounce off the springboard, double somersault and end up facing them, eyes glinting. Or shin up the ropes and twist himself into knots on the rings, swinging easily. Do triple backflips on the bars. Classwork was too hard for him but the others rather liked that. He was a facile sketcher and his quick cartoons of staff members made him an underground hero.

Now and again Misses Weber and Starck who had moved their mission to an Aboriginal fringe settlement outside the Taws called at the school and took Normie off for the weekend. Clarrie Somerdew noticed an improvement in his reading and upon probing discovered the two women were giving patient coaching.

'You should have asked me,' he said to the boy. 'It's what I'm here for.'

Normie stared at his feet.

'Would you like an extra half-hour each day?'

Normie's eyes looked up and sought the grey distances of the plains.

'Well, would you?'

There was some kind of chewed mumble.

'I'll take it that's yes, then. Heavens, Normie, after a few weeks you'll leave the rest of the class behind.'

But he didn't, though he was running faster than ever, played hooker in the junior football team and beat the senior boys in the mile. He was turning into a kind of glamorous mascot.

'Well, that's better than nothing,' Vine remarked to Clarrie Somerdew after a burning sports afternoon in October. The field day had been rounded off with air-raid practice that was suddenly prelude to reality. As the boarders got ready in the change-rooms for tea there was horrible excitement when the town sirens hooted out over the streets and roofs of the Taws.

Trembling with *schadenfreude*, the lot of them, on the edge of possible disaster.

In the blazing sunset two small wasp-fast planes flew over the score of boys crouched in air-raid trenches. The planes skimmed to the horizon, circled and returned.

'Heads down!' roared Clarrie Somerdew who had taken over command from a mysteriously absent headmaster. There was suppressed giggling. The stink of deliberate farting. 'Peugh, Darkie! Urk, you stinking pewk!'

'Quiet!'

The two fighter planes buzzed them once more and then vanished towards the coast while the boys crouched, heads between knees, waiting for the all-clear. Terror? Disappointment?

Vine marched them back to the schoolhouse, watching his son from the corner of his eye as he made a point of walking with Normie Cooktown. Matthew, he decided, was more of a Christian than he could ever be. Could ever, ever . . .

He thought of Normie's latest assignment, passed on to him by Clarrie Somerdew. 'How do I handle this?' baffled Clarrie, already braced for enlistment, had asked. The essay lay on Vine's desk, a network of red pencillings. 'My peeple joyn the army,' Normie had written, 'but they dont get payed as much. My peeple are the onlie reel Australians.'

'He has a point,' Vine said. 'There's a fighting political

178

spirit there not altogether fashionable.'

Later he had taken the essay and read it aloud to his senior history group and called for comments. Grudgingly the class admitted that Aborigines should be paid as much as the rest of the troops. 'But they go walkabout, sir!' On Normie's second statement they were silent. Vine knew he shouldn't have done it, but, 'Hands up,' he had asked mildly, unwisely, 'those boys whose fathers are in the forces.'

Only three hands out of fifteen rose. 'We're necessary industry, sir,' one of the graziers' kids explained patiently as if soothing a numbskull. 'Just about all of us. We're feeding the troops.'

'My dad's in parliament,' another said with sly emphasis. 'He tells the country what to do, how to do it. I don't think he'd like those remarks much. Sir.'

Warned.

'What's a boong like you,' one of them asked Normie Cooktown that afternoon, 'doing at a school like this, eh?'

Vine overheard this question on his way to duty in the shower-rooms. He saw Normie, plumped out by boarding-school stodge and the bravery that came with being the fastest runner, stick out his lower lip and he paused by the half-open door.

'My grandad . . .' Normie said. And stopped.

'Your grandad what? Witchetty George? Wurley Wille?'

'My grandad owned your dad's place once. Reedy Crossing.'

'Bullshit!'

'It's true. My grandad was Martin Pelham.'

The other boy reddened. 'What about your grandma, then? What about her? Some camp gin. Pelham doesn't count as your grandad.'

'He went to a better school than this.'

Vine held his breath. Other boys coming across from the playing-fields looked at him curiously.

'And what was that? Wombat College? Mulga Grammar, eh?'

'No,' Normie Cooktown said. 'It was a place in England.' He scuffled feet and memory. 'Rugby. My grandma told me. She was his *moodja*.'

'And what's that then? What's *moodja*?'

'His wife.'

'Not his real wife, mate. Just a camp gin like I said. Your grandad was a gin jockey, just a gin jockey, see. And what was the name of that posh school again?'

'Rugby.'

'Never heard of it,' the senior boy said, full of spit and contempt. 'I'll ask sir.'

Vine pushed the door wide in time to see Normie launch himself at the other boy's face. There were snarls and blood as he pulled them apart. Normie's face had darkened with old grievance and Vine knew that the inner anger would stay and harden and wait for its moment.

Sometimes, strolling through evening in the desolation of the school grounds, dodging Marcia, trying not to think of Marie Laroche, he wondered if he were truly alive. None of that *cogito ergo sum* stuff that merely planted the body in position. Not even *tango ergo sum* – clutching his fingers so tightly they bit into the palms of each hand. He was part of a dream in God's eye, as insubstantial as tumbleweed, flimsier, rolled every whimway. Although he'd chosen, hadn't he, this furrowed path – marriage, classroom death (yes, it was often that) with its petrifying repetition that greyed hair and mind – he had to hurt the flesh palpably at times to gauge whether he was or wasn't.

He wasn't.

Sometimes, too, when he mooched along the dying streets of the Taws, he kept seeing Tony Shell who had broken into his own fantasy, pushing that broken-down wheelbarrow piled with his few belongings, heading for the sea lanes on the margins of that dream. Years gone, yet there was no touching Tony Shell, no connection by flesh or letter to that handsome Apollo substitute, one hand on the shoulder of the captain of the first eleven, or at football practice crushed in a too enthusiastic scrum and, later, God knows what at shower time, his jolly voice raised in jokey hurry-up pep to the team, their genitals shrunken under the cold water.

Where should he start to begin?

I am alone, he told himself, watching Shell and barrow topple over the world's rim. Watching his wife resentful in the kitchen. ('Do we have to stay on here now we have Matthew? We need more room.') Watching his son move through napkins, infant classes, junior school, as if distanced from his aloof, awkward teacher-dad who could not, not ever, chum it up and play happy families. The job made him act out that same part daily with strangers.

That bogus idealism of extracting structure from chaos! There was an unalterable plane geometry to his movements: the clock the tea/toast the clock the bell the classroom the toted piles of exercise books the bell the repeated texts the stale jokes the texts the bell the common-room bitchings the clock/bell the ... the ... the ...

'I wonder whatever's happened to Tony Shell?' his tongue found itself asking as he sat at breakfast.

He watched his wife wrestle with the past, then tighten her mouth and nod warningly in the direction of their son who was wolfing toast. Her faint headshake barred further comment.

'He's teaching in Brisbane,' Matthew told them, working at marmalade. He was full of cheery candour.

They both nagged then: how did he know? He was twelve. That barrow had been pushed across the horizon more than a decade before.

'Apocrypha,' their bright kid replied. 'School legend.'

'But why would you want to talk about him?' his naïve father asked, curiosity niggling. 'So long ago now. What sort of things do you boys talk about, anyway?'

Matthew put down his knife and regarded his parents with clear and amused eyes. 'Whenever Parsons gives us his yearly pep talk on moral duty, special friendships. That sort of thing. That's when. The seniors who remember the seniors who filtered it down. What a scandal, eh?' It didn't even dint their son's aplomb.

Shrug shrug shrug. Incompetent at handling this. Was Matthew really his biologic child? Vine wondered. He had peered for traces of Doctor Quigley's broad and handsome Irish face and could find no genetic endowment. In fact, his son sported a junior version of his own anguished ascetic mug. But healthier.

'A fine lad,' Doctor Quigley would comment on those few occasions they ran into each other at the coast. 'A grand boy.' And he would chuck the resentful Matthew under the chin.

'My lad,' Vine couldn't resist emphasising.

''Tis a wise man,' Doctor Quigley murmured offensively, lapsing into a deliberate and rich brogue. 'Have you time, then, for a drop of the crayture?'

Vine felt doomed to remain in that inland mining town and soon after his son's twelfth birthday, yielding to his wife's complaints, rented a house on the town outskirts from whose creaking walls he would walk the dusty mile to school. His wife gave up her duties as matron and was replaced by a local war-widow. A resigned Pretorius took over as resident master.

The move did not stop him thinking of Marie Laroche.

183

At certain times of day in bright sun and at certain angles created by wind, the struggling eucalypts brandished daggers of light reflected off their oily surfaces. Dagger upon dagger. He was learning, too late in life on the treadmill, to find grace in the tiny beauties and amazements that came his way. Wife and son moved in separate worlds. He nourished a longing for tenderness.

There was nothing, he told himself and his wife one morning at breakfast, like the loneliness of marriage.

Behind them the radio blared carefully edited reports on AIF activity in Buna and Kokoda. Vine winced at the cultivated dispassion of Gerald Morrow, known locally as the Voice of the North.

'You're telling me!' Marcia rattled cutlery. She had picked up Yankee idiom in shopping forays at the coast. And what else? he might have asked. She had frequent mysterious appointments, absent midweek for days at a time. 'War work,' she would not quite explain.

He didn't want an explanation.

Surprised again.

'The garden mourns – *Der Garten trauert*,' Schwarzkopf sang one morning as Vine shaved, bracing for the day. '*Sommer lächelt erstaunt und matt in den sterbenden Gartentraum* – Summer smiles, astonished, weary, into the garden's dying dream.' And he realised – *he knew* – he was in love.

In love for the first time in forty-odd years.

Dismissing a misty film of the girl who sang '*Die Forelle*' as a warm-up prelude to this.

A middle-aged man's whimsy, he self-accused. Folly.

No. Never. He could have wept as Schwarzkopf sang those final five words: '*Ist dies etwa der Tod*? – Can this be death?'

Don't answer.

The love object was not but soon must be made aware. After all, they worked together, more or less, she with her classes in French, her sketchy assistance with the school choir. (The visiting music master had long gone and died at Lae.) Replacements came and left and the headmaster struggled with numbers and tried never to replace. 'Make do,' he kept saying. 'There's a war on.'

Vine had his private war. What *was* it about her?

Marie Laroche was small, almost invisible one might say but for the passion of unruly hair that shadowed her unemphatic features. She would sit quietly in the staff common-room, her head bent over butchered translations and exercises, to glance up, when her name was spoken, with a short-sighted blink of violet.

This day she was blinking at the wrong man, a pudgy army reject from the south who had come to take Clarrie Somerdew's place. He wrote poetry and had published a small collection of verse, copies of which he left lying about. His rich, world-weary accent was a source of mimicry to the junior forms but his cherub face below a crusting of black curls regarded his classes with an amused assurance. He was unashamedly bored by sport.

'Did you say something?' Miss Laroche asked, smiling at the cherub face.

'Not I,' Mr Warlock said. His own smile, directed at Vine, was too knowing, Vine thought furiously.

'I did,' Vine said. 'Nothing much really. Just that that must be even more tedious than the stuff I mark. More room for error.' An uncrossing of his skinny legs, discomfort in the stomach, a contraction of the heart.

'Not really.' She smiled. Her face became oddly pretty, slightly lopsided under the shadow of her hair. 'These things have their humour.'

'Do they? Do they really?' He was simply shoving the conversation along. Mr Warlock rose, gathered books ostentatiously and left the room.

'Of course. Look. Let me show . . .'

And earnestly she searched out some idiocy in the scrawled misinterpretation of vocabulary-weak juniors. But Vine wasn't listening. He was watching her hair, her mouth, the fragile curve of her neck, all in an imbecile and unexpected lust.

'If you have a moment,' she suggested shyly.

He had all the time in the world.

He began shadowing her movements, secreted a copy of her timetable in his desk. There was the music room emptied after choir practice where Miss Laroche, seated at the scabby Bluthner upright donated by the wife of the town clerk, would explain the follies of unpardonable chordal errors by the lads who had just destroyed a three-part version of *Nymphs and Shepherds*. But then she would add, might add, 'Still, frankly, I can't see why not.'

And she would play a sequence of chords. 'You see? It sounds, well, interesting.'

He would agree that it did. He would agree to almost anything.

'But this –' hands striking at too ordinary resolutions, 'this is what Doctor Parsons will expect on parents' day.'

He suggested she might have Stravinskys in the making, Messiaens. The violet washed to the edges of his encumbered world.

'You understand then? You like Stravinsky?' If only she wouldn't leave her lips so parted. He wanted to pop a chord between them.

'Only now,' he would have liked to answer.

Forty-seven, dear God, and in the throes of idyll, unexpected as rainstorm, as those rains that never came.

Yes, he could swear it was unplanned, unavoidable. That sudden stumble of the heart, a brief crippling that had not happened ever before, contracted from that first encounter a term ago at a staff meeting.

'And this is Mademoiselle Laroche.' Pretorius was ponderously making tea as they waited for Doctor Parsons to arrive. 'Who will be taking our laddies down cultural Gallic groves previously unknown to their tasteless skulls.'

She blinked with embarrassment, uncomfortable at Little Graph's heavy-fisted humour, and had gone to sit uneasily on the edge of a chair by the window.

'May I?' Vine had asked, rinsing out a clean cup for her at the sink. And she had nodded and taken the cup from him with a well-shaped hand that, later, he hoped might discover another confidence in his. Her smile was annihilatingly sweet. Madman!

It was inexplicable. Walking home that afternoon through the dust beside the yellowing paddocks, he could not even recall if she were pretty. He supposed she was. In any case, he reformed her so, moulded an object of worship that was faultless in contour.

He found he was driven by his ferocious obsession. He lent books, waylaid her in corridors, added biscuits to her saucer at morning tea, began once more translating suitable or unsuitable Horatian odes that he slipped shyly onto her desk.

He had to talk about it. Mention her name.

'There's a new member of staff,' he couldn't resist confessing at dinner one evening. 'A young woman.'

'Oh yes.' Marcia was dishing up vegetables. She didn't glance up. 'What's she like?'

'She's the new French teacher. A little music as well. The choir.'

He began eating, keeping his eyes busy on chops. If he looked up his wife might see the explosion of light.

'That's the last of the meat coupons,' she said, tackling her own meal. Displaying enormous uninterest. Their son looked from one to the other as if watching ball-play.

'You should be especially nice, Dad,' he said, 'to Ted Werner. His dad's the butcher. Old Parsons is always giving him special favours.'

'I'm incorruptible,' his father lied. He glanced over at his son and smiled in a way that was almost complicit. And from that moment Marcia was aware.

Abstracted by love.

He barely thought of Marcia, who had announced one desperate night after he shrank from her chafing fingers that she thought it time for her to think of her own sexual comfort.

Good God! What was she doing uttering words like that in the days of prudish pursed lips and euphemism – had the American presence brought with it a climate of *laissez-faire*? The weather certainly created its own equation with the passions and when Vine was informed by a noted town gossip (eyebrows raised, gobble-mouth downturned) that his wife had been seen driven coastwards by American staff cars – 'She does work hard for the war effort, Mr Vine!' – he felt nothing but relief.

'Ah, yes,' he had said to the gooseberry eyes of the local grocer's wife. 'Ah, yes. These are changing times, aren't they. Bully for her!' He gave a little bow. 'And bully for you, too!' A courteous afterthought that made the lady flush.

Envy, he judged. And he blanketed his own guilt.

So it was not difficult for him to announce as they washed up together some days later, 'Marcia, I'm afraid that we must separate.' He did not notice his son paused by the door.

She asked, lathering vigorously, 'Why? Why now?' After years, she added, of indifference.

There was nothing concrete he could offer, only infidelity of the heart. He gave the dinner plates an extra polish and put them carefully on the rack. He admired their bland circular neutrality. He rubbed between fork tines. He moulded the teatowel into every cup.

'You can't do this,' Matthew said, shocking them both. His hands, separate, were clenched in tight fists. 'Please don't do this.'

This rented kitchen in this rented house with its vertical timber walls, its picture-rails hung with the cultural loot of years – his and hers – as disparate as their owners. He had contributed two Renoir prints and a stuffed bookshelf, a pottery bowl he had picked up in Tuscany once on a walking holiday, and an anonymous pen-and-ink sketch of *palazzi* in Venice. She had an array of landscapes of never-to-be-visited European lakes and waterways and some terrifying rednesses of the wide brown land she had cut off butcher Werner's yearly calendars.

Vine put down the last cup as gently as if it had been formed of sand, hung up the towel, noting the obduracy of his wife's shoulders as she mopped last drizzles from the sink-bench, the startled and appalled eyes of his son.

'Oh Matt,' he said hopelessly, arms loose at his sides. Then quietly he let himself out the back door to stand beneath the guava tree.

How could either of them resist the essential loneliness

of marriage, that artificial marcotting based on paradox? As a couple – was 'grew' the word? – sweltered together, they also grew/sweltered apart. First rule of family. *Familiae regula prima: amor odium est.* Love is loathing. In a perverse way he was glad she had had her fling with a group captain, American colonel, whatever, and wished for his own sake it might have lasted longer. It exonerated him, he reasoned falsely.

But.

There was always a but.

I love you, he had confessed to Marie Laroche, trapped between piano and store cupboard. He noticed the yellowness of the piano keys, the permanent depression of one of them, a missing ivory, the flaking of polish from the front boards where the candlestick holders had been removed leaving permanent sores.

Three days before, he had endured an improving session in the school chapel while a visiting cleric harangued. Hello, boredom, he had whispered, safe at the very back of the room from reports of mutiny. Hello.

Should he pack a bag?

Should he move to a downtown hotel? (He had caught sight of his son's expectant profile at that point.)

Should he do nothing?

What could be more and less attractive to his natural sloth than that?

If only Marcia would leave.

The silence surged out from his rented house one mile away to pummel him there.

So, I love you, he had admitted, but without much force.

The young woman did not know what to say. The abruptness of his words shocked. She thought, perhaps, that he was old enough to be her grandfather, a *grandpère* with fanatic eye.

She began stacking music sheets.

I am serious, he insisted.

She watched her hands shuffling and ordering torn pages within folders. All those little attentions of the past month had meant friendliness, she believed. Not this.

Say something! he demanded. Please! (Animation at last!)

What?

You must have known, he floundered. Since you came I . . . We could leave here. (Eagerness took over.) There are other schools, other places. We could go away now, next week. Oh soon!

Excuse me, she had said, pushing past his groaning body to shut the piano lid and place herself on the forte side of safety. Samuel, she added.

His first name came as a surprise. It seemed years since anyone had used it. The young woman's face had flushed a terrible red that just as quickly drained away, leaving freckles startled by his declarations of love.

Please, he begged. He felt tears scorch his eyelids, a gulp clamp the air in his throat.

Not now, she said gently. We can't talk about it now. She could have wept for him. She made the mistake of placing a consoling hand on his arm and in a second he had her clutched to his bony frame that shook with the despair in his blood. Her response was small cries of fright, of struggle and shove. The piano stool crashed against his elderly shins and almost as quickly he released her, humiliated, shamed, to begin the endless apologies that would dog him till he died. He heard her protest that they were little more than strangers, that she would have to love him as well. She did not.

Then he was alone in the afternoon classroom where spiders had spun dangling scales played out in the oblique sun of five o'clock, where the room jangled with Czerny exercises and Clementi sonatinas, where his damnation was complete and as perfect as a Bach prelude.

He raised the lid on the piano, staring at its mute keys, then he sat down and struck two notes. Their undamped harmonics buzzed like flies.

Thirty now. Father Donellan tell him thirty. He tell about war in Europe, in Pacific, and he organise them on Doebin go help out on farms on the coast where the men sent away.

Don't want to leave Jeannie. Got three kids now and she have to do all that work. Mumma dead and dadda too old to help much. Some of the men join army. Don't like that idea. But say okay, I cut cane all right. And then three of them, Willie Omba, Hector Fourmile and him, they go over mainland in mission launch and Father take them up to big cane farm north of Townsville.

Them people Italian. Look little bit like them, like Willie, like Hector. But the lady she smile, eh, and show them rooms in shed and Father say, You be good chaps, now, and work hard. And Hector say, When we ever do anythin else, Father? and they all laugh then and the lady she make Father tea up on the verandah and she give them theirs to take back to shed.

It real hard work, all day slashin that cane, jumpin away from snakes. Early up all right and work work work till sundown.

Father come sometime see how they doin. He say, How are you, Manny? Hector? Willie?

Okay, they tell him. But they want to go back Doebin, see their folks.

You will, he tell them. Just as soon as cutting's finished. Take you back myself, he say. Maybe you come back planting time.

He forget that year but the next he take them and when they see their wives an kids everythin all right.

They got pay too, more than they ever got on Doebin workin for the gubbamin. That make Jeannie happy. Then he remember mumma say, Happy don't last.

HE LIKED TO THINK HE CREATED A THREAD

HE LIKED TO THINK HE CREATED A THREAD, a unifying factor in all those lives he touched.

A chant-line.

On the other hand . . .

'Och, Father O'Flynn, you've a wonderful way wid ye, all the young childer are wild for to play wid ye, all the old sinners . . .' et cetera, et ceter-rah!

He was lovable, kind, caring, generous with his time.

'They're truly nature's ladies and gentlemen,' he often said, speaking of the island's blacks. 'Day by day I grow more fond of them.' And he meant it.

Yet Father Donellan had no trouble with conscience when it came to seeing those missionary rival proselytes on their way, despite their own good nature, gentleness and caring. When he arrived on Doebin on his second visit a year later, he found the boarding house empty and no replacement for that efficient Mrs Curthoys. Disaster left its stain, its ghosts. He borrowed blankets and pillow and some cans of food and emerged, not quite guiltily, from the larder to find lanterns waving in the dark along the beach and moving steadily up through the scrub as welcome.

He couldn't believe they remembered him from his visit there the year before when he had offered that first Mass, a Mass of portent sketched in blood, a presage of catastrophe. But Moses Thursday rushed forward, his face cracked into a grin, the lamp swinging from dark to light to dark.

'You hungry?' Moses asked. 'You get tucker long our camp, eh? My missus she cook bush pigeon.'

Donellan walked away from the empty boarding house to Moses' grass hut on the back road, urged on by giggling and singing islanders.

'You be quick,' Moses urged. 'Curfew at nine. Still the same, eh?' He liked his own humour. 'My missus she make curfew too.'

The priest marvelled at the human need for order in this world of leaves.

All those years, he thought, of spiritual persuasion in the far west, walking miles when the train broke down or paddling through mud in an early Wet, borrowing a cow cocky's truck and celebrating Mass on the buckboard, the wafer no less consecrated for being blessed in cathedrals of air. In the recesses of his mind lay the soft rains and greens of Ireland, the damp-stained walls of his seminary, the valley mists and hill folds. He would ring down this curtain to blot out the saltpans, the reds and ochres and gaunt scrub of his then landscape, and whistle as he trudged or clambered on goods trains or hitched rides in delivery vans, hoping for a welcome at distant stations where at last he could murmur, '*Introibo ad altare dei*,' in the comfort of a settler's living-room.

Fortitude kept the flesh in order.

Years of it.

And now the move east had brought him again to Doebin for a second, more permanent, time, for tucker at Moses Thursday's, courtesy requiring him to doss down there in a lean-to out the back.

No one had mentioned Uncle Boss. There was a new man now, a humourless disciplinarian, a public servant with a narrow face and narrower views who enforced segregation and ran the island like a barracks. There were more bells, more prohibitions.

'Don't you think,' Father Donellan asked cautiously that first week, 'that we,' he was careful to say 'we', 'might treat all the people here as if they were ... well ... people?'

The new director leaned back in his office chair against a brochure view of coral waters and stared. He found churchmen pests, especially this Irishman with his egalitarian notions.

'What do you mean exactly?'

It was hopeless. Father Donellan gave a shrug, rose, and went away into the morning.

It was dark blue heat, tide-threat nuzzling the islands and the beaches under black air. '*Go-ah!*' Moses Thursday said in language. And suddenly the priest's alpaca was spotted with rain, large drops whacking on palm and coral dust. Father Donellan fought his umbrella open. 'Big Wet,' Moses said, guiding the priest out on the road to the prison. 'He jus start, eh?' He smiled with pleasure and nudged the other man's elbow, point on point, bone-touch. Donellan didn't mind. 'You got permit, brother?'

'Got everything,' Donellan said. He patted his pocket. 'Even got cigarettes for your cousin.'

Moses giggled. The rain burst above them like a tap and they began running along the sandy track to come to a gasping stop outside the island gaol where one of the black boys, crazily armed, stopped them to examine the permit.

'You won't like this, eh?' Moses said confidently, walking ahead down the narrow passageway between the cells.

Donellan could hardly bear to look. The floors were moving with cockroaches that gorged on the smeared grey blankets of the prisoners. Dark, ill-ventilated like the detention rooms in the boys' barracks, the cells stank of shit and despair.

'Here's Willie.' Moses peered through cyclone mesh.

Willie Omba and the priest stared at each other, one man chained by the system, the other by his collar. Outside there was a world of rain and sea-pound. Donellan wanted to plunge into its freshness, seek baptism. He saw Willie's eyes glint in the half-dark. 'How long?' he asked.

'Two months yet.'

Moses Thursday interrupted indignantly. 'He got six months for cheekin the boss.'

'I should have got twelve yesterday,' Donellan said, trying to make a joke, to show fraternity, partisanship. Teeth flashed in the gloom.

'Fella next door, he got twenty-one days bein caught after curfew,' Willie said.

'Why was that?'

'Him courtin his girl. They want get married, eh. Like me. Same thing.'

'And can't they?'

'Not without boss say yes. Give paper sayin yes. Like you gotta get me, Father.'

There was violence apart from the weather, even standing still in this fetid corridor. Outside, axes of wind and water chopped at landscape. That was less than this violence to the heart. Floggings mattered little beside the permitted lash of thwarting, the grinding of spirit that was practised daily in this visual paradise.

Under the Act almost every form of patronage became assault.

'I'll ask. I shall declare the banns. Would you like that, Willie?'

Willie Omba's face came close to the wire mesh and he frowned.

'You still gotta get that piece of paper, bro. Still get.'

'Don't worry,' Donellan said, worrying. 'I'll get it.'

Waiting.

Days moved slowly. The priest on U-millie left unexpectedly, and while the lazaret waited for a replacement Donellan went there twice a week in an outboard piloted by Jardine who dropped him off and returned in the afternoon to pick him up. Donellan said Mass, heard confessions and visited the sick in the lazaret. There was only a handful of patients now for the new director had plans to close the hospital and move everyone to Doebin.

'Don't know what you buggers get out of it,' Jardine said.

'Don't you?' Donellan couldn't help feeling fastidious. 'And what do you get out of being here?'

'I'm wife dodging,' the boatman said. 'No woman in her right mind would want to come to this arse of a place.'

'You've been dodging a long time, then.'

'Maybe.'

In the evenings Donellan and the teacher, Pop Wesley, played chess for hours, listening to the spaces between the rain squalls. His days were consumed with the care of his flock. He visited the invalid hostel where some of the lepers transferred from U-millie rotted quietly along with the coughing skeletons with TB. He spoke to Willie Omba's sweetheart, her head shaved for being caught in the long grass with Willie, her dress a bulging sack. She wouldn't raise her head before him.

'Bless you, Essie,' he said, and he put out a hand to pat her flinching shoulder. 'Don't worry now. There's no shame. The shame is with the gubbamin, you understand? It's not your shame at all.'

She shook her shaven skull while tears rolled.

'The shame belongs gubbamin,' he insisted. 'I've asked. I've got your piece of paper, see?' He waved in front of her the form the director had reluctantly signed. She put out one finger to touch the paper but wouldn't look up.

He trudged his way back to the priest-house through a fluid scaffolding of rain holding earth to heaven. His umbrella was buffeted by fists of wind as he slushed through the last half-mile, head lowered before curious settlement houses whose louvres were a-gape for air in this water world.

How, he marvelled, could everything be so beautiful and so ugly, so simple and so complicated? He loosened his collar and decided his only release would be to become stuffed with the substance of good works that, like this rain, would dissolve to allow replenishment and the calm that was the cup of cold water given in His name.

Donellan stood dripping in the doorway of his tiny sitting-room and found Wesley on his verandah working happily through the pages of a month-old newspaper with as fervent a dedication as he might give to the office.

What were the words they exchanged? Did they matter? Even as he stripped off his sodden and peculiarly cheap-smelling garments in the shower-room and began towelling his body dry, even then he couldn't remember. There was something he wanted to say to his visitor, some quick-wit words of cheer. He came back to the sitting-room dry, changed, comfortable, and there was a cup of tea and sandwich waiting for him.

'Well, now,' he said to Wesley – and gave his shoulder a friendly slap as he passed – 'you do understand what it's all about, don't you?'

Minor victories. The director grudgingly allowed a fortnight's remission of Willie Omba's sentence and Father Donellan married him to Essie in a packed church, the largest congregation he had had since his arrival. Flowers. Singing. Smiles.

After the ceremony, unable not to notice the proud swelling of Essie's waistline under the cotton wedding dress, he whispered as she wrote her name slowly in the register, 'I blessed the baby too.'

Doebin was to be his home for the next seven years.

During all that time Father Donellan never yielded in trying to plough democracy into autocratic ground. His successes were minimal. After that he was moved back to the mainland with the outbreak of war, to cope with parish wives of interned Italians, women left alone to run cane farms and rear kids. He organised workers from Doebin to help on the farms, where harassed wives swore the blacks worked harder than whites.

Father Donellan's bishop fretted about all these social changes. Most of all he was appalled by the obvious competence of women who coped alone.

'The trend is worrying,' the bishop said at an area conference of parish priests. 'Women,' he added, the two syllables conveying a certain bitterness, 'are driving cars, working in factories, dressing like men. And now, when they leave the kitchen, they must, of course, expect to face the real world and all that that implies.'

'You mean,' Father Donellan suggested rather impertinently, 'how will we get them back?'

'I don't follow you. Get them back where?'

'Into the kitchen.'

The bishop tutted and looked away. He had enough trouble finding a housekeeper. He decided to ignore this humblest of his workers. He found the demands of the teaching sisters in his empire of parishes sufficiently irritating, but was forced to tolerate them. They did the humdrummery none of his lieutenants could or would easily endure. He stared past Father Donellan's amused face while he spoke of Aboriginal labourers on Italian cane farms. He spoke graciously but distantly. He thanked Father Donellan for organising the mission launch *Avila* to bring the young men across from Doebin. He thanked him for driving the workers along the coast to the Fiorellis, Gambinos, Petrocinas. Father Donellan refrained from telling him that overwrought housewives wept with gratitude.

Several hundred Italian men had been rounded up

after the fall of Singapore and shipped to Brisbane in closed trains. The bishop, in a political quandary over this summary treatment (for many of them were his parishioners), did a Pontius Pilate and kept his mouth closed. As discreetly as he could, fearing government rage, Donellan visited farms, gave communion and conducted sessions of the rosary. 'It's the Masons,' the Italians muttered, seeking a scapegoat for this disruption to their lives. 'It's the communists,' the clergy said, who could only see red.

Signora Pergolesi's twelve-year-old son was furtively moved to a boarding school west of Townsville where he was bullied and ostracised for three years. There was no room at the Catholic establishment in the Taws but by string-pulling Father Donellan had him enrolled with Doctor Parsons a month after Normie Cooktown, whose half-caste skin placed him in the same category as Giovanni Pergolesi.

Ecumenical before it was fashionable. Diversity.

So there were pastoral visits to the green farms of disgraced Italians, to country schools of a different persuasion, as the diehards said, who had taken in evacuees, and, best of all, long tea-drinking sessions with now-befriended Misses Weber and Starck, still surviving with their Bible classes in a humpy outside the Taws.

Chaos, Donellan murmured guiltily and happily. Chaos gave a sudden zest to life. There were makeshift classes run in presbyteries and Country Women's Association halls, in schools of arts, in warehouses and shearing sheds. His world became a replica of his early evangelism but now he had a car, grudgingly supplied by the bishop and topped up with gas every week or so by generous American GIs.

Then a Japanese bomb split a palm tree in Townsville apart.

A pre-disaster bravado nourished those townsfolk who elected to remain despite government pressure to evacuate the north. The notion of abandoning the state to the enemy sickened them. The Brisbane Line, that proposed last ditch of fortification, became a dirty joke.

On one of Donellan's visits to Doebin to see how his successor was handling the situation, the *Avila* was inspected by a low-flying American helicopter. There was an onslaught of pentecostal wind. Father Donellan waved and pointed elaborately to his dog-collar, stood air-slashed in his greenish-black suit while the chopper hovered. A face looked out at him, grinned and flapped a hand. Something dropped and hit the deck of the launch. 'Jesus!' the launchman cried. 'What the hell!'

Donellan picked up a carton of cigarettes from the deck and saluted thanks to the retreating helicopter. 'I need one myself,' he said to the launchman, breaking open a pack.

It was more than six months since he'd been back. The sea still rimpled green around the jetty piles. The timbers creaked in the same spots. The track up to the settlement had been widened. There were more women and children. Some of the young men had enlisted but most of them had been drafted for land work. Yet still those left remembered him. A foam of names and faces.

This was the place his heart hid, he knew. Not in that hot timber town huddled under Cootharinga with its ugly orange escarpments, twinned riverfalls of rock that looked as if a gross explosion had cleft the hill in half, the residue of earth running east to form barren foothills for the scrubbiest of trees. And below, the houses and two cathedrals, rivals for souls.

It was all too tiring. He thought momentarily of Starck and Weber who had pointed out to him without words how everyone was headed the same way, after the same thing: the kindliness of the godhead discovered in a cup of tea and a stale biscuit offered with simplicity in a broken-down hut.

From the island he looked across at the coast, the town, that ugly place, that *jolie laide*, no longer visible. Only the Great Divide that in early morning or late afternoon stretched deceptively delicate folds and pillows of grey-blue haze and violet. That lay before him; and behind, the hump of the island menacing the blue channel.

Once this island had been his purgatory.

All through the war he returned to Doebin as relieving pastor but only for a few weeks at a time.

Back and finding it as enchantingly beautiful and as spiritually loathsome as ever. The latest director (change of face, no change in attitude) was authoritarian, racist, dogmatic. Deputy Leggat was deputy still, his weedy frame and moustache unchanged by years and a vanished wife. There were drinking bouts now to temper the weather. Handyman Jardine appeared to be in a permanent state of semi-intoxication. The dregs, Donellan told himself listening to the boatman's handling of the native boys as they unloaded cargo onto the wharf. Then he asked himself was he any better in his crumpled priestly garb, collar grimy already from sweat, his intolerance clipped ragged to the verge of sin, Hell being the swinging blue waters of Shippers Cove.

Deputy Leggat was there to oversee.

Donellan could hear Leggat fussing and screeching on the jetty's end, urging the boys to watch it, watch it, as they lifted a chest of drawers to the top of the rail, readying it for the waiting workers. Sun slashed at them all like a sword.

It's valuable, Leggat was yelling, words meaningless as air. Careful! Careful! Oh God, you stupid buggers! Watch it!

The boys observed the deputy sideways, casually, avoiding eye contact, and Donellan saw Billy Cooktown give a little smile. At Leggat's last screamed warning they raised the chest and slammed it down neatly against the railings, so that eight expensively turned knobs flew off like eggs and floated away. As the chest thudded onto the jetty planking, its frail end-boards splintering, its eight abscesses facing the sea, the runtish deputy danced on a tightrope of rage. 'Fetch them!' Jardine bellowed, pointing to the bobbing drawer knobs. 'You get in there and fetch them!'

All that power play.

It was worse than ever in the settlement, he discovered later. Far worse. Since his first visit, his first Mass, so many years ago, the population had trebled, swollen by refugees from violent marriages on the fringes of white coastal towns, by half-castes dumped from everywhere, by black men with records of petty crime and drunkenness, unwanted by the army, incapable of working on the farms.

The sottishness. The rapes. The misery.

A mere half-dozen attended his first service the next day and then only with permission of the director. '"I will go unto the altar of God."'

'This place,' he said to the public service red-face in his office the morning after, 'is like Alcatraz. You hate them, don't you? You hate all these people. At least Brodie was fond of the poor devils.'

Outside the world was measled with rain.

He pondered what devices could, if he were writing a fiction – which he wasn't – incorporate the diurnal drudgery and dredge meaning from the pettinesses that tracked landscape towards some ultimate event. Would it be a dreary canto of tribulation? Was ordinary living only ever a series of minor climaxes, each poised on its own plinth of dubious history? Was it necessary to have climax upon climax in what ultimately led to the vertex, the chorus vanished, the lone soloist before the emptied orchestra pit, and the gates of the next world opening upon a panorama of – what?

Of what? He was close to loss of faith and only

discovered affirmations of belief and trust in the menial offices of his day. He remembered admitting to another priest that he found organising a bed or a meal for some town black or white derelict more meaningful than the Mass.

'But,' his colleague had replied, nonplussed, 'when you do that, it *is* the Mass. It's simply another version.'

Ritual and brotherly love should not be inseparable.

Again and again he decided that ritual was empty without being enriched and amplified by practical application. 'Do this in commemoration of Me' became talismanic words.

Was that cruel and rigid collar he wore another version of the *halos*? The threshing floor of the Greeks? Nimbus? The light around the body? Long before Christians took over this emblem of eminence, he had read once, heathens used it to decorate representations of deities and emperors.

Nimbus. *Halos*. Aureole. Dog-collar.

He ran a loosening finger about his neck as he confronted the director in a late afternoon painted dark already by the sky's own nimbus of storm and raincloud. This, too, is the Mass, he wanted to say, resolving to a series of pleas or prayers to the thick-skull opposite for betterment of conditions that now enforced segregation, rigorously observed: the privileges for whites only; the curfews; the nagging bells; the young women kept pure behind wire in their dormitories; the prisoners in the island lockup with their rags of blankets, the stench of piss and faeces.

'The women have to be locked up at night. It's for

their own protection. You must understand this. We have had enough attacks here by drunken men.'

'Then how do they get the liquor at all? I don't understand. I thought this was a dry island.'

'Boats. It's smuggled in.'

'Your own staff don't supply it, I suppose. After all, you do have one or two with . . .'

The director could never forget the god of the public service. He straightened behind his desk, his eyes becoming stony.

'How dare you!' He could lash himself into a rage from ice-cold to fever-hot in seconds. 'How dare you, sir! Don't come here with your pious cant and presume to tell me my job. There is no one on my staff who would do such a thing. No one.'

'Yet the white staff may drink, may they not? Naming no names,' Father Donellan persisted, his voice at its silkiest, 'but you employ sots, God forgive me for the word, and they aren't black. Don't you find it odd at all that the moral exemplars should be allowed to indulge, brutishly, from what I hear and see, what they forbid the poor wretches they control? What an example!'

'Get out!' the director roared. 'Get out, you impudent Roman.'

Father Donellan took his time about getting up, edging his chair back slowly to the tempting rim of the abyss.

'You're wrong there. I'm not Roman. I was born in Donegal.'

The director began banging viciously at a desk-bell until a frightened young face poked round the door. 'This man is –' he almost choked, 'leaving. Immediately. Take him out please.'

Donellan replaced his lumpy panama, straightened his alpaca coat and went into the side office with the clerk. 'You couldn't possibly be training for that job,' he said to the lad. There was a shake of the head, a voice whispering as they went out onto the verandah. 'I'm temporary. A casual. Everyone's temporary here, well, except for the old hands. If they can be.' He added the last words bitterly. 'Who'd want to be permanent?'

'Why are you here then? Why do you stay?'

'Oh, I had notions, notions of service. It's a holiday job until the war ends.' He pulled a face. 'I'm on school holidays. Idiot stuff, I suppose, coming here. But my father – he was here once, only for a while. Teaching. Vine. You might have heard of him, though he wasn't here long. It's a kind of emotional suicide, I guess. But I thought I could do something. It's hopeless, you know.'

Donellan smiled his old perky smile and patted the bony shoulder alongside him. 'Offer it up,' he advised, 'as the good sisters used to tell us. Perhaps they didn't tell you. But it's not bad advice. Store merit. Grace.'

'That might work for you,' the kid objected. He was little more than an adolescent. 'There's too much here to offer up.'

The weight of it all kept them both earthbound.

Donellan walked back to the priest-house set on a rise behind the little chapel and found Paddy Cullen, the curate from U-millie's leper settlement, brewing a pot of tea. The curate had been on his tour of duty for two years, moving between the islands. Like the clerk, he was too young for this. He had returned too soon from sick leave. His hands trembled as he measured tea-leaves into the pot. A tic bounced at the corner of his mouth.

Donellan dragged a deckchair up to the door that looked out at the mainland. His heart filled with pity for Paddy Cullen as for the young clerk, for the unendingness of bodily service that the world could inflict on those who believed only in the immortality of the spirit. 'This man's new,' he said, meaning the director, 'if three years means new.'

The curate came out with the tea and placed it on a table beside Donellan. He shrugged, his emptied hands now looking hopeless. 'It was all right before. The director before him was better. And that other, the one who . . .' The curate hesitated. 'The blacks loved him. They would do anything, anything. Maybe he was a bit easy-going, I've heard. But life was better. This one's a tyrant.'

'I know, I know, Paddy. But let's forget him for a moment. I've splendid news for you.'

'What's that then?'

'You're getting a break, lad. It's official. Straight from the bishop's mouth. More or less permanent. I'm taking over for a couple of months until they find someone older and more case-hardened, my boy. You're off for a stretch in Brisbane, in fact. How's that for news?'

It shocked him to see the sudden light in Father Cullen's eyes, the glow of sacrifice doused, understandable though it was. 'Oh God!' the curate whispered. 'I've got to confess I prayed for it.' He picked up his cup and the

216

cup rattled on its saucer, the saucer bucking in his hands. 'When?'

'Within the month,' Father Donellan said. 'Now, never let me hear you say, Father, that prayers aren't answered, will you?'

He didn't expect the shaking that followed and then the tears.

Imprisoned by water. Paddy Cullen tossed in his sweaty sleep and gabbled. Donellan could hear his mutterings through the thin walls of his room, through the rain-noisy dark, through the muffling of the mosquito net and the whine of mosquitoes. Another fortnight had gone by. The supply barge couldn't reach the island in the high seas running from the Cape. The *Avila* was port-bound in Townsville.

'But why?' Paddy Cullen had asked earlier that evening as if listening to a bedtime story. 'Why? Why would Brodie do it?'

A few days before, they'd been chewing over that fifteen-year-old horror. The vibrations it had left quivered in the young priest's soul. He talked of nothing else these last days.

'Despair,' Father Donellan tried to suggest. 'Who knows what it can drive a man to. I only met him the once and he seemed a good enough fellow. The natives liked him.'

'But his children,' Paddy Cullen said. 'How could he?'

He was obsessed by the permutations of guilt.

What's done is done, Donellan wanted to say. There were other troubles brewing on Doebin. Manny Cooktown had been punched witless by the boatman. It was difficult to find the reason. Manny's brother Billy said there had been a fight because Jardine was beating his common-law wife Betsy, Manny's daughter. Well, hardly wife, Billy said. She only thirteen. She go there as housegirl. Clean up, eh? Cook meals. He jump her, bro. All last year, he jump her. The boss, he know. He say nothin.

Donellan had wandered down to the boatshed with some trumped up reason for calling so that he could inspect Jardine's flattened nose and black eyes. The damage gave him an uncharitable thrill that sped his query about the possibility of a boat to take Father Cullen to town. The boatman was angry and sulking. 'You can see the way I am,' he said. 'I couldn't steer a bloody tinnie.'

'Tell me,' Father Donellan said, seating himself more or less comfortably on a work-bench, 'about those Cooktown boys. Didn't one of them shoot Captain Brodie?'

Jardine blinked and began rolling a cigarette that he placed delicately between puffed lips. 'You're going back a long way, aren't you?'

'Just curious. I'm wondering if Manny still suffers from the memory of that. If he can't get rid of his ghosts, you know.'

'Just a trigger-happy boong, if you want my opinion. Couldn't keep his fuckin finger still.'

'Ah,' Father Donellan said, letting the vowel roll out

218

slowly like an expelled breath. 'But he was released, wasn't he. He came back a year later.' A flat statement. 'They brought in a verdict of not guilty after all.'

'Where's all this getting us?'

'Nowhere, I suppose. Nowhere. I was just wondering.' And he hesitated. 'I was wondering, too, where all the whites on the settlement were when all this was going on. You see . . .' and he presented a face of the blandest innocence to the boatman, 'I never really heard the full story, not coming back for a year. There was a – what do you call it now? – a conspiracy of silence from the holy of holies. From the administration section, that is. It was as if they had all been struck dumb, you understand. You do understand, don't you?'

Jardine blew smoke directly at the priest in a tiny gesture of contempt. 'He was acting on orders, mate. Leggat's, if you want to know.'

'But you just described Manny as trigger-happy.'

'In a manner of speaking, he bloody was. They gave him the gun, see. But he could've shot Brodie in the leg or whatever. Didn't have to finish the bugger.'

'Maybe he panicked.'

'Maybe. And what's all this got to do with the price of apples, eh?'

'Oh, a little. Something.' Father Donellan eased himself off the work-bench. 'I mustn't hold you up.' He walked to the door of the shed and looked out to the water and the jetty fifty yards away. 'And where were you, Mr Jardine, while all this was happening? You were pretty close, weren't you? You could have done something.'

219

'Ah, piss off!' the boatman said.

He was a man no longer afraid of death, poor Paddy Cullen, sent off on the *Avila* at the end of the wet season to some kind of recuperative retreat house in Brisbane for religious overcome by rigours.

'Bless you,' Donellan had said automatically to the leached figure of his colleague arched painfully over the rails of the mission launch in the same agony as the stained-glass saints in the cathedrals of his childhood. Cullen had refused to understand where he was going or why. Donellan knew. Donellan understood. Keep chipper, he had whispered. And had said again to himself 'keep chipper' as he hustled his rugby team of islanders into place with the scowling visage of the director filling the whole island sky.

In the spaces before sleep lately, his brothers and sisters would float across his dream world, dead now, but still alive in those last dockside snaps he had brought away with him and brought out now and again to remind himself. There was Daniel stamping into the barn in a fragrance of milk and cow dung, arrogant and disgraced because he'd got Shally Burke into trouble and there'd be a wedding he didn't want any day. And Eris, gone, vanished overnight on the Liverpool boat because she couldn't stand milking and packing spuds any longer, disappearing into the back streets of that foggy port to become a statistic among the streetwalkers. Ah-ah! he lamented aloud in his sleep. And Denis who'd made it and gone to Dublin to work for a lawyer and taken out articles himself and become a big man with a lousy marriage and three ungrateful kids who had given him hell. Ah-ah!

All gone now. Where was the point of it all? The slipshoddery of this brief span.

And poor Paddy Cullen who resisted torments of the body with bouts at the bottle and when that failed became a nervous jerking tic-ridden fellow plagued by guilts, furtive lusts and the closer-licking flames of a damnation in which he fervently believed.

'It's too hard being human,' the curate had admitted one evening to Donellan. 'It's the greatest punishment of all. That first bloody bite of the apple!'

'I know. But there's always dignity. The dignity of endurance.'

'Dignity! Dignity!'

Father Donellan bent over the chessboard. He'd been teaching the curate the rudiments of the game.

'Yes.' He moved his queen into an invincible position and then regretted doing it. Was he too small to let this sad man have some victory? 'We have to, well, swaddle ourselves in it, use it as a protective garb.'

'Like the director?'

'If I were a charitable man,' Father Donellan said slowly, 'I could say yes. I could make excuses for him too, perhaps. But no, Paddy, not like that. Never like that. That's where your sense of humour comes in, me boy. Every now and then as you feel your *dignitas* taking over, you have to step back and have a good laugh at the sight of yourself.'

'I can't do it,' Paddy Cullen said, realising checkmate and shovelling the pieces together. Then he was shamed by tears.

'Me poor boy,' Father Donellan said. 'Oh me poor boy.'

And he couldn't either. Sister Cornelius had arrived from U-millie a month before, outraged with complaint. Father Cullen was having trouble saying the Mass. The words of consecration stopped him in his tracks. He could not bring himself to pronounce *hoc est enim corpus meum* as his unworthiness rose and choked him. At night he was bombarded by the little fleshly sins of his penitents that swept across his mind like a swarm of bees. He had tried not listening at confession, had closed his ears to the gabbled repetitions and then was seized with guilt as to whether or not he had actually absolved. He was not fit for the words of consecration. He was not fit he was not he was . . .

Mass was taking up to an hour, an hour and a half, in the hot makeshift chapel on U-millie, the sick slumped or restless on the hard benches, and work to be done.

'Father Cullen,' Sister Cornelius had reprimanded, aware of the young man's torment but brisk with her obligations, 'you may have time for the luxury of scruples.

I simply haven't. I have patients to see to, a clinic to run. The people here simply don't understand. You'll have to pull yourself together.'

Father Cullen had looked at her hopelessly. 'You're right, of course. You're right.' And then he had gone down to the little beach and the jetty and sat there all day in the heat-blaze until he, too, was a cot case, stiff with baked skin and running a fever.

'You must do something, Father,' Sister Cornelius demanded and Father Donellan had said he would write to the bishop.

'I mean now. You must do something now. It's not that he has much to do, you know. A daily Mass. Communion. Benediction once a week. The sisters and I are busy all day. We are simply not getting the spiritual consolation we need. And more importantly, neither are the islanders.'

'Where's your charity, Sister?' Donellan demanded.

'I haven't time for that,' Sister Cornelius said sharply. 'In addition to the nursing we try to run classes. We supervise meals, cleaning, cooking. What would you know about it? In fact,' she added intemperately, 'what would the bishop know either?'

Father Donellan wanted to smile. She had a point. He understood both sides. He said, 'I don't know which is worse, you know, the pain of the body or the mind. Somehow I think it's the mind. Do you pray for him?'

'When I get time,' Sister Cornelius said abruptly.

The bishop was an aloof man who had once stated that he could not abide any dominance of women in

Church matters. That he needed their assistance in running his network of parishes and schools was another matter. Donellan was tempted to repeat the story of the first parish priest in their mainland town, who was so incensed at the arrival of the first nuns come to establish a school he had let them carry all their possessions, including awkward plaster statues of the saints, up from the wharf themselves. He began, 'I suppose you know about Father O'Mara who –'

Sister Cornelius interrupted with, 'I know what you're about to tell me and I am not amused.'

Donellan pushed back his chair and rose. 'Very well,' he said, 'I can see you have a problem. I'll write, as I said I would, and the best thing you can do for now is to send the lad back here. I'll come over myself once a week until we can find a replacement.'

He had watched her go, walking steadily away along the road to the jetty. She was a tall woman, middle-aged he guessed, but with an energy that seemed to brush aside the encumbering quality of those medi-aeval white garments, the steaming effect of coif and veil. Even as he watched he saw a group of islanders who had been waiting under the coconut palms come out to greet her, shyly, then with laughter, crowding round her, touching, talking. She bent to pick up one of the children and cuddled it for a moment, her hand caressing the girl's hair before setting her down. He saw that the sister's face was transfigured with smiles.

No, he knew, she simply wouldn't have time. Every

swabbed sore was her practical form of prayer. He was ashamed.

And felt shame again now, as he sat in the kitchen on the morning of Cullen's departure.

The young man had not slept the night before. Long after midnight Donellan heard him rise from his bed in the living-room, heard the screen door squeak back and footsteps plod to and fro along the garden path. Then a rain squall drove him in and finally Donellan got up himself to find the curate sitting beside the open door staring out into darkness.

'What's the matter?' he asked.

There was no reply. He boiled up water for tea and encouraged Cullen to drink some but the young man's hand shook so fiercely that half the contents of the cup spilled on the matting.

'It will be all right,' Donellan comforted stupidly. 'Everything will be all right.' He removed the cup from Paddy Cullen's hands. 'You'll be seeing your family in Brisbane soon. How about that, then?'

Silence. Donellan remembered too late the curate had no family. His father had been killed during the war at Milne Bay. His mother had died not long after seeing her boy ordained. Now he had added another vow to those already taken: silence. The darkness stretched and weakened into light as Donellan dozed in his chair. He awoke to find the curate had not moved but was absorbing the new morning with indifference.

Donellan made some kind of breakfast. The curate broke a piece of toast into small pieces, took a few sips at black coffee and uttered his first words in eight hours: 'Is it time to go?'

Despair was the unforgivable sin.

Cullen reeked of it.

Donellan seized the curate's small grip stuffed with his few clothes and books. 'Take these,' he offered, handing over some tattered novels that had lain unread for years on the priest-house shelves. He glanced at them. The author's name, Sanford Rim, was prominent among whorls of dust, horses' hooves and lassos. 'Someone left them in the boarding house years ago. Look, they're even signed by the author. Quite a little collector's item, eh?'

'I don't want them,' Paddy Cullen said. 'Thank you.'

'Come on! They might cheer you up. They're good for a laugh.'

The curate took them without argument and shoved them in the pocket of his alpaca and began the long long endless never-ending walk to the jetty.

Another was leaving as well, the director having begged a last-minute place on the mission launch for boatman Jardine, dismissed at last for affronting that puritan's moral code. Staff wives had protested. The director could no longer ignore.

Jardine was already ahead of them, jaunty, untouched by disgrace. He was leaving behind three half-caste kids as well. Or was it more? He'd lost count. He gave the priests a vile wink from a still blackened eye. 'Nice day for it,' he commented. 'Travelling.' There was no one there to see him depart. He wasn't sorry to go, even after all these years. There were plenty of jobs going along the coast for a man of his skills. He smirked as he moved away from the priests and stepped on board. The boat shuddered under him. No one answered his asides. He slouched into the small cabin, settled himself with his luggage and began smoking.

On the jetty Father Donellan was telling Paddy Cullen to keep in touch, drop a line. All the platitudes. The curate had passed well beyond heeding/hearing under the cloud-choked sky. Father Donellan took his hand. It was limp and cold, frail as a shell. 'Cheer up, lad,' he said, too heartily, shaking the hand, then patting the young man's shoulder. 'Cheer up now. Even if you don't owe it to yourself, you owe it to God.'

'God!' the young man whispered. He turned away and stepped onto the launch. The helmsman sent the *Avila* out in a wide throbbing curve while Donellan stood there watching it draw farther and farther away. He could see Paddy Cullen still standing rod-straight and bleak in the stern. He waved but there was no response and the launch rocked into distance until it was a toy and Donellan, still straining, saw the ant figure in the stern clamber onto the rail and project itself like an arrow over the side and begin swimming.

Or not begin.

Life no different here from them old days, eh?

But things changin over on mainland all right. Normie he tell them bout everythin, bout the cars, bout soldiers from America, bout school. He say school bit like bein on Doebin, white bullies all the same. Still, he get ideas then. He see things done different. Maybe, he say, things get different for us, eh Manny?

Some things change. Grandma Rosie she dead now, three years back. Jericho he gone down to reserve at Woorabinda but Billy stay on here. Sometime he went mainland like me to work on them sugar farms too. Got real money then. The boss here glad to see him go. But he always come back. Troublemaker, new boss call him. Like Normie. Real troublemaker.

Stay clear, Manny, Normie tell him. You got wife an

*kids. You gotta keep an eye out for dadda an that Billy,
now Jericho gone. Dadda gettin old.*

Like me, he tell him.

*You had your trouble, Manny, he say. Don't want no
more.*

*These days, this place got funny feelin. Bama jiba-
yararri. People frighten, eh? An they angry.*

I THINK I'VE BEEN BORN BEFORE MY TIME

I THINK I'VE BEEN BORN BEFORE MY TIME.

I don't fit.

I mouth off.

This narrow-minded town!

After the island – pretty phrase that. I repeat it: after the island. After the island we settled, Mother, Claire and I, more or less comfortably in yet another boarding house Mother was invited to manage, a hostel of sorts with half a dozen boarders. Claire and I returned to boarding school, 'to be finished' as they quaintly put it in those days. Well, yes!

We hardly met the cast until a year later, though I can say Mr Morrow, whom I remembered from the island, moved out virtually the day Mother moved in. I thought she'd terrified him. I was wrong.

I am twelve years' wiser. Events are so bland and yet remain so muddled. If I say Thomas and I yawn in each other's face, you'll know we're married, my husband's brief lust long sated, mine merely awakened.

'Whatever you like,' he is fond of saying, fussily dabbing traces of breakfast from his mouth. 'Do whatever you like. Take a lover. But I must remind you, 'cushla, I have a position to maintain in this town.'

What town?

At the height of the Pacific war he is trying to persuade me, for a variety of reasons, most of which I suspect but don't care about, to take our daughter south and rent a house in Brisbane. He fusses about our safety. I shy away from the thought of unfamiliar landscapes. Besides, this one is peopled with exotics from the New World, gleaming boys in tight uniforms and easy accents that, despite their fluidity, also fit like gloves. I should be ashamed, thinking this way. I'm not. I meet them at hospital socials, at the dinner parties of town worthies determined on giving our newcomer rescuers a good time before they are sent off to be slaughtered in the Coral Sea. I also meet them at bus-stops.

For the first time I've noticed how similar my husband's accent is to that of the American troops, and wonder if this synonymous charm is being exercised as easily on probationer nurses.

'Of course it is,' Tinker, my best friend, tells me. 'He can't help himself. Two can play at that game. Why don't you?'

I nod, pretending indifference, wise with nearly a dozen years of wedlock to counterbalance the flippant and preposterous urges that overtake me when I saunter through wolf-whistles and chiacks along Flinders Street.

I don't look my age. I am twenty-nine going on three hundred. But the actual digits ahead of me huddle in a warning of mortality.

Forget it!

I am ready but I don't know for what. And I am weary of a Celtic charm that is shaken like spice over any dish within gulping reach. We bore each other rancid. That is the very word. It amazes me to see the empurplement of rage that washes over Thomas's neck and face. You're too plausible, I once told him. Too ready with soft and easy excuses. You – I had searched for a killer word or phrase that might explain or resolve the situation, especially for me, and heard myself protesting – rot my will.

Back on the island he had said to me, softly, gently, just as my fingers were picking out the last notes of a Debussy prelude on that rotting boarding-house piano, Let me tell you about Madame de Montespan. ('Let me tell you about Emma Bovary, Anna Karenina.' I was doomed. My seduction was complete.) There I was, a virginal slender thing who had once glimpsed the hairy bag inside his bag of a bathing-costume as he sprawled immodestly on the beach at Shippers Vale. (*Veux-tu te baigner, Leonie? Veux-tu nager, petite?*) Petite had shut her eyes against the horror of his gaping groin and splashed delicately in the tide below the casuarinas. But then his dapper Irish face erased the memory of his private parts and his voice vibrated with poetry.

I never knew anyone to know so much verse.

Let me say now it was an oral seduction. That voice!

That accent! (That blarney I would have said had I been older.)

And that charm, no matter where he showers it, still hasn't diminished even towards me. It's like a bad habit. It's simply that watching its dissemination from such suffocating quarters, I suffer from constipation of the soul.

Walking through the troop-crowded streets of our town, uphill, downhill, is my attempt to arrest the creeping grittiness that is attacking me from the head down. Smile, nudge, whistle. Those signals act like anti-toxins.

Thomas and I do all the dutiful things. We both love our daughter. We both bore her. Annette is a tremblingly intelligent seven-year-old. Thomas and I attend canteen dances, fundraising dinner parties. We meet only officer class, gloriously laundered men with manners that could give Thomas a run for his money. I want a bit of rough. Isn't that natural after all these years of phoney courtliness?

Last week when he was called away to Brisbane (airforce transport provided, glossy WACs!), I was invited to another fundraising dance held by the wives of town burghers. It was a scrubby affair. There was a makeshift band playing Glen Miller numbers but nobody was really in the mood. We danced, we drank, we decorously flirted.

Late in the evening a curly boy whose hair was so blond it was almost white cut in on me while dancing. My elderly banker partner disappeared.

'I've been watching you,' curlylocks said.

What is the reply to that? I smiled.

'All night.' The prod!

'Oh yes.'

'You're a pretty girl. Why don't you make more of yourself? You've got the basics. Great bones. Great body. You need tarting up.'

'Do I?' I was tempted to say, You're pretty rude! and wriggle from his too close hold. Back there was the safety of the bank manager and town councillor and their wives.

'If you want a good time,' he suggested in my ear. His eyes were an electric green, his skin fresh and pink. There was a feral quality in his unblinking stare.

'I'm having a good time.'

'Not my sort of good time. Let me take you home.'

'Certainly not,' I said, all fake uppity outrage. The dance ended then and he didn't bother seeing me back to my table.

Over coffee afterwards at the banker's home, a low shrub-hidden sea-gazing colonial in Belgian Gardens, I mentioned the young man but touched only the perimeters of our conversation.

'Gatecrasher,' the bank manager pronounced. He was a tall eaten-away fellow who kept a mistress in a northern coastal township and was consequently righteous and conversationally puritanic. 'Never seen him before. He was with a group who came in late, a bunch of LACs from the base who made things unpleasant for the doorman. Forget it, my dear, if he offended you, because he's definitely not our class.'

'What *is* our class?'

'What? What's that? I don't understand you.'

I didn't understand either.

Pestering phone calls followed. How had he discovered me? I flirted with disaster. The voice at the end of the wire was so persistent. Thomas was still away.

I take tea with Tinker, my repository, my confessional for marital plaint. Once-hidden wishes flutter out unguarded. Tinker is a tall unrestrained young woman who works in a government office. We were at school together for that last year. She is a splendid violinist who went straight to the second violins in the Brisbane Symphony Orchestra where she had a brief but passionate affair with a cellist. He was a married man. Gossip. Scandal. Horror. Tinker was removed. Brisbane was like that. She returned north and married one of several applicants rather as if she were buying a handbag. The lucky groom is now somewhere in New Guinea fighting fever, leeches and Japanese. She is philosophical about his absence but after Brisbane has learnt caution and takes her pleasure where she can, as discreetly as this small town allows.

I am painting toe- and finger-nails magenta. (There's a message in that! I read somewhere that whores in the later Roman Republic dressed in purple!) Tinker watches as I wave and wriggle digits to dry the lacquer. From her mantel radio a soprano is whooping her way through a Strauss waltz and achieving a terrible climax.

Tinker says, 'But you don't even know this fellow. You know nothing about him.'

'I don't know anything about Thomas. Or rather, I know too much, I suppose.'

'At least you know he's not criminal, violent.'

'Who said anything about criminal? You're very careful all of a sudden. Very picky.'

'You suggested he had a feral look. I think "magnetically feral" were the exact words. Did he give you a name when he rang?'

He had given a name.

'But can you check? The draft's pulling in all sorts now. It could be any name, for Heaven's sake.'

'Oh God! Do you want me to go out to the barracks and get a list of all serving men? Of course it's all right.'

'And where does this charmer plan taking you?'

'Kissing Point. Pallarenda. I don't know.'

Tinker makes a face and slumps back in her chair.

'Not even toasted sandwiches at the River Rose! At least he certainly won't be involved in any courting expenses.'

'You're talking like a whore, Tinker.'

I grin, to soften those words.

'And how will you get there?' she asks, ignoring me. 'Walk? Hitch? Swim along the coast?'

I tell her not to be like that. He has a motorbike. I will ride pillion.

'You're out of your mind,' Tinker says flatly. 'Don't go.'

Well, I have a week to think about it. Why a week? Where's the urgency? More to the point, his urgency? I go over and over that scatter-brusque invitation to meet behind the post office (why behind?), to hitch my leg across his pillion and throb off for a joyride out of the war-darkened town. Against the foolhardiness of this ragtag invitation my mind hollers grudges fermented by the latest communication from Thomas. A bad line. His voice tinny and divested of charm over eight hundred miles of wire. 'Not for another week, mavourneen. I'm trying to tee up a lift.' The phone goes dead.

Tais-toi, tais-toi. On n'aime qu'une fois.

In flattening heat the afternoon of the tryst – that word is a scoffer – I trudge to Tinker's house, catching her at her palm-infested front gate as she is emptied out of an American jeep. The officer, who waves nonchalantly, is a mass of badge and braid. She glares at me.

'Come in. You did not see that. Not.'

I repeat those nostalgic and corrupting words of Laforgue.

'What's it mean?' Tinker asks rudely, stripping to her underwear and vanishing into the shower.

'"Silence,"' I call through the shower curtains. Tinker's neck is blackened with lovebites. '"Be silent! You love only once."'

'Bullshit!' Tinker yells. She steps naked from the shower. Her thighs are bruised as well. Thumbprints? 'Don't go.' She slams the bathroom door in my face.

From her living-room window I see Dagoombah squatting in cobalt. Closer in, the tottering houses weighed down by mango trees and just beyond them, on the front, the boarding school where Tinker and I and later Claire had been dormitory-bound. Claire, of course, tried to fight the bonds. She went south. She plugged her way through a university course, driven to escape the drear of it all, and ended up teaching in some four-street town in the south-west of the state where despair led her into marriage with another pub-owner's son. She is merely repeating the cycle. Poor Claire. We write. We exchange dutiful letters. But these days it's as if we are barely related. Mother, unchiding, uncommenting (she has her own private scandal!), rattles between our unhappy ménages on duty visits.

Back then, then, Tinker and I, that chaste pair, had planned other lives. From Tinker's window I watch uniformed day-girls trailing out the gates and along the Strand in the afternoon release. And there I am once more in a hushed assemblage of prim-faced boarders as Sister Assumpta slides onto the assembly-hall stage and stares down the chattering mob into dumb delicious terror.

It took only seconds. The geography of her face, the pattern of that well-known landscape, became frozen.

'There is a girl,' she informed us with her careful speech that spaced each word so softly she had us all straining, 'who has had an unfortunate accident in the dormitory. I am sure you know what I mean.' Our eyes sought each other. There were small and knowing smirks. 'She has,' Sister Assumpta continued, fondling her beads, 'spent some time switching mattresses from her bed to another, to that of an unoccupied one in the junior wing.'

241

(Instant vision of some weak-bladdered girl lugging the guts into the neighbour room – we did know our Shakespeare! – around midnight.) Tinker let out an unfortunate snort of mirth until quelled by Assumpta's eye as I shook beside her. 'Would that girl ...' Long pause. 'See me at the end of assembly.' Another terrifying hiatus. 'And also that other young lady who made that extremely rude noise.'

Our exits. Our entrances. We understood only the smaller dramas.

As we filed out Tinker nudged my gaze towards an unfortunate in the form below. 'She always looked like a kidney problem. Bet it's her.'

We all hung around the hall doorway longing to see who might confess. Charity hadn't claimed us yet.

Nor had it claimed us when wretched Father Brimstone, as we called him, came to take our senior class for apologetics. He was a delicate and nervous young man who cringed from the critical eyes of six adolescents. Somehow Tinker always steered the discussion to infringements of the sixth commandment. Impurity was the only sin that concerned us. It racked our days. Sins of the flesh in thought, word, deed! the mission saviours thundered in the incense-filled candlelit chapel. Of course I realise now I didn't know how to commit any of them. But Tinker ...

'Any questions?' Father Brimstone would foolishly ask after twenty minutes of boredom on *ex cathedra* infallibility.

Tinker's hand – she was stunningly pretty then, despite a persistent splash of acne – would wave a languid fiddler's-bowing arc.

'But not all rules can cover every case, can they, Father? Not in the real world? There are circumstances.'

'I don't understand,' the unfortunate Father Brimstone would say. They had chopped words before.

'Imagine,' Tinker would propose – and we all imagined – 'a shipwreck on a desert island. Two survivors – a man and a woman. There is no possibility of rescue. Just exactly, er, Father, what is their position?'

Someone giggled. No one dared say 'missionary'.

Father Brimstone dropped his eyes before Tinker's bland knowledge-seeking earnestness. She was achieving a delicate and fervid curiosity. He adjusted his collar. It was very hot in the classroom.

'The Church is quite specific on the matter. There could be no . . . um . . . congress.'

'Congress?' persisted Tinker, her eyes wide.

'Relationship.'

'But years and years? After all, the Church does teach that the contracting parties are the celebrants of marriage.'

Father Brimstone looked at his watch. Twelve eyes watched him look.

'The marriage must be blessed by an appointed minister.'

'There is no past, no future,' countered Tinker, irrelevantly as we all thought then. 'Only now. We only understand now. Which is gone even as I say now.'

'You're too philosophical for me,' Father Brimstone said, managing a slight chuckle, 'and anyway I can't see . . . Look, girls, I think that's enough for this morning. There's Sister Assumpta at the door.'

Tinker smiled. 'Next week. We'll talk about this next week, Father.'

'Of course, of course.'

Sister Assumpta's eyes drilled through the six of us impeccable in our navy uniforms, our white blouses, our slyly curling mouths.

'I hope the girls have been behaving.'

'Indeed. Indeed.' Father Brimstone on the run. He dreaded the ritual of conventual politeness. He wanted to dodge morning tea: the best china, the slice of sponge cake.

'I will speak with you girls later,' Sister Assumpta threatened with a cool knowing eye, then hurried after Father Brimstone to uncover imagined lodes of misbehaviour.

Tinker never did discover what could or might happen on her deserted island. She cut a swathe through the conservatorium she attended in the south. She played violin with an elegant effortless careless passion and after her unfortunate affair with the cellist wed, on a recuperative holiday at home, after a weekend's courtship (What kept you, Tinker!), a baby-faced local whose parents owned several stores in downtown Sugarville – Gerald Morrow's ironic name for this town.

'Are you in love?' I asked.

'I don't know what you mean.' Tinker had stared

gloomily about the empty rented house crammed with appalling furniture that her father-in-law had donated from the slow-sales section of one of his stores. There was a threatening double bed in brilliant orange high-gloss, a fake cedar dining-table with six matching chairs, and a squat and uncomfortable three-piece cliché of Genoa velvet seatery complete with inset arm protectors of wood veneer.

'Jesus!' she had said on my first visit to the love-nest, 'I didn't know it meant this.'

'Then why did you do it?'

'Oh God! Who knows? Who'd damn well know!'

She began making up for it as she thought of the now, the vanishing present.

I think *I* mouth off! What about Tinker? She was a feminist apologist before her time.

Not long after Tinker returned north, that ugly phrase, that arithmetical summation of females – vital statistics – began to appear in print and resound from the lips of cheapskate radio announcers salivating over beach-girl competitions. Thirty-six, twenty-four, thirty-six had greater authority than $E=mc^2$. Our saviour pals from the New World weren't shy about using it. One day at a bus-stop in Flinders Street as I waited with Tinker, a cheeky GI with an engaging grin sauntered up and lingered. 'Say,' he said, breaking the tropic ice, 'you girls have terrific vital statistics!'

Tinker looked at him coldly. 'And what are yours?'

'What are my what?'

'Your vital statistics. Eighty? Sixty-five? Two?'

'I don't know what you mean, sugar,' he said moving a little closer.

'The largest number is for your intelligence quotient,' Tinker said smoothly. She smiled.

'And what about the others?'

'I think you can work that out.'

'Ah c'mon, lady!'

The bus was just pulling in. Tinker moved forward to follow my nervous flight and with one foot on the step turned and said clearly, 'IQ, height, dick.'

After the island, as I said, and after I finished school, I became part of a cast: two bank clerks, one wharf foreman, an elderly teacher and a junior from Burns Philp. Mother cooked and cleaned, doing a Martin de Tours, patron saint of reformed drunkards and innkeepers. Not that there were any reformed drunkards. They were quickly shown the door. Two young girls helped in the kitchen and with the laundry. We weren't a cheerful lot and I was unmoved by any of those lumpy boarders who sat apart from us at mealtimes below the lazy ceiling fans. By eight o'clock each morning they were already sweating into their shirts.

Outside this louvred building perched on the lower slopes of the hill, trees plotted and spied upon our half-shuttered evening windows, sending leafy warnings to the lonely men sprawled with their sticky dreams upon their bachelor beds.

I tried resolutely never to think of our last weeks on Doebin, of the horror, the killings. Yet the house and its tenants repeated some kind of pattern. I, too, would have to marry to escape.

Would that be escape? Already Claire was planning flight to Brisbane and a university course. Would that help? Would anything break apart those conventional constraints?

The piano had come back from the island, jangling across on a barge. Now it stood like a carved trophy in one corner of the sitting-room whose windows gaped downhill towards the wharves and the jangling waters of the bay. Schumann in the tropics! Mozart! Grieving joyous crystals of pure white!

'Och, you don't want to be playing that any more, mavourneen,' the good doctor had cried when he bounced in one day not long after we had moved there. He was still limping, but attractively, from the wound in his groin. (We did not discuss the wound. We did not discuss that fearful night. It was as if we had all taken vows of silence.) He tossed *Kinderscenen* on top of the piano and began to rummage in his bag. 'Here! I have a little something for you I had sent up from Sydney. It's been a while coming at that.' Deftly he adjusted two volumes on the piano rack. I picked up the first. Fauré. The music appeared different, difficult. I sighed and replaced it beneath the second volume, *Cinq poèmes de Baudelaire*.

'Let me tell you,' jolly Doctor Quigley said, 'about Baudelaire.'

Ah, the avidity with which I absorbed the lurid gossip, still biting, of another world, another time. Baudelaire's then. (My now.) 'So you see,' Doctor Quigley murmured, one fatherly hand upon my fatherless shoulder, ' "*mère des souvenirs, maîtresse des maîtresses*," you are becoming aware. There's another world altogether beyond this place, this flat boring pancake of a country.'

Those words prepared me, of course, for attendance at a concert the next week at a theatre in town. A chamber music group was travelling through the north (were they lost?) raising funds for the unemployed at the more populous centres. Everyone doing his bit, as it were. Half-heartedly I accepted an invitation from one of the bank clerks, an earnest lad, a reader with a permanently blocked nose who appeared at breakfast one morning, two tickets anticipatorily in his hands. 'Go, darling,' Mother urged. 'There's so little here.'

The bank clerk dinked me into town on his bicycle. My best dress flapped in the darkness as I clutched at the handlebars, feeling his boyish arms encircle me. His phlegmy breathing honked in my ear. There was a short, horrifyingly fast ride downhill before we spun dangerously into the main street to skid to a stop right outside the theatre where he wedged his bike between two parked trucks and chained it to a hitching-post – survivor of horse-and-buggy days. He was so young, so enthusiastic.

In the dim light of the foyer his blond stubble glinted. Already he needed a shave. He sucked in air and smiled at me with a kind of triumph but all I could think of was the now of his mucus-ridden snorts, the pimples, forgetting the enthusiasm that was so moving. (He was wearing his best tie.) The now of it all.

Now. It affects me.

We edged our way past those already seated. In the row behind were Doctor Quigley and Matron Tullman, already recovered from a gunshot blast to the neck and smiling stiffly as the acute doctor spotted me and leaned forward to make quacking sounds of welcome and pleasure. (Even the words I chose those days of sharpened awareness seemed to have a derogatory flavour.) Old charmer Quigley looked wonderful in a dinner jacket that smelled slightly of mothballs. There were only three men in formal evening wear in the whole concert hall.

All through the Haydn I could feel the doctor's eyes warm the back of my neck. There is no magic in a young woman being aware of who is aware.

At interval my snuffling partner raced away to purchase synthetic orange juice for us while the town's cultured spoke confidently and informedly about the players. Well, some of them. You could see most of the husbands were hating it as they shuffled and fiddled, dragged there by wives anxious to display silk and beadwork. Bank clerk Dennis genuinely loved music and was so excited at the prospect of a Beethoven quartet in the second half he almost forgot my presence as he guggled his soft drink, and not even the swooping of Doctor Quigley as I modestly sipped alerted him to the possibility of a senior, more sophisticated attention.

Matron Tullman's blazing coolness simply breezed past to burnout.

'Enjoying it?' quizzed Doctor Quigley, leaning to catch my reply, a little too close. Both of us were all eyes. 'Quite a cultural explosion for this part of the world, eh? The man next to me was snoring through the Brahms. But only softly, mark you. His poor wife kept nudging him awake.'

'He'll be worse during the Beethoven.' Dennis grinned, exposing large healthy teeth. He blew his nose vigorously. Shamed and delighted – yes, both! – I dropped my eyes and stared into the orange flare of my waxed paper tumbler. Not drinking but drowning.

'Nasty cold you've got there,' the doctor commented. 'You need an early night.' Mock-warningly he smiled at the pair of us, me in my best skimpy blue and Dennis with his strangled Adam's apple bulging above an unaccustomed tie. Doctor Quigley was playing concerned uncle while Matron Tullman dropped a light but possessive hand on his arm and began steering him away. 'Time!' she cried girlishly. 'Time to go in!' The doctor rolled put-upon eyes at us and made flippant protest gestures as he was led off.

'He seems a nice chap!' Dennis, too, was a nice chap. A pity about the acne and the permanently blocked nose. Wiser, now, perhaps I would settle for those negatives. But I said, 'Yes, yes he is.' I said I would tell him later about our first meeting, about Christmas, about the

250

horror. I whispered, as we edged back to our seats, 'He was witness at a murder trial,' and was energised by the exhilarant gulp beside me, the sudden electric tension in my companion's arm who now could not wait for the concert to end.

'Shh!' People around were scolding as he pestered with half-questions. 'Shh!' The theatre lights were already down.

That was my only outing with the bank clerk. What is left of that evening but the recollection of a chaste and dry-lipped peck on the cheek and a copy of *The Man Who was Thursday* left at my breakfast place? He persisted, of course, with invitations, other books, but Doctor Quigley had swung into courting mode within the week, dazzling me into partnering him to a number of private dinner parties (where was Matron Tullman?) and mind-numbing musical soirées at the homes of old Sugarville families. I would shock them with the *Waldstein*, all three movements, while they shifted sweaty legs and attacked my prestissimo with coughs and Doctor Quigley beamed sadistically. Afterwards I would ask, 'But Marcia?'

'Never mind about Marcia,' he would answer. 'She'll be taking up a post at the Taws. Don't worry your adorable – and it is adorable – little head.'

I feared I was going to enjoy being someone's pet.

Mother was not altogether pleased with this turn of events. She gave minatory eye-rollings.

I hadn't even begun to grow up.

My head is not so little.

When, on one of those evenings of pearl and ash so common during the cane burn-off, Doctor Quigley suggested marriage, I accepted. Partly I was charmed by his continued attention; partly I wanted to escape the boarding house and the stream of elderly deadbeats the Depression had brought, men who stayed one night or two, then slipped away without paying. Mother could hardly afford that. But, 'Poor things,' Mother said. 'How could they pay? There's so little work. All they can do is keep walking.'

And that was true enough. Those gaunt faces still float across my memory alongside a picture of Mother buying cheap cuts from the butcher and spoiled vegetables to keep a giant soup simmering just in case more half-starved desperates should come by. Mother was softening, softening.

'The classic *pot-au-feu*,' Doctor Quigley announced, tucking in and not minding at all sharing the kitchen with a tramp whose trousers and shoes let in the weather. I liked him for that. I wanted to soften too. That was the day I said yes.

'You're a grand woman,' he told Mother. 'Grand. Women should be soft.' (I know now he meant malleable!) 'I like a soft woman.'

Mother, of course, was soft and hard. An interesting amalgam of opposites. Maybe tough would be a better word. There she was, a tall fair-headed woman with fine bones and a sufferingly determined mouth and chin. Handsome was the word others used and even her foolish refinements had been knocked askew by levellings tempered to the winds of pre-war. Not that any one of us was aware of war looming. The purges in Germany meant little to us south of the equator. After all, as Doctor Quigley pointed out, we were still doing our own purgings, working off our own guilt-driven cruelties on the indigenes. Who cared? There was general silent approval. 'The buggers,' as the manager of one of Sugarville's banks said over dinner, 'aren't even human.'

Yet a few days after I agreed to marry Doctor Quigley, these general concepts received a blow in a surprise visit from missionaries Starck and Weber who had come into town for some kind of spiritual sustenance.

They had no trouble running Mother to earth and had a favour to ask. I was banished from the sitting-room and went to twiddle fingers in the kitchen, peeling endless piles of potatoes and pumpkin pieces for dinner. After half an hour Mother fetched me back and the missionary ladies exclaimed with delight over my health, my proposed marriage. All the usual politenesses. They, I must confess, looked worn out from their work in the field. But they glowed with a terrible zeal.

'Look at this,' Mother said, producing a small photograph.

I see a draggle-line of chained Aborigines being driven through scrub by a gentleman on a horse. No! Look closer! Two gentlemen. The blacks are tethered by the neck. Neck to neck. If one jerks away, the rest suffer. Abominable! Behind them, equally hopeless, trail their wives. The desolation and acceptance of white vileness is scribbled over the faces of the women. One of them is holding a baby, close, close.

Suddenly, I wanted to cry. But worse, I recognised one of the men.

'That's Jericho Cooktown, Billy's brother! Why are they doing this?'

Starck and Weber nodded in the hot twilight created by the shutters. Flies buzzed and whined outside the windows.

'That's right,' Miss Starck said. 'But don't ask me why. No "why" will ever explain hatred, will it? It's true you never forgive the people you have treated badly.' She shook her head. 'This could go on and on.' She looked from the photo to me and smiled. 'We need people of goodwill. And there are so few.'

Miss Weber interrupted, her hands knotted in an earnest lump on her faded skirt. 'If they have a job, you see, a home, the Act will give them an exemption.'

'But where are they going? Where are they being taken?'

'Back to Doebin.'

'Is that so terrible?' I asked.

'You don't understand,' Miss Weber said. 'They go there. It's little better than a prison. You know that. What's the latest word from Europe? Concentration camp? They know no one. They're separated from their own tribe. These are Kuku-Yalanji. Except for Jericho whom they took in when he ran away. They won't be able to speak the language of the others. They certainly won't understand whiteman talk. When they don't understand they do things wrongly. They're punished and still they don't understand.'

She hesitated and dropped her eyes to watch those weaving fingers. 'I need your help.'

'How?' Mother asked, knowing.

'Even if only one,' Miss Starck pleaded. 'Even one can make a difference.'

'I don't know,' Mother said. 'Is it Jericho you mean? Or his young brother Billy?'

She worried about that. What school could he attend if she took him? The black–white laws were rigorous. The social codes more rigorous still. Billy was once boxed soundly by Mr Leggat when we were on Doebin for playing with a piece of stick on Coconut Avenue. He'd run snotty and yowling into my arms, screeching for his mum and quivering with terror.

'Put him down, you stupid girl!' Mr Leggat ordered. 'Do you want to catch something?'

I remember my reply. I had continued rubbing my nose across Billy's taffy curls. 'I hope I don't catch what you have, Mr Leggat.' And I'd walked off cuddling Billy, walking him back to the girls' dormitory to hand him to his mother. How was it, I wondered now, Jericho had run away from family responsibility?

'That's not his *moodja*,' Miss Weber said, pointing to the woman at the end of the sad little line. 'Not number one, you understand. That's not Jericho's child. He paddled from island to island, he told me, in a bark canoe along with Jimmy Friday. But the canoe fell apart. So they swam. It took them a week, resting up on the

255

islands. And then they walked, walked all the way, first back to the Waluwara tribe and the tribe moved on. And then they found some people of the Kuku who took them in. And all that time, the bullimen hunted them down. You mightn't remember Jimmy. He worked all day on the sawmill at Doebin and lived on the other side of the island.'

A silence fell. Then Miss Weber said, 'Annie took the photo.'

Mother stared beyond the cracks in the louvres and was back in the boarding house at Shippers Vale. So that I was the one in the present hearing the afternoon footsteps along the footpath outside, the coughing of trucks, the smack of a ball bounced by kids playing. It was Mother who kept a supply of old but clean shirts and trousers for the men travelling through. Mother who made sure they had a filled tuckerbag and a few shillings to put in their pockets when they left. And Mother who sighed finally and said, 'Of course, Mitzi. Annie. Of course.'

'*Ngayu bambay*,' Mitzi Weber said, her face all smiles, '*yurra nganya ngulkurrduku kujin*.'

'And what does that mean?' Mother asked, smiling back.

'I was sick and you looked after me.'

There followed what I can only call a litany of poor

blacks whom Mother helped and nurtured.

Ruby Fourmile and her little boy. Pray for them.

Tommy Sweetcreek. Pray for him.

Esau Friday. Pray for him.

Billy Cooktown. Pray for him.

The years they had with Mother gave them respite from Doebin, the chance to save their small wages which were normally taken over by government officials, and a minimal education that made Billy Cooktown, at least, literate. Claire worked with him at weekends and wasn't happy until at last he could pick up the Sugarville *Bulletin* and read news items aloud to her. On his return to the island he became a teacher's assistant at the native school.

During the litany I married and did all the expected things. I visited other doctors' wives, gave morning teas, played tennis and watched Claire matriculate and then vanish south to teachers' college and university. Would, I thought, passing around sandwiches and badly made butter cake, that I had done the same. ('Just because I have a uterus it doesn't mean I can cook!' I told Thomas. He smiled slyly. 'No. But it means you have to.') Illusion. Disillusion. Thomas's obsession with me receded in direct ratio to possession. No one, but no one, tells us these things.

Nor did it occur to any of us that we were waiting for war.

Thomas ceased visiting the Taws the moment we married. Someone else took over his honorary medical visitations to the school. I think he imagined I was unaware of his attachment to Matron Tullman and it was only through Dennis that I heard she had married one of the staff and had a child of her own. Or of Thomas's. (Let me tell you about le Comte d'Espinay!) Perhaps I was ageing too rapidly for a man who took pleasure in the soft nubility of youth.

One year. Two.

Once he had fussed over what I wore, how I dressed my hair. Now he seemed much too busy in his practice and his work at the hospital to notice whether I painted my nose blue.

I painted my nose blue and presented myself at breakfast like a clown. He was plunged in newsprint, his hand automatically extending his cup for a refill.

'This is pretty boring,' I commented.

'What is?' He refused to look my way. I knew he had seen my nose.

'Marriage.'

'No one ever pretended it wasn't, 'cushla. It's boring for all parties. You need a child.'

Three years. Four.

Sometimes we went south for holidays: Brisbane, Sydney, Melbourne, cities so different it was as if their founding fathers had markedly different cultural genes. Or was it the climate in each place that made the hearts of cities strangers? We were in Melbourne for the state's centenary celebrations and joined the crowd on St Kilda Beach to watch the large ship bringing a sottish member of the royal family to give his ducal imprimatur to the festival. We were crushed by unmoving mobs on Princes Bridge. We just managed to jump clear from a sinking overcrowded houseboat on the Yarra as gogglers rushed starboard to ooh and ah at fireworks. We visited relatives of Thomas, and I remember his fiery sister knocking off a man's hat during a Eucharistic procession near St Patrick's. 'Show respect!' she shouted, face and accent twisted with anger. 'Show some respect, you great oaf!' Thomas sidled back into the crowd, drawing me with him, doing a Saint Peter, rejecting kinship, until brogue and working-class rage faded. We took the train to Ferntree Gully. We sat in Wattle Park with a cut lunch. We visited Williamstown and ate fish in a bayside café.

'I like it here,' Thomas told me. 'I like the weather. It's a bit on the Irish side. *"Il pleure dans mon coeur"*. Do you think we should move south?'

'What about Mother?'

Thomas sighed. The sound came deep from the gut.

'She could join us. She must be tired of raw-boned northerners by now.'

'And what made you choose the north then?' I hid from his answer by picking out bones from my lunch.

Thomas hesitated and joggled one knee while he looked across the grey waters.

'Now, that's a different story altogether.'

He never did tell me.

And the next year, Brisbane.

The overgrown bush town was populated by women

259

in floral dresses and men in braces and stinking serge suits. The sun. The trams. The coil of river under the high cliffs of Kangaroo Point. We trailed past a miniature zoo, pausing to inspect the wretched monkeys. One of them reached a skinny rubber arm through the wire and snatched Thomas's ice-cream cone. I removed myself from outrage and mired tweed and wandered off to sit by the river until Thomas tottered back with another ice.

I was pregnant but had not yet informed him.

Strangely, as I sat being absorbed by those orange cliffs across the water struggling towards sky and plunging into their river doubles, I found myself wondering if I still loved Thomas – the ferry beetled across the waterway and herons strode through immeasurable gulfs of air above the gardens and their secret pockets of palms – and if, between pastoral interludes, he loved me. I watched his portly but impressive figure pace back from the kiosk down the sloping lawns. In seven months he would be a father. This third person would bind us even more tightly.

What else was there?

Pal Tinker had announced one day to Father Brimstone during a religious discussion class that she thought marriage an unnatural relationship.

'What's all this,' Tinker asked, 'about a woman being subject to her husband? Say if he's a moron? You mean she's got to do what some pinbrain tells her?'

Bubbles of the purest excitement rose in all of us, floated their perfect blue spheres into our bemused noddles and held us on the edge of our seats.

'Look, Father,' horrible smile, 'why is it that the sex which commits 90 per cent of the crime – murder, rape, bashings, to say nothing of legalised killing in war – has the right to lay down all the rules on moral behaviour? Bit much, eh? Teeny bit illogical?'

Father Brimstone quickly summed up the fallacy she was committing, that of arguing from the particular to the general – speaking fussily, the flustered old dear, through our unuttered derisory hootings. But Tinker came back to the attack just as Sister Assumpta entered at the end of the period.

'At least women should have some representation on panels of moral jurists, don't you think?' She offered her most winning eye-flap and smirk. 'After all, we're the persecuted ones, told what to do by men, punished by men, bullied by men. And never a voice! Now Father, is that Christian?'

'Leave the room!' Sister Assumpta said softly, swishing down the passage between the desks. Rosary beads rattled. Habit shushed and shushed. Sister Assumpta must surely have had sympathy for those words. The diocesan bishop bullied his curates and couldn't tolerate nuns having opinions at all.

Tinker was expelled.

Mentally I step down the slope into the river that merely mirrors those stunning blue northern waters and flounder in the empty spaces Tinker left behind. Three years later when she had returned north after her hectic southern rites of passage we met again. I had been walking along the Strand, a newly married confidence,

261

so I believed, to my step, and had sat for a while on a bench near the grassed foreshore in the late afternoon to read more of *Alice*, which I hadn't opened since I was eight. Through my own looking-glass and eleven years later I was still frightened by the Red Queen even though I smiled and read and turned pages and smiled and read and smiled, being adult now, initiated now. A series of laminations.

My hat brim hid me then from the outer heated world and left me alone on the far side of the mirror. But not stranded.

'Off with her head! Off with her head!' a mocking voice shrilled above me and I looked up to find Tinker staring, amused. 'What! Reading that old closet child-molester? Really!'

Where? I asked. How? Why?

A lover, she explained briefly. Abandoned. Her grammar fazed me. Her or him? I didn't like to ask as I crashed through glass barriers to the present. Tinker was looking older, the prettiness worn at the edges. Her hair was cropped into a shingle and her shoulders were still slightly hunched in violinistic stoop. Hugs. Kisses.

'Come on home,' she urged. 'I've got a flat just round the corner and Jerry can drive you home.'

Jerry?

There were bedraggled others asleep in the sun along the front, sprawled on benches, on grass, thin pallid men with three-day beards. Their roped blueys lay on the turf and served as pillows. Their hats tipped over their eyes.

'Who's Jerry?'

'Ah well,' Tinker said.

Thomas settled heavily beside me, finishing the last of his ice. Carefully he licked each creamed finger. I watched him lick, reminded of the fastidiousness of a cat.

'I'm pregnant,' I told him. For a moment all the trees stood still.

'Ah well,' Thomas said.

All these things engaged me in those days: my newly acquired conservatism, Tinker's dashing post-flapper (in a scrubber of a township like ours) rebellion. Even Mother had escaped the dominating prejudices and constrictions that were applied to female behaviour. She developed a casual admirer in Gerald Morrow, broadcaster, Voice of the North. He became her lover, I discovered on a steamy afternoon during the Wet when I popped into her bedroom to borrow a trinket. We were all shocked. Outside the invaded boudoir, rain suddenly collapsed on the town in a solid block. 'A purge,' Mr Morrow said elegantly from his prone position. Mother refused to marry despite Mr Morrow's request (he had reached the age where he needed to be looked after!), despite gossip, despite confessional autocracy, despite . . .

No one, she said one evening not long after she learnt of my pregnancy, was going to intrude on her lifestyle or her financial security, such as it was. She'd worked hard. She'd paid off the bank despite those hard times. She owned the building and it was something to leave for her ungrateful daughters.

Once I would have pleaded with her not to destroy her reputation or her happiness because of me or my sister. I was changing. I admired her stand.

'Maternal care means more to me than a tumble in the hay,' Mother continued tartly. 'That is simply a diversion to stave off loneliness. The heart . . .'

She stopped there but I knew, I knew she was going to say 'the heart isn't involved' or 'the heart doesn't come into it'. And now I wonder about myself. 'Since when,' Tinker once asked a horrified Father Brimstone, 'have women been trained to be anything but economic whores?'

She always did have a nice turn of phrase.

Now I sit in Tinker's awful living-room with the Genoa velvet bagging and the cane furniture coming apart on the tatty rattan matting, waiting for her to emerge from the shower. The years. The years. Mother cast out lover-man some time back in a genial parting and settled to late middle-aged respectability and grandma duties when my daughter was born. As the war struck our shores she became a Red Cross stalwart, working in canteens, hosting the Church's Evenings for the Boys. I think of her as I sit in this unloved room of Tinker's and wonder what she would advise if she knew my adulterous strategies.

On Tinker's radio someone is singing mournfully:

Aint got the change of a nickel,
Aint got no bounce in my shoes,
Aint got no fancy to tickle,
Aint got nothin but the blues.

'You and me, baby,' I say aloud while apprehension grows, watching the door, waiting for Tinker, watching the clock hands creep on to my trysting hour.

I decide not to wait and shout goodbyes at the bathroom where the shower has now stopped pumping. 'Don't do it!' shouts the unbelievably non-reckless Tinker. Outside my folly consumes the whole town.

At home I make myself a scrap meal (Thomas is still away) and settle down to listen to heavily censored war news from the Pacific front. I watch the clock. The hands stagger to six. To seven. I begin to dress, to paint my lips, brush my hair and organise it into a captivating series of rolls. I look through this looking-glass, another Alice, and my restless eyes are seared unexpectedly by orange blaze, by an island alight, my husband staggering through pallid moonshine pursued by a prancing maniac. These are memories I have resolutely thrust down into some dusty box, resolutely never spoken or thought about. I open the box and dust those memories off.

I used to be a sassy girl. Years have taught me something

about the unmoored behaviour of humans.

Beyond the shutters night rattles its clamps and trees conspire at the windows. A watery, fluctuating ledger of debits and credits swims across the glass. I am twenty-nine. I have a husband, a seven-year-old daughter now dumped ('Protected!' roars Thomas) at his protective insistence in a southern boarding school where we both whimper ourselves to sleep at nights. And a desperate case of boredom.

This world, my world, is now so dark even the hump of the island has vanished. I am frightened of the dark. Play your hunches, someone once advised me. Was it Tinker? It's always safest.

I play mine.

I scrub the paint from my mouth, brush out those provocative starlet rolls. Irrationally I find myself tense with fear and lock all doors and windows. Branches tap and try to force an entry. I lie huddled on the other side of that looking-glass in a fiery glare of fright and sweat waiting for daylight.

The week crawls by. While I wait for a bus in town I hear my name called and turn into the glass eyes of that curly boy. He has a smile that never reaches those eyes. In fact, it barely touches the planes of his cheeks.

'I waited.' It is an accusation.

I fumble parcels and excuses.

'Never mind,' he says, interrupting me. 'Maybe you were right.' He smiles again. 'A cautious girl.'

There is something about his smile. He watches me steadily as I wait, a challenge implicit. 'Some other time,' he suggests or not suggests. Then he struts past me, roughly brushing my loaded arms and stalks to a motorbike propped near the kerb across the road, throws a muscular leg over and kicks the machine into horrendous life. I watch as he pulls goggles down but he doesn't look once in my direction. And then he swings the racketing bike out from the gutter and speeds off, swerving between pedestrians and army jeeps, down towards the front, the blue, the blue. Have I failed or won? And what?

Thomas returns, jovial and sated.

'Listen to this, 'cushla,' he says to me two mornings later, looking up from his breakfast paper which he absorbs like cereal and peering lovably over his bifocals, 'there's been another attack, assailant unknown.'

'What do you mean, another?'

'They don't print everything, you know. This is the fifth I'm aware of. Official policy is don't frighten the locals. It could be one of our God-given Yankee saviours. It could be one of ours. Mustn't offend the troops. Maybe they feel by now things have gone a little far.'

I wait until he has left for the surgery before I open the paper. I am filled with misgiving. I make domestic excuses to postpone reading. My hands puddling dishes in soapy water develop an uncontrollable shaking. My knees buckle. I make beds and sweep leaves off the verandah and watch the hands of the clock move on to nine.

The house rings like an empty shell placed to my ear. As if I am placing the house. I bolt back and front doors before I finally confront what I know I will read.

There is a picture of Kissing Point and the blurred, print-distorted face of a young woman watching as I read. 'The badly battered body of an unknown woman was discovered late yesterday afternoon on the sand at Kissing Point. If anyone can identify . . .'

I stop reading. I see superimposed on that drab little snapshot eyes without a smile, lips stretched into the lineaments of a smile. And I shudder as if someone has stepped on my grave.

In our living-room the Church committee meets informally to discuss the establishment of a home for fallen girls. (My libido has been curbed by certain events but Tinker screeches with vulgar laughter when I tell her the committee's endearing plans.) Thomas bustles about with drinks for the banker, another doctor, and the bishop's assistant, Father Brimstone – now translated to higher things.

I am barred from the discussion, banished to the kitchen for supper-making: ('That won't be any trouble at all, 'cushla. Just a sandwich, a biscuit or two!')

Sitting there reading, confined to barracks as it were,

I can hear that important male mumble going on and on and on with an occasional laugh brought to boardroom order by Father Brimstone's authority to speak dogmatically. Around ten I go in and smile politely, adding a social comma to a periodic clerical sentence. I am irritable with heat, mosquitoes and, above all, a sense of exclusion.

'Why fallen?' I demand abruptly. 'Why must men regard pregnancy as a fall, for God's sake! Why do you use that term? I thought the Church taught motherhood was woman's noblest function, in fact her only function. One big yawning uterus!' (I am turning into Tinker.) 'Aren't men fallen, too, for Chrissake, or is there a special dispensation for male sins of the flesh? How about,' I add, 'a home for risen men! That's the nub of the matter, isn't it?'

But they are not disturbed, that's the rub. They are disgusted. Thomas rises and says, 'My dear, the supper . . .' Banker Gilham lights a cigar, puffs languidly and gives a smile whose tolerance maddens while Father Brimstone's lips pinch briefly and relax. His fingers keep playing with his fountain-pen.

'Now, now,' he says soothingly after a long silence, 'we can't have you giving opinions like that. Not on such a serious matter.' He seems to have lost that nervousness that dogged him in his weekly confrontations with the senior religion class. 'You just be off, like a good woman, and attend to those matters that concern you in the kitchen, my dear.'

Neutered! Checkmate!

There is an even longer silence. Banker Gilham coughs

gently. The men refuse to lower their eyes, and watch me. I watch them back. My anger is choking me. Finally I say, 'It's like talking to apes.' Then I turn, slam the supper into the trash bin and bang the door behind me, hoping they will hear the outside door crash as I leave the house, running scared and unsafe through the blackout to Tinker's. Perhaps Thomas attended to supper.

I sleep that evening on a stretcher on Tinker's side verandah, anaesthetised by the smell of damprot.

'Of course,' Tinker says, pouring tea next morning, 'you must realise that most men never have to prepare a meal from birth to death. That's why they marry, for Heaven's sake!' She grins wickedly. 'Leave mother and find another charley to set food in front of them. It's why they're paid more in case they don't marry. The extra money's for eating out.'

Tinker trots out memories of family Christmases: mother sweating in a 90 degree kitchen over the roast chicken, the steamed pudding, the stirred custard, the washing-up (the men have their quiet time then, with beer, to discuss races and football), and then on to preparing the evening meal while the men go off to the pub for their loud time to return drink-sodden, argumentative, picky and chair-prone while mother and the girls serve food, watch them gorge, then clear up to sag back wilted and exhausted listening to the snores.

Happy Christmas, everyone!

Tinker – a tenor sax sounds at left – has a greatly enlarged photo of Doebin black boys carrying the bishop on a litter, the *sedia gestatoria*. She has this record of class distinctions hanging on the wall above her dining-table where we sit drinking our tea. The natives are barefoot with their trousers rolled up. The bishop is wearing a pith helmet above his canonical garb in tropical concession. The litter is followed by admiring lay Sugarville gentlemen, also barefoot and with trousers rolled up. One of them is suckass Gilham. Tinker thinks it is the funniest thing she has ever seen. 'Couldn't he fuckin walk?' she screeches. Language, Tinker! These days she's practically an outcast from the stuffier town groupings but still cuts a swathe through GIs. The Church needs her every now and again to perform at fundraising concerts, for she is still a captivating violinist, the best in these parts. Billed as the big number for a St Patrick's evening, she was stopped by the bishop's secretary as she was about to go on stage. Father Brimstone's late revenge! 'Excuse me,' the embarrassed but maliciously delighted priest said, looking everywhere else but, 'the bishop thinks your ... um ... dress is a trifle ... um ... immodest.'

Tinker's basic black was dashingly scooped. She glanced down at her sumptuous décolletage and snapped her violin back in its case. 'Tell the bishop,' she said with her most ravishing smile, 'to play his own shitty sonatas.' She walked out the stage door.

Olé, Tinker!

271

We fortify ourselves by recalling that moment. I feel better every minute.

'More tea?' Tinker asks.

After that supper contretemps, Thomas and I are teetering on the brink of marital wreck. Thomas spreads his charm over the female population of Sugarville – ancient, middle-ageing, sprouting, toddling. What a nice . . .! Isn't Doctor Quigley a . . .! I bend forward and crush my moan. He spreads it more particularly in ways I don't care to think about with at least two other women who are or were patients. One is actually the wife of banker Gilham. (Doesn't he know? Or care?) The other is a nubile buddy of Tinker's.

I have reached that stage where I can't even be bothered talking about it, though for his last birthday I gave him a copy of *Les Fleurs du Mal* inscribed with his favourite sentimentality, '*On n'aime qu'une fois.*'

'Darling girl . . .' unwrapping the gift, ''cushla!' And he began to sing, '"She was just the sort of craytur, bhoys, that nature did intend!"' I wish this were a music roll, this paper, like the old pianola munches, and then you'd get – we'd all get – the tune if you don't know it already, you and me singing along with a chorus of adulterous husbands. *A cappella* shrilling from the double-bed club.

Only this morning in a shopping arcade I was passed by a strolling couple, tall, elegant, legs stretching from

272

here to there. He was bearded, sailor-capped. She was a grey-blonde stunner. They glided, carnally, casually between the grocery aisles, talking and holding hands, for God's sake, her right swinging in his left, easy, easy, and they emanated – it was coming out like gamma rays – sexuality, and sated sexuality at that and my God they're fifty-plus if they're a minute. Envy glued my feet to the floor. Then I heard what he was saying: 'He'll piss himself when he finds out about us!'

Do I need help, the expensive therapy of some zestful Freudian with his psychoanalytic drivel?

I remember Mrs Brodie and her gentle servitude. I remember Mother and the coolness with which she severed herself from Gerald Morrow. I think of Thomas and wonder if this is to be for life. My daughter Annette will understand if I flee south, scoop her from her dormitory nightmares and start making a life for us both. Throw ourselves on Claire's mercy, perhaps. Start the same old cycle.

Shall I?

In the meantime I have Tinker to sustain me while I work this out. I don't need a psychiatrist.

Tinker's cheaper!

Tinker doesn't cost!

Tinker's motif – a sax in the wings – driving its lonely aching beat even as we sip tea, cuts in with its heavy four-four!

*All them years, eh? Still rememberin Uncle Boss. And **now** this new man he cause real trouble.*

Twenty years gone since then. More maybe.

*Normie goin to make strike. He talk about it all **the** time. Normie he educated two years at that inland **school** where they bully him, eh, bein blackskin despite all **that** white he got. Like they bully here.*

Normie good speaker. He talk and talk to them. Twelve-hour day, he say, for rations!

Separate schools, he say, for whites and blacks!

Areas for whites only! he say.

*White boozers, he say, spewin up the drink we **help** unload. Then we clean up the vomit!*

No good, he say, all that! There more of us!

Normie goin to make trouble. He mad bout everythin.

275

Got wife, got kids. Talk all the time bout unfair.

Don't say nothin, Manny, he tell. Somethin big goin to happen here. And soon. The world changin out there. It goin to change for us too.

THERE WERE PATTERNS TO FOLLOW

THERE WERE PATTERNS TO FOLLOW. There were always patterns, Matthew Vine knew, Normie Cooktown knew, each of them understanding the predictability of things, the lack of real variance in the human span.

After fourteen years to meet again on home ground. Or was it that?

See them. See the players lined up for the final curtain. Offstage: Quigley, Tullman, Curthoys and her daughters, schoolmaster Vine and Morrow. Dustily behind dusty scenery move Misses Starck and Weber. Enter stage right: Normie Cooktown and Vine's son.

There were links everywhere.

Young Vine kept remembering his father's disappointment at his decision to use his law degree working on Doebin as one of the government officials he had himself learned to loathe. 'Thrown away' was the phrase. He thought of his father, a dour retiree barely managing on the pension, sad and uncertain; he thought of his mother grown powerful as a rock, risen from that long-broken marriage and for years, until her retirement, running a country hospital hundreds of miles away from the bleak dustbowl of the Taws. He tried to blink away memory.

But why? his father had asked. Why?

I'm there to buck the system, Dad.

But are you? Are you bucking or submitting?

No. Not that. Not submitting. Never that.

You'll find it impossible, Matt.

In a small way, his idealism had argued, in a small way I can do something. I've made friends with a lot of the families. Normie Cooktown's, of course. The Ombas. The Fridays.

Then you won't last long.

I've been threatened with dismissal twice, he had said with ferocious pride.

And then what happens?

Who knows, he said. I'll move on. Up the Cape or out to the Kimberleys. There's work to be done.

Then you'll be classed as a paternalistic do-gooder. You'll lose both ways.

At least I'll have tried. At least I'll be learning to decline the gumleaf, conjugate the seasons.

As here, he thought. Now, he thought. Treading in my old man's shoes. The pattern.

Normie and Matthew, excited by encounter, had squatted under the trees near the jetty to talk over old times.

'I won't have this,' the director told new hand Matthew.

'There must be no fraternising with the natives, do you understand?'

'We were at school together,' Matthew protested. 'He's a good chap.'

'No more,' the director said. 'I want to hear no more. Is that clear?'

What was clear were the links between them, however tenuous, sorted over in secret evenings at Normie Cooktown's house. He was married to Cassie Friday and had a son and daughter. He was big and strong and filled with a sense of his own worth given him by those missionary ladies so long ago.

'Where are they now?' he asked. 'Still preachin?'

Matthew smiled remembering. 'Miss Weber died two years ago. Miss Starck's in a retirement home in Brisbane.'

'And Missus Curthoys?' Normie asked. 'Them Jesus ladies,' he grinned, 'took me to see her couple of times. Not long after that Leonie married the doctor. She was a good lady, all right. Looked after my brother Billy for a while.'

See them, still on the proscenium, the lights going down, the hall emptying. Father Donellan is praying in the wings. Oh God, young Matthew Vine thought. His father here first, now rotting his days away in a rented flat in Townsville, disappointed into silence. His mother retired at last to a unit on the Gold Coast, still plump with officiousness, irritable with lost authority.

All the players on stage, in the wings, yet paradoxically scattered.

His connection to all of it went through Annette

Quigley as well, whom he had known at university, fresh-faced Annette who had vowed never to return to the north and was working as a dogsbody in a Brisbane legal firm, trying not to know, not to remember, even if obligation demanded that now and then she should visit her mother and Aunt Claire, sitting their days out in a south-western country town. 'Things are changing,' Annette had insisted. 'God, I can't tell you how tired I got of Father – jocular of course and worse since he's given up practising, that's how he got away with it! – constantly battering me with the feminine principles. A suitable marriage. Appropriate boredom.'

Matthew had to laugh and stuffed away any ideas he might have had about pursuing Annette. Irresistibly the north had drawn him back to a public service job on Doebin and a burning sense of sacrifice that might have pleased a missionary. At night on his bedside radio he heard the well-bred tones of Gerald Morrow still enriching news histories of the area. He would burrow his fury at the palliative lies beneath the sheet.

The islanders' restlessness was increasing. There were constant complaints of mistreatment to which no one listened.

'I'm gunna call a strike,' Normie Cooktown said.

Normie Cooktown brooded over old hurts.

But it was the present that stuck sharper barbs than

those humiliations he'd felt at twelve.

After all, they didn't matter, they didn't matter at all, Normie had decided all those years ago, watching in that dry inland an eagle stroking through immeasurable gulfs of air and spinnakers of cloud caught on the high winds.

He had been swooped on, picked up and deposited by letters and recommendations from schoolmaster Wesley to Anglican Church dignitaries – whose clout was more than the director on Doebin could deal with – at that school in claypan country where somehow or other his skin, his cultural disabilities eventually found a way of coping. 'You move,' one of the teachers, Clinger Vine, had advised him, 'your emotional colour to another tense.'

'I don't understand.'

'Don't you?' Clinger's face was all thin and wrinkled and worried and gentle. 'Don't you? Well, it's like this. Take all your certainties from Dreamtime – is that what you call it? – past imperfect, past finite, whatever, and make it present continuous.'

Normie didn't know what the old bugger was on about, but he looked kind. He asked the master's son.

'I think Dad meant,' Matthew said, measuring up for a practice goal on the frost-dried oval, 'you take all the confidence you would have in your own surroundings – I mean your natural ones, I guess – and use it in your present. Get me?'

Normie made vague gestures with his head and scuttled in front of the other boy to kick a bullet shot straight between the posts.

'Bull's-eye!' Matthew commented without resentment. 'Selfish sod!' and gave him a friendly shove and rival hoot.

Days carved in dust so that they lost their shape instantly: classwork, games, friendlessness, friends – of a sort. How strong? How loyal to a half-caste? He had scraped through the junior examination with six Cs. His mumma wept with pleasure. And the war was over with no jobs for a brownskin, only a return to Doebin to help his old man, getting older quicker and his mumma fading. Helping the old man catch turtles, sometimes twelve, fourteen, to sell to the rest of the settlement who needed the meat. And working. Mainly that.

He'd married with the director's permission. He'd had kids. 'Wonder I didn't have to ask for permission for that,' he would say bitterly to Freddie Sweetwater, to Hector Fourmile.

Nothing had changed. There were still the dormitories, the ration lines, the bells, the segregation.

White staff came and went. One bully director was like another. There was electricity now but mainly to the houses of the whites. There was piped water – to the whites. There was a mission school, a new church, a government school, another store.

Once old Clinger, who had maintained a more or less correspondence, had written to him suggesting he keep a diary, a journal of what pleased, what hurt. It could come in handy, he advised, if ever . . . If ever what?

There was a time, Vine wrote, I felt deeply about something – someone, actually – and I put that down, all of it, as if it were fiction. Oh, I can't tell you the pain and hurt of the reality. But after it was written, and the years had passed, I found I couldn't even remember the faces – the face, to tell the truth – or the words or the events. Not with any clarity, that is. It was as if the whole of that period had lost its reality and become absorbed as fiction and was as fragile and unmemorable as most fiction is. It had ceased to exist.

'Fuckin fiction!' Normie said aloud and bitterly, looking around the crowded shanty he shared with his family, four of them in a room twelve by ten. He was angry with the letter when he had managed to work out what it was Vine was trying to say. That wouldn't work for me, he thought, seeing how it goes on and on, how it lives each day with me and my kids and the rest of us.

Still, something had happened to him then.

Normie brooded, wondering why he had ever bothered with that lousy school. What good had it ever done for him except those few moments of victory on playing fields? It done somethin, his eldest brother Manny said. You can talk to the bastards now. You aint scared.

The other young men who worked with him on the roads, on the buildings, complained about the pay, the rations, the limits to their freedom, and Normie found a new voice as he encouraged their complaints. We must do somethin, he whispered as they sweated, unloading crates on the jetty under the eyes of the bullmen. Gotta do somethin, he urged round nightly cooking fires, heady with revolt. We must show ourselves men, eh? We're worth somethin.

He wrote back to old Clinger a month later, just one line: This fiction, it don't go away.

They had patterns to follow, poor feller blacks.

There had been a long-running strike of Aboriginal workers in the Pilbara where they sought to lift restrictions on where they should live and how much they could earn. Rumours spread across the Cape that at reserves and missions their brothers might take a stand against the Act. Three years under this new man on Doebin were more than they could bear.

A new lockup was being built and the director had his work-gang toiling Saturdays and Sundays without respite. After an argument with the overseer, Normie Cooktown walked off the job and was soon followed by the rest of the gang. In the hot evening a group of Normie's friends gathered at his house to discuss tactics. See them: Willie Omba, Moses Thursday, Hector Fourmile.

Gambling was forbidden.

A tactical presumption of gambling.

Willie Omba, given the gift of rhetoric before the director, became heated in his denials. He was ordered off the island along with his pregnant wife and the rest of his family. Three days later, Hector Fourmile was arrested. Then their spokesman, Normie Cooktown, was ordered to leave. Normie refused. 'I'm an island man,' he said to the director. 'What are you?' He walked out of the office, refusing to go to gaol and even the black police boys refused to arrest him. Rumours spread and spread like wait-a-while, spread and caught their tiny barbs on decades of resentment. Normie strode arrogantly in public view down Coconut Avenue, outraging the whites.

'We scrub their houses,' Normie complained to Matthew Vine in his capacity as legal adviser for their grievances, 'for nothin. The men won't do island dance for the tourists and they get put in the lockup. If they go up the mountain with their girls, they get twenty-one days. The girls get their heads shaved and have to wear bags. Did these buggers learn from the Nazis?'

No difference, Matthew Vine thought. None.

'How can you do this?' he demanded of the director.

'Don't you dare teach me my job,' the director said icily. 'Are you promoting immorality as well in your capacity as counsellor?'

'No. Charity.' It was hopeless. 'Simply charity.'

A week after the arrest of Hector Fourmile a regular supply barge was due in. Normie Cooktown led a group of ten men to the jetty for unloading. In the mid-morning heat Matthew strolled down to the cove and found Normie's workers busy but unloading food supplies only: meat for their families, the hospitals, the dormitories, the doctors and nurses. They left the rest of the cargo untouched and any bottles of alcohol they smashed or threw into the indifferent waters.

Normie was beyond laughter as he tipped flagons of gutrot into the bay. The barge master tried to intervene

287

but was held back by angry blacks. Meat for the administration staff rotted on the deck in the boiling afternoon and every attempt by the master and his assistant to lug the crates ashore was stopped by groups of shouting men. Finally the barge was forced to back water and pull out into the channel.

Matthew Vine, watching from the trees on the shoreline, found the director had come up behind and was watching as well, his face tight.

'Happy?' he said to young Vine. 'Pleased about this? Spreading your communist notions to people who can't understand them.'

'Oh, they understand, all right,' Matthew Vine said. 'They understand only too well.'

'You're finished here,' the director said.

Inertia spread.

For days a standstill.

Men failed to turn up at the sewage works, the sawmill. Slop buckets of the whites remained unemptied. House-girls neglected to clean administration quarters. And all of them, all of them, men, women and children, encour-aged by Normie Cooktown, sauntered openly along Coconut Avenue, stopping to chat or simply sit in places barred to them.

At last, after a week of frantic pleas from the director to the mainland, a posse of white police was brought over by launch to guard the homes of whites peering fearfully through shutters as blacks strode the streets.

There goes Moses Thursday! There goes Freddie Sweetwater! There goes Normie Cooktown! All of them deliberately rousing rage behind those shutters as they squat beneath mango trees in the main avenue to smoke and laugh. White mind envisaged plots and stratagems. Black mind saw lotus-eating, chewing the rag, and only now and again gave amused thought to those white bosses forced to clean up their own droppings.

'Ah shit!' Freddie Sweetwater said. 'This is the life, eh, bro!'

'That's it! You said it! Shit!' cried Moses Thursday as he remembered the unemptied goona buckets of the whites and they rolled about laughing in the mango shade, looking up briefly as Matthew Vine came along the road to squat beside them. He felt hidden eyes scorch as he accepted a cigarette and lounged back on the unmown grass beneath the trees.

'How long, eh?'

'As long as it takes,' Normie Cooktown said, moved from laughter to bitterness quick as a flash. 'And how long you got?'

But their surmisals were wrong. For the start. The police wandered about the settlement talking casually to the strikers, dropping in at their homes, offering cigarettes, drinking tea, asking questions, storing replies.

'They're checking you out,' Matthew warned Normie Cooktown. 'They're trying to catch you off your guard.'

The director and his staff remained indoors, skulking behind shutters. It was like a replay of that other time, old Leggat told the director. Those two nightmare days when the superintendent had terrorised the island. 'This is now!' the director shouted at crumbling Leggat. He was a stupid man who understood nothing but the raised voice, the instant application of force. On the jetty the stink of rotted food finally drove two of the burlier white staff to go down and shove the crates into the bay, where there was a frenzy of shark activity.

There were spies. There were whistle-blowers.

No gubbamin man came to discuss islander complaints.

The director refused consultation and sucked in breath and rage behind bolted doors, holding out, holding out, while the bullimen prowled the streets and even the islanders grew tired of inaction and the insecurity of waiting.

After another five days the director, on the advice of the roaming policemen, made a further insistent call to the mainland demanding reinforcements. Matthew Vine shuffling paper in his little office heard the call, heard the busy consultations and knew his loyalties lay only one way. That afternoon he walked down the avenue looking for Normie Cooktown who was sprawled in his usual place beneath the mango trees.

'Well,' Matthew said, answering a week-old question, 'not long now, I guess. Anyway I came to tell you something. There's trouble today. The mainland's sent over reinforcements. They arrived an hour ago. There's a boat with a team of police anchored in one of the coves.'

He stayed there with the men, finishing his cigarette,

lighting another, and even while they talked he saw from the edge of his eye two of the previously pally policemen marching down the road from the administration block, hands on batons, revolvers bulging at their hips like misplaced genitals. He said softly to the three men, 'Don't look now, but it's on. For God's sake don't resist. Don't fight, you hear? They'll use that against you. Just get up quickly and saunter off. I'll keep them busy if I can.'

Shadow into shadow. The avenue emptied, islanders slipping away, becoming invisible, as they had learned from childhood to avoid white presence.

'Hey!' one of the bullimen yelled, starting to run. 'Hey, you black buggers! Stop, you hear!'

Big men running through heat heavy as canvas, pushing through fever-folds down an empty road to an unruffled young white stubbing out midday with his cigarette.

The night is filled with the splintering of wood, the thuds of kicked-in doors, shouts and screams, the howling of kids and women, the three a.m. raging of bullimen rattling handcuffs and chains.

In the muddling dark the ringleaders' huts are torn apart and the men, shackled before their terrified families, are dragged out as a warning, a symbol of what follows defiance of white codes, of the retribution of noncompliance.

See them – there goes Moses Thursday, there goes Freddie Sweetwater, there goes Normie Cooktown – prodded at gunpoint through the streets of administration along the avenue to the sea-front.

The whole settlement is awake and Matthew Vine flings from his bed and drags on clothes before racing outside. His work colleagues huddle with their wideawake eyes, interpreting the purge, with their ears absorbing the cries and shouts of angry islanders. They obey the rules. They maintain distance.

Despite the anger of police, Matthew follows the shadowy procession of prisoners as they stumble and trip in their leg-irons. Behind the men trail wives and children, faces snotty with fright and tears, their clutching hands struck aside by batons, pleading bodies thrust roughly back. More and more of the blacks come from their huts to thicken the crowd, keeping up a wailing in language, a fearsome night-ghost of unknowns that worries the bullimen and now even the director who has emerged from his house and is striding at the rear, impatient to see the finish of this act played out in starshine and the cold phosphorescence of the sea.

Normie Cooktown is at the front. Blood runs down his face and clogs his lips. One eye is swollen. He keeps his head high and looks neither left nor right, does not bother to check his shackled feet. Fifteen years since he went, full of hope, to that school on the mainland. Fifteen years since old Clinger told him to maintain his dreams, his sense of self. He spits in derision and a gobbet of blood and sputum lands on the face of the bulliman by his side.

'You filthy bastard!' the copper shouts. 'You stinking black bastard!' He mops at his face and delivers a hard punch to the side of Normie's skull. Normie trips and falls sideways, smacking the ground with a thump. 'Get up!' the bulliman yells. 'Get up, you bugger!' He stands there and watches as Normie struggles, lurching upright for a few seconds only to topple off balance and pitch to the ground again. 'Maybe a boot'd help,' the copper says and he pulls back one foot and delivers a massive kick to Normie's guts.

The mob has come to a standstill.

Matthew finds himself bawling, 'Stop that, you hear! Stop that!' He pushes through the knot of women and children until he finds himself standing above his friend's body. 'Hey, Normie,' he says bending over and ignoring the copper's wrenching arm, 'it's me. Matt. Let me help, mate.'

'Leave him!' screams the copper. 'Leave him, you stupid faggot!'

Matthew turns and looks the policeman straight in the eye. Someone is playing torchlight on them and its wavering beam catches jungle that has become enemy, battalions of leaves against which the terrified faces of the actors swing like masks. The director has trotted up pussy-foot behind.

'I saw that,' Matthew accuses. 'I saw you kick a prisoner. I'm a lawyer, friend, and I'll give sworn evidence against you. I'll see you charged with brutality. I'll fix –'

'Ah, piss off!' the copper says. 'Pick the bastard up and piss off!'

Matthew bends over his friend. 'Come on,' he urges. 'Let me give you a hand, see you down to the boat.'

He pulls Normie upright and gives his arm an encouraging squeeze. 'Like old times, isn't it?' he says, not wanting to enlarge, but both of them remembering the cement floors and walls of the change-rooms, the cold-water showers, the school bullies, the snide cracks, the knotted towels and fists. 'Don't worry. I'll see you get a fair go. Promise.'

Behind him Normie's wife and babies are gulping with terror, afraid to let out the cries that are shaking their bodies apart. The little girl is trembling so much she can hardly stand. Normie's wife Cassie gathers the child up and begins moving again and Matthew continues walking with his friend down to the beach, the jetty, watched every step of the way by the police.

Surprisingly, old Leggat, the deputy whose malice like wine has aged with him, is waiting by the steps that lead to the police launch and when renewed wailing bursts from the wives and children he crams them onto the boat as well. 'The lot,' he says spitefully. 'Take the lot.'

At the back of the crowd under the witnessing trees and shaded by his own sour victory, the director stands impervious. With narrowed eyes he watches Matthew Vine and then walks down to the landing.

'I heard what you said. There'll be no trial.'

'What do you mean, no trial?'

'Exactly what I say. You and your promises! They're

being taken to another reserve where their troublemaking abilities will get no sympathy, believe me.'

'Where exactly?'

'A long way from here.' The director half smiles. He feels he has handled the whole thing pretty smoothly. 'And as for you, you can start packing the minute you get back to your quarters.'

Matthew turns away from his rancour and runs along the jetty. The launch motors snarl and catch and the propeller churns the pre-dawn water into a foam of ghosts and links and memories.

Dry-eyed he looks at the sad little huddle of prisoners and he shouts, 'Normie!' once, twice. But Normie, looking straight ahead, indifferent to manacles and leg-irons, wobbles to his feet and raising his voice begins to sing in language, making a new songline for all of them, and just as suddenly the wailing and lamentations of the watchers on shore cease, the crowd silent dark shapes against the dark.

Normie stares blindly across the bay, his wrecked face stony, body rocking with the rocking boat.

'Shut that bastard up!' one of the coppers yells, maddened, but the noise of the motors drowns the order.

Yet still Normie Cooktown sings and sings for all of them: for his wife and children, his two friends and their families trapped with him, for the grieving blacks on the island.

Ngana dungaydu
Ngana kari binal

Yinya burrir bama-mu
Ngana kari binal
Yinya ngangka ngulkurrijin
Marri marri marri
Yinya ngangka nganjay
Ngana kari binal.

It is not one of his people's songs. He is weaving words
learnt from Moses Thursday and Freddie Sweetwater in
a gesture of brotherhood. As the boat churns the sea-
miles he becomes a poet:

We are leaving now
We do not understand
That island belongs to our people
We do not understand
Those flowers were beautiful
Long time, long time, long time
Now they are wilted
We do not understand.

And as he sings Moses and Freddie join in the refrain.
Ngana kari binal – we do not understand. Nothing stops
them.

Over and over he sings the words. *Jirrbu-jirrbu*. Lonely.
Sad.

Over and over and over, eyes fixed on the looming
coast, he sings all the way to the mainland.